It was twilight as they descended the hills into the outskirts of the capital. The lights of Athens were blinking on below them. Indy was tired, thirsty, and hungry, but most of all he was anxious to get to the palace. It was the one place he felt they would be safe. *If* they could get through the front gate.

But Conrad interrupted his thoughts. "Take a look at what's ahead," he said.

Indy grimaced. "Swell. A roadblock."

Nikos leaned forward. "I bet this is where it gets dangerous."

Indy frowned at the impetuous kid. "At least one of the places."

"Look," Conrad said. "Let's reason with them. We'll explain that we have important information for the king."

There was no time to argue. They were fifty yards short of the roadblock when one of the soldiers pointed. Several others raised their guns. They fired and the windshield shattered. "I don't think they're open to conversation," Indy said.

THE INDIANA JONES SERIES
Ask your bookseller for the books you have missed.

AND THE

PERIL AT DELPHI

ROB MacGREGOR

BANTAM BOOKS
NEW YORK   TORONTO   LONDON   SYDNEY   AUCKLAND

INDIANA JONES AND THE PERIL AT DELPHI
A Bantam Book

PUBLISHING HISTORY
Bantam mass market edition published February 1991
Bantam reissue / June 2008

Published by
Bantam Dell
A Division of Random House, Inc.
New York, New York

Bantam Books and the rooster colophon are registered
trademarks of Random House, Inc.

ISBN 978-0-553-28931-2

Printed in the United States of America
Published simultaneously in Canada

www.bantamdell.com

OPM   18 17 16 15 14 13 12 11 10 9

For Trish

Special thanks to Lucy Autrey Wilson of Lucasfilm, who refused to let go when Indy's life line started to unravel.

"*The bravest are surely those who have the clearest vision of what is before them, glory and danger alike, and yet notwithstanding go out to meet it.*"

— THUCYDIDES

Prologue

Delphi, Greece—1922

Indy hung in the darkness like a quarter moon, suspended by a rope that burned into his chest and armpits. He heard shouts above him, but couldn't make out the words. When he dropped his head back, the aperture high above him offered no more light than a twinkling star.

"Dorian!" he yelled. "Send down another torch!"

His voice bounced back and forth against the walls of the crevice; he didn't know if she had heard him or not. He rubbed his cheek against his shoulder and peered down. Blackness was everywhere, an inky veil that disoriented him, dizzied him. Nausea rolled through him. He squeezed his eyes shut and moved his hands a fraction of an inch upward on the rope, fearing that in the next second, it was going to snap and he'd follow his first torch into the fathomless darkness below him.

There was no space, no time, only the pull of

gravity, the suction of the void. He couldn't have dangled more than a few minutes, but it seemed he'd been hanging here for hours, waiting for light to redeem him.

"Jones," Dorian shouted.

His name reverberated in the pit. He glanced up and saw a flickering light dancing toward him. The rope that held it coiled and uncoiled, serpentine, its tongue hissing fire. Indy ducked as the torch darted past his head, then grabbed the rope and snared the end of the torch.

He gripped it, his breath erupting from his chest like hiccups. He peered at the wall in front of him, no longer certain if it was the right wall. Maybe he was too far down. He tugged on his rope twice and Doumas, Dorian's assistant, lowered him another two feet. Then he was directly opposite the tablet. It jutted out from the stone wall like a tombstone in a graveyard, and was tilted slightly downward.

He pulled a four-pronged clamp from his knapsack and pounded it into the wall with a mallet. He was about to place the torch into it when something caught his eye. He held the torch in front of the tablet and leaned forward for a closer look.

He'd been told the inscription would be caked with dirt and that it would have to be cleaned once the tablet was taken to the surface. But he was staring at parallel rows of glyphs that were not only clearly recognizable, but were written in ancient Greek, a language he could read.

His eyes skipped over the words, devouring them.

Excitement knotted in his gut. He put the torch back into the holder on the wall, and pulled a notepad from a side pocket of his knapsack. Quickly, he scrawled the translation. He couldn't believe it. They were right. The crazy bastards knew what they were talking about.

He wanted to yell up to the top, but decided to conserve his energy. He stuffed the notebook back into the pack, pulled out the net, and carefully covered the tablet before fastening the drawstrings to a hook at the end of the rope.

He was about to start chiseling at the wall to loosen the tablet when the rope suddenly jerked against his chest. He dropped several inches; the rope tightened under his arms.

"Hey, what the hell is going on?"

His voice ricocheted about the crevice. He was directly below the tablet now and saw pick marks under it. Someone had not only cleaned the inscription, but had tried to remove the tablet. But who?

The rope jerked again. A weird creaking filled the crevice and he knew what it was. His rope was fraying. He pulled the torch from the wall and held it up. "Aw, Christ."

Easy does it, he thought. He placed the torch in his mouth, and reached for the rope above the spot where it was unraveling. He heard a resounding snap, a sharp, terrible sound that echoed in the crevice. His fingers snagged the rope.

He dangled by one hand, the frayed end rubbing against his wrist. The torch burned the hair on his arm. His face was contorted in a grimace as he stretched his other hand over his head. Sweat beaded on his brow, trickled into his eyes.

He felt a hard yank from above, and the rope slipped through his fingers. He reached desperately with his other hand, but his fist closed on black air.

He fell.

1

COLLEGE CAPERS

Chicago—two years earlier

The night was still and tight as the two men lumbered down a narrow lane, limp bodies draped over their shoulders. Rain from a spring shower puddled in hidden depressions, shadowed by the tall buildings on either side. They were nearing a corner, and beyond it was the grassy mall, their destination.

One of the men was tall and rangy and bobbed as he walked as if constantly readjusting the weight of the body he carted. The other one was sturdy and muscular. Coils of rope hung from both sides of his belt, and he moved with the nimbleness of a mountain climber. Suddenly, he stumbled in one of the ruts and lurched to the side, almost losing his balance. Nimble, yes, but also afflicted by occasional spasms of clumsiness.

"Damn it," he sputtered as he recovered his footing. It was almost over, and he was edgy.

"You okay?" the tall one asked.

"Fine. Let's stop a minute. I've got a bad feeling about this."

The tall one unceremoniously let the body slip from his shoulder, then pulled out a flask from inside his coat. He held it out, but his partner shook his head. "No?" The tall man shrugged, then took a long swallow.

"Take it easy on that stuff," the rope man hissed.

"It takes the edge off."

"Fifteen more minutes and it'll be all over," the rope man said. He hugged the shadows of the building as he moved ahead, the body still draped over his husky shoulder. When he reached the corner, he looked both ways. In spite of his concern, he was determined to complete his mission, and he wanted every detail perfect.

He turned to signal his partner, but the man was already standing behind him, the other body slung over his shoulder. They headed down a rain-slick sidewalk, the glow of street lamps reflecting off its surface. They stopped when they reached the first light, and slid the bodies onto the grass. Barely visible under a nearby hedge were two other bodies they'd left there half an hour earlier.

"Call your tune," the tall one said.

"Get Paine ready. I want him first. And make sure his hat is on straight." He loosened one of the ropes coiled on his belt. A hangman's noose was knotted at the end of the rope, and with a graceful swing of his arm, he tossed it over the arc of the lamp. The noose danced in the pale light.

"Okay, slide it over his neck, and make sure his name tag doesn't come off."

The tall man lifted the body and worked the noose over the head. When it was tight, he reached into Paine's vest, pulled out a three-cornered hat, and fit it firmly over his head. The other man, meanwhile, had scaled the lamppost, and now raised the body into place. He deftly tied the rope, then dropped to the ground.

"Hey, he looks great. Now, just three more to go."

The tall man tipped the flask to his mouth once more and again he gestured with it to his partner.

"We'll do Georgie next," the rope man said in response. "God, I can't wait to see the reaction tomorrow morning."

A headless figure wriggled beneath a dark gown like a magician struggling to free himself from chains and locks. Then the top of a head, a brow, and a face emerged from the dark cocoon. He straightened the gown over his bare legs, and gazed at himself in a full-length mirror. He ran a hand through his thick hair, which was parted in the center, then placed his mortarboard and tassel on top of his head.

The intricate lithographic lettering on his diploma would say he was Henry Jones, Jr. But those who knew him called him Indy—short for Indiana, a name he'd used since his early teens. "Henry Jr." was consigned to use on official documents, and by his father, who still called him Junior.

In fact, the only visible remainder of his childhood was a scar on his jaw, which he'd gotten in a scrap with thieves he'd stumbled on in a desert cavern as they uncovered a relic of the Spanish conquest.

But even his father, if he were here, would see that he was no longer a kid. He was handsome in a rugged sort of way, with clear, determined hazel eyes and the broad shoulders and musculature of a halfback. But he wasn't a football player. Although he was well co-ordinated, he preferred horseback riding and skiing to sports like football or baseball. He was also proficient at the use of a whip, an odd skill he rarely talked much about. Not that any of that mattered today.

"I'm a college graduate," he said to himself, and smiled at the image those words conjured, but his smile revealed more than a hint of irony. He was grad-uating in spite of everything. He'd missed so many classes last fall, his grades had nose-dived and he'd nearly been expelled. For several weeks, he'd simply lost interest in his formal education while he was at-taining another sort on the street.

He and Jack Shannon, his wily roommate, had spent their nights at barrelhouse piano saloons on the South Side, listening to musicians with names like Pine Top Smith, Cripple Clarence Lofton, Speckled Red, and Cow Cow Davenport pound the keys on their uprights. The music was called barrelhouse pi-ano because the small bars where it was played served liquor directly out of kegs. At least, they had until Prohibition started a few months back.

Most of the jazzmen had come up from New Orleans, the hometown of jazz, in the last five years, and more were arriving every week. Living conditions for Negroes were better in Chicago; there were jobs in clubs where they could make fifty dollars a week com-pared to a dollar a night in New Orleans. And

Chicago was where the recording studios were making jazz records.

When the bars closed, Indy and Shannon often headed to freewheeling rent parties where the music continued until dawn. Shannon would bring his cornet and play along with the likes of Johnny Dunn and Jabbo Smith. Not only was Shannon one of the few whites Indy had seen play jazz, but he was undoubtedly the only economics student playing the music. Most of the jazzmen in the barrelhouse saloons were uneducated. They didn't read music, didn't follow the rules, didn't know the rules, and didn't care. They didn't even know their music was unusual, and all of that contributed to its power and integrity.

"Hey, you ready? You said you wanted to get there early, right?"

He looked up, snapping out of his reverie. Shannon's red hair looked as wild as ever. His gown was draped over his arm, and he wore a coat and tie. The coat was too short in the sleeves, but he knew Shannon didn't give a damn about it. He had a habit of nodding his head when he was excited or nervous and he was doing it now. But Shannon always seemed a bit edgy, as though he weren't really made for this world. The only time he ever seemed perfectly at ease was when he was playing his cornet. Then his lanky body seemed to flow with the music and you no longer noticed his size twelve feet or his long neck with its bulging Adam's apple.

Indy glanced once more at himself, then removed the mortarboard. They were only a couple of blocks from the grassy mall where the ceremony was being held. They'd be there in a few minutes.

"Okay. Let me get dressed. I don't have my pants on yet."

"Dare you to go just like that. Graduate without your pants, kiddo."

"No thanks. Don't see any reason to do it." He watched Shannon through the mirror, knowing that he would make an offer.

"Tell you what. I'll buy you a bottle of hooch. We'll get plastered."

Indy shrugged. Hell, with the gown on, no one would know the difference. "All right." He wasn't exactly looking forward to the ceremony; he just wanted to be done with it. Not wearing any pants would at least make it somewhat interesting.

"I can just hear ol' Mulhouse now," he said as they left the house. " 'You are a new generation, a generation of hope.' " His voice was deep, authoritative, mimicking the university president. " 'The war is over. Go out into the world and show others who are less fortunate that America's young people are hardworking, productive individuals who get the job done, whatever that job may be.' "

Something like that, he thought. No, the ceremony wasn't the reason Indy wanted to arrive early.

"How is it with no pants?" Shannon asked as they headed down an oak-shrouded street.

"Cool and breezy. You should try it."

Indy expected him to laugh and make a joke, but Shannon wore a pensive expression. "Is your father going to be here?"

Indy shook his head. "He's busy. Hell, he didn't even bother to apologize."

"Really?"

"Yeah. That's how he is. My father, the esteemed expert on grail lore, is a man with little time for anything or anyone outside of his scholarly pursuits."

"He always been like that?"

"Only after my mother died when I was young. Ever since then he's become more distant from me, no matter what I do. I guess I majored in linguistics just to get his attention."

Shannon glanced at him. "How would linguistics get his attention?"

"For as long as I can remember, he's said that language is the key to understanding mankind. But so what? How can he expect me to understand mankind when I can't even understand him?"

"I wish *my* family were staying home. Hell, I wish I weren't even graduating."

"What're you talking about, Jack? You've got a job and you'll be making good money." Shannon had been hired as an accountant with a Chicago trucking company for the salary of two hundred fifty dollars a month, a sum that seemed astonishingly high. When Indy asked how he'd gotten it, Shannon's only response was "family connections."

"And you'll still have time to play in the clubs," Indy continued. "Hey, remember that night we went down to the Royal Gardens and saw King Oliver? Authentic New Orleans Creole jazz. It's all moving right up here into your own backyard. What more could you ask for?"

Shannon didn't say anything as they crossed the street. "You *are* going to play, aren't you?" Indy asked as he watched a shiny new Tin Lizzie motor past.

"I made a deal."

Indy noted the dour expression on his face. "What kind of deal?"

"I have to stop playing jazz. That's the price of the job."

"That's crazy. Why?"

"It's not 'respectable' music, Indy."

Indy knew that jazz was slow to catch on. And many whites thought the syncopated beat—accenting notes when it wasn't expected—and improvisational style were "jungle music." *It causes the listener to move in strange, suggestive ways,* he'd heard one radio commentator say.

"That's bullshit, Jack, because I think you could be as good as Earl Hines or Johnny Dodds. You watch; things will change as the music catches on."

"I don't know if that'll ever happen." Shannon swayed from side to side, his gangly arms moving to their own beat. "You know, they're even blaming jazz for those riots on the South Side. Can you believe that?"

"The rioting had nothing to do with jazz." But the city's race riots were a sour note in a nation that was feeling good about the Allies' victory. They created a sad contrast to the big parades that marched along New York's Fifth Avenue, celebrating America's role in the triumph.

"It's not marching music, Indy. You know what I mean. Nobody feels like a goddamn hero when they listen to it. That's the problem. It's coming from a different place, and so am I."

Indy chuckled. "You could always go to Europe with me, and start a new life."

"Don't think I haven't thought about it. I'm jealous as hell. You're going to love it."

Paris, Indy was sure, would be fascinating, but he wasn't so certain about becoming an expert in ancient languages. "I guess. But studying old manuscripts in libraries isn't my idea of an exciting time."

"You keep saying that. Why are you doing it?"

"The opportunity was there, and I wasn't going to pass it up. Simple as that."

Shannon abruptly turned down an alley, and motioned for Indy to follow.

"Where you going?"

"C'mon," he said in a hushed voice. "I said I'd buy you a bottle. Let's get a pint and take it with us. There's a guy close by who's got it."

"I don't know, Jack." Prohibition was a bad joke, but Indy was anxious to get to the campus.

"It'll only take a minute. C'mon."

He shrugged and followed him. Although the two men got along well, they differed considerably in their consumption of and attitude toward alcohol. Shannon had been a heavy drinker since he was seventeen, and Prohibition hadn't slowed his habit. Indy, on the other hand, had a low tolerance for alcohol and could take it or leave it.

Halfway down the block, Shannon opened a gate, and strolled along the walk to a back door. He rapped out the universal code for "it's me"—BOP; bop-bop-bob-bop; BOP; BOP. A dog answered, yelping from inside the house. Shannon glanced back at Indy as if to make sure he was still there.

A moment later, a short, frumpy man with a cross look on his face opened the door. A two-day stubble shadowed his jaw and his white hair was mussed, as though he'd been sleeping. He shouted at the dog, then asked what they wanted.

"A bottle of juice, Elmo, what else?" Shannon said with a smirk.

The man motioned for them to enter. Indy smelled whiskey on his breath as soon as he stepped into the cramped kitchen.

A wiry, mixed-breed dog growled from behind his master. Indy kept his distance and looked around the kitchen. Green paint was peeling from the walls, revealing patterned wallpaper. One of the cupboard doors lay on the floor where it had apparently fallen some time ago, and the room stank of urine-soaked newspapers stacked in one corner.

"Just a quick pint, Elmo. We're in a hurry."

"Good for you." He looked past Shannon and frowned at Indy's black gown. "Who's this guy, a judge?"

"Don't you know a college graduate when you see one? We're on our way to the big time."

"Is that right? This professor who visits me says I deserve an honorary degree. How do you like that?" Elmo grinned, his teeth lining up in his mouth like a picket fence that had yellowed in the sun.

"A degree in what, moonshining?" Shannon asked.

"No. Chemistry."

Indy laughed, but he felt uneasy, and wished they hadn't stopped.

"You got it or not, Elmo? We don't have all day."

"Fifty cents."

"Fifty?" Shannon threw up his hands, enraged by

the price. "How about a break for the new graduates? C'mon, Elmo."

"Fifty cents," Elmo retorted, and crossed his arms over his chest.

"All right, all right." Shannon turned to Indy. "You got a quarter?"

"What about our deal?"

"I'll pay you back. Don't worry."

Indy dug into his pocket. He earned expense money by tutoring high school students in Latin and French, but never had much extra. He grudgingly handed Shannon a quarter.

Elmo dropped the coins in his pocket, ambled across the kitchen, and descended into a cellar. Indy glanced at his watch. "I hope he doesn't get lost down there."

Shannon waved a hand impatiently, dismissing Indy's concern. "Relax, we'll be there in no time."

Indy saw that the dog had bared its teeth and was growling again.

"What's his problem?" Indy grumbled.

Shannon pointed at the mongrel. "Shut up, pooch."

But the dog charged past them as someone banged on the door. Shannon looked toward the cellar, shrugged, then opened the door a couple of inches. "Who is it?"

"Ya mudda. Open up. I'm here to see Elmo."

"Who's there?" the old moonshiner called out as he emerged from the basement. He slipped Indy the pint, and the graduate-to-be stuffed it inside his mortarboard.

The door swung open, and a man in a dark coat,

tie, and hat filled the doorway. He had a grim, menacing look on his face and a gun in his hand.

Aw, hell. A damp chill raced up Indy's spine.

Elmo took one look at the new visitor and bolted toward the front door. The man yelled for him to stop, but Elmo kept moving. The man charged through the house, the dog yelping at his heels.

Indy and Shannon exchanged a glance and rushed for the kitchen door. At the bottom of the steps, Indy tripped on his gown and fell to his knees. He scrambled up and raced after Shannon, who was sprinting across the yard. Indy couldn't help laughing; they were getting away, escaping the danger, and he even had the whiskey. But then Shannon stopped abruptly, and Indy crashed into him. At the gate were two cops just waiting to nab them.

"Hey, you two!"

"Shit."

Shannon spun, dashed across the yard, and ran between two houses. Indy didn't wait around for directions; he darted after him, hiking up his gown as he ran. He passed Shannon as they crossed the street. They fled across a succession of yards and in between houses. He was almost sure they had gotten away when he realized he'd run into a yard enclosed by an eight-foot wood fence.

"Damn," he hissed.

"Watch out!" Shannon shouted behind him.

Indy's head jerked around; he expected to see the cops. Instead, a pair of Doberman pinschers were dashing toward them. "Christ," he breathed. He dropped the pint, pulled on his mortarboard, and scrambled up the fence. Just as he was about to lift a leg over the top, he was yanked back. One of the Dobermans had snared his gown. The dog snarled and shook its head from side to side as Indy struggled to get away.

He reached back and jerked hard, ripping the gown from the dog's mouth. He leaped over the fence, and dropped to the ground where Shannon was already waiting. They crossed another yard, ducked around a garage, then pulled up short. The two cops were standing in the alley with their revolvers drawn.

"Nice going, boys. Hold it right there," said the shorter cop.

Indy froze. Now they were in trouble, and it wasn't even his trouble.

"Billy?" Shannon said, rocking forward onto the balls of his feet. "That you?"

"Jesus," murmured the cop. "Jack Shannon. What're you doing here?"

"I could ask you the same thing. We were getting a pint. We're on our way to graduation."

"Christ, Shannon." He glanced at his partner. "It's Harry's brother." He jerked his head toward the alley. "Get out of here and watch who the hell you do business with from now on."

"Thanks, Billy."

"Don't thank me, Jack. Harry's going to hear about this. You can count on it."

Indy had no idea what Shannon's brother had to do with the cop. As they hurried toward the campus, Indy's torn gown flapped like a flag behind him. "Your brother's not a cop, is he, Jack?"

An angry scowl tightened Shannon's face. "No, but

he's got friends. Billy Flannery is from the neighborhood."

"But what were they doing?"

"Putting a small-time competitor out of business. Harry's got territory to maintain."

"The cops work for your brother?"

"Wake up, Indy. They all work for the organization, and Harry's a charter member. It runs in the family."

2

HANGING HEROES

The back of Indy's gown was in shreds, and he held it together with one hand as they passed through the gate of the campus. But he didn't give a damn. He was just grateful to be free of cops and crooks and dogs. He was graduating and that was all that mattered.

He glanced up at a banner fluttering in the breeze. CELEBRATE FOUNDING FATHERS DAY—MAY 23, it read. At the sight of it his stomach knotted, and his sense of relief vanished. With everything that had just happened, he'd almost forgotten about last night. What had seemed like a notable way to end his college career no longer felt so wonderful.

As they reached the end of the lane leading to the mall, they stopped. A crowd of black-gowned students and their families were gathered on the sidewalk. Above them, bodies dangled from ropes high up on lampposts. From where they stood, the hanging mannequins looked like actual corpses dressed in American revolutionary garb complete with loose white shirts and vests, tight-fitting pants, and three-cornered hats.

"Well, look at that," Shannon said with a mischievous grin. "Georgie, the two Toms, and Benji."

Indy stared glumly at the sight. The thrill had definitely worn off. "I don't know. It's sort of grotesque in the daylight. I guess I didn't really think they'd still be here."

On a weekday the campus maintenance workers would probably have cut them down and carted them away by now. But it was Saturday, midmorning, graduation day, and everyone was stopping and staring.

"Well, I think it's great." Shannon grinned and slapped Indy on the back. "We pulled it off." There wasn't a trace of concern in his voice.

"Yeah. Swell."

"Look. The press is even here. It's your chance to tell them all about it!"

That was his original intention, but now he wasn't so sure he wanted to take credit for the deed, much less boast about it. Maybe it hadn't been such a good idea to postpone it from the night before Founding Fathers Day to the eve of graduation. Maybe no one would understand.

Shannon punched him lightly on the shoulder. "There're my folks. See you in a while."

Indy watched him drift into the crowd, then walked over to where photographers were snapping pictures of "Tom Jefferson." Several people were talking at once, and the words struck him like blows to the gut.

"Who could have done it?" he heard someone ask.

"What was the point?"

"No point."

"It's horrible."

"Must have been a Bolshevik. I've heard they were on campus."

"Maybe it was a Royalist. I'm sure they must hate Franklin."

"A mad Englishman."

No one seemed to find it humorous or to grasp its meaning. Now he was barely able to contain himself. He felt like shouting that it was just his Founding Fathers Day exhibit, and didn't they understand what these men stood for, anyway?

"It's a disgrace to the university," an authoritative voice boomed from under the next lamppost. "An outrage of the worst sort."

Mallery Mulhouse, the university president, was surrounded by reporters, students, and parents. His face was ruddier than usual, and his brow was covered in sweat.

Founding Fathers Day was Mulhouse's inspiration. It involved a day of speeches and patriotic ado, and although no one was forced to participate, it was considered a gaffe for undergraduates to ignore it. During Indy's first two years, when he'd lived in a dormitory, the floor captains had been responsible for getting everyone involved in making floats for the parade or other related projects.

Last year, when he'd moved into an apartment off campus, he'd avoided Founding Fathers Day. But this year, Mulhouse had required everyone taking a history or an English course to write a paper on the Founding Fathers or fail the course. Indy had grudgingly abided, but in his own way.

"Anyone who would hang effigies of our nation's founders from the lampposts of an academy of higher learning is clearly a dangerous, unbalanced individual," Mulhouse continued. "I consider this an act of sedition, an affront to everything this nation is about."

A frown furrowed Indy's brow as he worked his way closer to Mulhouse. He'd expected controversy; he'd wanted it. But he hadn't counted on Mulhouse considering it some sort of high crime against the nation.

"Don't you think it was just a college prank?" one of the reporters asked.

Indignation seized Mulhouse's face, reddening it even more. "If it's a prank, it's in extremely poor taste. Whoever was behind it will be found and proper punishment will be meted out."

"Are you saying that hanging these dummies could be considered a criminal act?" another reporter called out.

"The university police have been notified, and our lawyers are looking into the legal aspects at this moment. Right now I'm not discounting anything."

"Dr. Mulhouse, isn't what we see here simply an example of freedom of speech as professed by our founding fathers?" asked a student Indy recognized as the university newspaper's editor.

Mulhouse pointed to "Georgie" behind him, who was now being cut down by one of his assistants. "Young man, hanging an effigy of our country's first president on a lamppost of a university is not an example of freedom of speech. On the contrary, it's a threat to it."

Damn. It wasn't going well at all. Indy looked down at the mortarboard in his hand, and wondered if they could still take away his diploma. Then what? He'd be out of luck, that's what. But he should have thought about that last night.

"What do you make of it, Jones?"

He turned to see Ted Conrad, his history professor. He was in his early thirties, wore an old-time handlebar mustache, and was Indy's favorite instructor.

Indy shrugged and gazed at the nearest dummy. "Someone went to a lot of trouble."

"Looks like a parting shot at Founding Fathers Day to me."

A hint of a smile shadowed Indy's mouth. "Could be, I suppose."

He admired the professor for his forthright manner as well as for his compelling ideas. Conrad had repeatedly told the class to stand up for what they believed, to question authority. Freedom of speech, he'd said, meant expressing yourself any way you wanted as long as it did not harm anyone else. That was what democracy was about. Conrad had also poked gentle fun at the exalted stature of Founding Fathers Day, and when he'd assigned the required class paper, had prodded them, saying: "Keep in mind when you write this paper that you are attending a university, not a church."

Indy had done just that, and now Conrad suspected him; he was sure of it.

"What I see here, Jones," he said, smiling as he motioned toward the hanging figures, "looks a lot like what you were suggesting in your paper."

Indy suddenly realized he was as transparent as

water to Conrad. "I didn't say they should've been hanged. My point was that if the British had won, our great Founding Fathers would have been branded traitors and probably hung."

"Oh, I know your point. I liked that paper. Gave you an A."

Great. He understood.

"Then you can appreciate what I did here," Indy exclaimed. "This was my parting Founding Fathers Day project. Democracy in practice."

Conrad nodded. "Only a week late, but still nicely timed to coincide with your graduation. I admire your boldness, Jones. But you're still going to have to face the consequences, you know."

He looked down at Indy's torn gown, and the white, hairy legs which protruded from beneath it. "Nice outfit, by the way."

Indy felt like an insect trapped on flypaper, still alive but ready to be squashed. He stood at one end of a long conference table in a richly paneled room on the fourth floor of the administration building. It was smack in the gray, cold heart of the university, a place few students ever ventured. Seated around the table were the dean of students, the history department chairman, a member of the university's board of regents, two university lawyers, and Ted Conrad. Except for Conrad, who'd turned him in, all were severe-looking older men in gray suits.

Suddenly, the door opened and President Mulhouse strode into the conference room. He greeted everyone around the table, then looked up at Indy. "Take a seat, Mr. Jones." Mulhouse pointed to a chair at the opposite end of the table.

He'd been roused early yesterday morning by two university police officers and questioned in their office. He'd confessed everything, except Shannon's participation. Dean Williams had been present and after the police were finished, he questioned Indy for another half hour about his personal life. The dean, a distinguished white-haired man, had once been a psychology professor, and his questions reflected that fact. Finally, he'd been ordered to appear here today at ten sharp.

" 'The Nature of American Patriots and Traitors,' " Mulhouse mused, tapping his finger against Indy's Founding Fathers Day paper. "Well, that's better than 'Hanging Heroes,' as the press calls this episode." He peered at the new graduate over the rims of his pince-nez and stroked his chin, one of those practiced academic gestures at which he excelled. "Did you think you could really get away with this, Mr. Jones?"

"I...ah..." Indy cleared his throat and tried to overcome his nervousness. "I'm not trying to get away with anything. My paper is about the fine line between popular heroes and treacherous villains. If the British had won—"

"But the British didn't win, Mr. Jones," the history department chairman interrupted. "And when you hung the effigies of our national heroes, our Founding Fathers, from those lampposts, *you* were acting like a traitor. And that's precisely how most people see it."

"I think we need to consider some mitigating circumstances in our judgment of Mr. Jones," Dean Williams said. "I had a long talk with him yesterday morning, and I believe that he is a disturbed young man. His act was not so much an attack on our Founding Fathers, as against his own father, his only living relative, the renowned medieval scholar Dr. Henry Jones.

"As I understand it, Dr. Jones is a very busy man, and unfortunately he did not have the time to travel from New York for his son's graduation. There apparently has been some resentment on the son's part regarding his father's aloofness, and what took place the night before graduation is a manifestation of those feelings."

It annoyed Indy that the dean discussed him as though he weren't in the room. And what was he saying? Sure, he felt resentful toward his father, but that wasn't why he'd hung the Founding Fathers. He was about to say so when Ted Conrad spoke up.

"That's an interesting analysis. Dean Williams, but I'm not sure it has much to do with Mr. Jones's actions. His motives were obviously related to his Founding Fathers Day paper. The paper itself was well thought out. Rewriting history is, at best, speculative, but the events he described were well reasoned."

Mulhouse's mouth pursed with disapproval. "Are you condoning his actions, Professor Conrad?"

Indy sat forward. "Excuse me, but—"

"No, I'm not condoning what he did," Conrad said, ignoring Indy. "He went considerably beyond what was required or allowed for such a project. I'm just explaining what I think motivated him."

It was obvious that Mulhouse wasn't buying any of it. "Of course you can look at it psychologically or academically. But the fact remains that Mr. Jones was illustrating his disrespect for our nation's founders, and his distaste for Founding Fathers Day, an institution at this university."

They talked a few minutes longer about his motives with everyone agreeing that, whatever they were, he was wrong. Then Indy was asked to leave the room. "Can I say something, please?" he asked as he stood.

Mulhouse frowned at him. "Go ahead, young man, but keep it brief."

"All I want to say is that my father has nothing to do with what I did. I never once thought I was symbolically hanging him."

With that, he turned and walked out of the room and took a seat in the outer office. He sighed heavily. He imagined them continuing their conversation, talking about the alternatives, deciding his future, and trying to dissect his personality in the process. At the very least, he was sure that Mulhouse intended to take away his diploma.

What would he do without a degree? He wouldn't go to Paris. That was certain. He'd have to find a job. But what kind of job? Without a degree he couldn't even teach French or Latin. He didn't want to think about what he might do, because he didn't know.

Several minutes later, the door opened and Dean Williams nodded for him to rejoin them. As Indy sat down, Mulhouse's gaze flicked toward him. "Now, Mr. Jones, you are fortunate that I am someone who listens closely to what others have to say. First of all, our attorneys and I have discussed the possibilities of prosecuting this case. It is our consensus that there will be no benefit for this institution if we carry the matter any further, at least in a legal sense. We prefer to put this behind us."

C'mon, just get this over with. Say it. Say you're taking away my diploma.

"The easiest way of handling the matter would be to simply expel you. But you've already graduated. Lucky for you." His smile was cold and hard. "However, we understand that you are planning to attend the Sorbonne this fall. We can easily refuse to send your records, and it's doubtful whether you would be considered a legitimate student." His pause was deliberate, to let the significance of what he was saying sink in. "But we're going to give you a chance to redeem yourself."

Mulhouse glanced among the others, and they nodded approvingly. "I would like you to apologize to everyone here for what you did, then write a letter of apology, which my office will submit to the press."

Every eye in the room turned toward him as the men waited for him to reply. But he didn't have anything to say. Why should he apologize for something he wasn't sorry for? What about standing up for what he believed in? What about democracy?

Conrad was staring intently at Indy and the message was implicit: *Accept what they're offering you.* Indy looked away from him, irritated that Conrad—who'd betrayed him, who couldn't even stick to his own principles—should now presume to advise him. But if he didn't apologize, he knew Mulhouse would make good on his threat to withhold his records. The lesser of two evils, he thought, and said, "Fine, I'll do it."

Mulhouse nodded, and smiled thinly. "Well, we're waiting. Let's hear it."

Indy looked down at the tabletop. "I apologize to all of you. I'm sorry . . . sorry I did it. Your office will have my letter of apology tomorrow."

Then he pushed away from the table, stood, and walked quickly out of the room. He descended the stairs two at a time until he reached the first floor, then headed across the mall. He didn't know where he was going. It didn't matter. He was literally seeing red.

"Jones, hold on, will you?"

It was Conrad. Indy kept walking.

"Jones."

He stopped, turned. "What do you want?"

"I want to talk to you."

Indy realized he was standing just a few feet from the lamppost where he and Shannon had hung the first mannequin. "I suppose you'd like me to climb up there and hang myself," he said, stabbing a finger at the lamppost. "Or maybe you just want me to apologize to you personally. Is that it?"

"Calm down, Jones. You did just fine in there. Just fine."

"Sure. I did great."

"Listen to me. You made your point. Believe me, you did. I talked to Mulhouse at his home for almost an hour yesterday, and he conceded that he'd overreacted."

"Well, I didn't hear him apologizing."

"No, but you didn't find yourself arrested, either. Those lawyers could have drummed up any number of charges from vandalism to treason. Don't you see?

You won. Hell, if booze were legal, I'd buy you a drink."

"I won, but I had to apologize? What kind of victory is that?"

"Look, Mulhouse has to maintain his cloak of credibility. If you had ripped it off by refusing to apologize, he would have had no choice but to ruin your chances at the Sorbonne."

Indy knew Conrad was right. "What about this apology I have to write?"

"It's your chance to explain to everyone what you were doing. Just don't gloat; say you know it was a mistake."

"Yeah. I suppose."

Conrad clasped him on the shoulder. "That's the spirit. Good luck in Paris. I envy you. I'm sure you'll do well and find what you're looking for."

As Conrad walked away, Indy thought about what the professor had said. What *was* he looking for? He didn't know, but he had the feeling that he'd recognize it when he saw it.

3

LADY ICE

Paris—October 1922

It was a brisk fall morning and Indy bundled his
leather jacket around his throat as he traipsed along
the boulevard St. Michel. Unlike most of the
Frenchmen he passed on the street, he wasn't wearing
a scarf. Madelaine had given him one last Christmas,
but he hadn't seen her for several weeks and wearing
it reminded him of her.

He leaned forward, pulled his hat low over his
brow, and picked up his pace. He not only wanted to
escape the cold, but he was looking forward to the
lecture this morning in his Greek archaeology class.
The topic was Apollo's Oracle, and he was curious
about the approach Professor Belecamus would take.

He crossed the campus, heading directly to the
classroom building. After two years of studying at the
Sorbonne, he felt he knew the city almost as well as a
native Parisian. But, of course, he would always be a

foreigner here, and oddly enough he liked the feeling. He was an outsider, on the inside.

He was in his third year of a Ph.D. program that focused on ancient written languages, and was taking his second course in classical Greek archaeology. It fit well with his study of Old Greek, but there was also something else about the course that particularly captivated him—the professor.

Everything about her, from the clothes and perfume she wore to the way she talked and walked, was distinctly feminine. And yet, beneath this veneer he sensed a strength and self-possession that intrigued him. The dichotomy hinted at the mystery of this woman and also defined the boundaries of her personal area. *Too close and you're in trouble,* it whispered.

So far that had not been a problem. He was midway through his second course with her and was excelling in it. His knowledge of Old Greek as well as his thorough understanding of Greek mythology made him something of a standout among his peers, but she had acted as if he didn't exist.

A few days earlier, he had approached her after class and asked a couple of questions about her lecture. She'd answered in a brusque tone that matched the cold indifference in her eyes. He refused to be intimidated, and had told her how much he enjoyed her lectures.

"That's nice," she'd said, then excused herself and brushed past him.

Dorian Belecamus was Lady Ice. That was the way he thought of her. Yet, ice could be melted, and somewhere below her thick protective coating there must be a warm, friendly woman who longed for intimacy.

Or so he fantasied.

Lost in thought, he collided with someone as he entered the classroom and realized it was she. He dropped to one knee to retrieve the notebook that had slipped from Belecamus's hand. His eyes shifted to her trim legs, which were just inches from his head. On most days she dressed in a long skirt and a white blouse covered by a sleeveless velveteen waistcoat. But today she wore a shorter plaid schoolgirl dress that made her look as if she might be one of the students rather than the instructor.

She crouched and plucked up a paper that had slipped out of the notebook. They stood at the same time and their eyes met; hers were lovely, wide and dark, almost black. "Sorry, Dr. Belecamus. I didn't see you."

"Thanks, Jones." She flicked a hand at her thick raven hair. It was tied back with a bow and set off her compelling eyes, high cheekbones, and full mouth. "Nice running into you. See me after class. I have something to talk to you about."

Abruptly, she turned away and walked to the podium. Indy gazed after her, astonished that she'd actually smiled at him. He glanced around the classroom, expecting to see looks of envy from the men, knowing glances from the women. But no one seemed to notice. He'd broken, or at least cracked, the cake of ice that encased Dorian Belecamus, and no one cared. What was with these guys? Their expressions were as inscrutable as the mugs on the skulls that stared out from the cases that lined the walls of the room. The

French were supposed to be lovers, but none of them seemed to think there was anything special about their instructor.

He sat down at a desk on the aisle, opened his notebook, and tried to think of reasons she would want to see him. He could think of none. A plain-looking girl with stringy brown hair and wire-rimmed glasses leaned over toward him from the next seat. "God, did you see how she's dressed today?" she whispered. "Like she thinks she's one of us."

No comparison, Indy thought. Worlds apart. Worlds improved. "She's not. Not even close," he said in a commiserating tone. He turned back to his notebook, cutting off the conversation.

"The topic today is one with which I am intimately familiar," Belecamus began. Ironic, he thought. She was intimate with a dead city.

"As a child I visited the ruins of Delphi during the early years of the modern restoration, which began in 1892." Her eyes darted to the door and a late arrival squirmed under her gelid stare as he found a seat. "As a high school student and later in college, I spent my summers working first as a volunteer, then as a paid assistant at the site. Delphi became the focus of my graduate study, and my Ph.D. thesis. Before coming to teach here, I spent five years as the chief archaeologist at the ruins while associated with the University of Athens."

She looked down a moment, and smiled to herself. "One of my assistants once made the mistake of jokingly referring to me as Pythía. As we all know Pythía was the name of the succession of women who served as Apollo's Oracle, or the Oracle of Delphi. To become Pythía a woman had to be from a poor farmer's family, more than fifty years old, and not particularly intelligent." Her eyes roamed around the room. "I hope you can understand why I did not feel particularly charmed by the comment."

This elicited a collective laugh from the class. Belecamus definitely fit neither the age bracket nor the intelligence quotient, and she most likely was not from a poor family, Indy thought.

"Pythía made her pronouncements from the altar in the Temple of Apollo, where she sat on a copper-and-gold tripod set above a fissure in the earth. Intoxicating vapors supposedly rose from the aperture, causing the woman to enter a frenzied trance." She smiled again, as if at some private joke, and her gaze settled on Indy. "One witness from the first century A.D. described Pythía's transformation this way: 'Her eyes flashed, she foamed at the mouth, her hair stood on end.' Then she would reply to the question which had been put to her."

Indy suddenly felt as though she were speaking only to him, that the rest of the class no longer mattered. Heat crept up the back of his neck. His eyes remained riveted on her, taking in the way the light slipped over her black hair and glinted in her dark eyes.

"Her answer was always an incoherent babble of words and phrases. Incoherent to all, that is, except the temple priests, who interpreted them for the petitioner." Belecamus looked over the class. "By the way, does anyone know what the word Delphi means? Mr. Jones, our Greek scholar, how about it?"

So, she *had* been looking at him, and she *was* aware of his study of ancient Greek.

"It means 'place of the dolphin.' "

She nodded. "Okay. But tell me, why is it called that?"

Indy had learned the mythical history of Delphi as a child, long before he even knew that Greece was a country. "Apollo arrived at the shrine in the form of a dolphin."

"And what did he find there?"

He suddenly felt as if he were twelve years old again and his father was drilling him on the myths he'd assigned him to study. But Dorian Belecamus was hardly his father. "A dragon named Python. It was the serpent-son of Gaea, the earth goddess and Poseidon, the earth shaker. Python lived in a cave on the mountain and spoke prophecies through Pythian priestesses."

"And what happened?"

"Apollo killed the dragon, and tossed him into a crevice in the earth."

"Thank you, Mr. Jones." Her eyes flicked away from him and darted around the room. "Now let's move away from the mythological aspects to our historical knowledge of Delphi."

She explained that for more than a millennium, from approximately 700 B.C. to A.D. 362, the mountain retreat had been the site of an oracle. She moved away from the podium as she continued talking. It was obvious she didn't need any notes. "At the height of its influence, Delphi was the seat of power in the Mediterranean, virtually scripting the political history of the region. Hardly any action of consequence was taken by the rulers without consulting the oracle. Even skeptical philosophers including Plato and Socrates held the Oracle in high regard. Over the years, Delphi accumulated a vast treasure of gold and marble statues, paintings and jewelry, all tributes from clients."

"Were the predictions actually accurate?" one of the students asked.

"I was just getting to that. The predictions were often worded in ambiguous phrases open to varying interpretations," she said. "However, one of the possibilities usually was accurate. Let me give you a few examples."

When asked how the Greeks would fare against a Persian attack in 480 B.C., the Oracle said to trust the "wooden walls." Although the meaning of the walls was debated, the Greeks successfully defended themselves in their wooden fleet of ships even though they were surrounded. "So those who interpreted the 'wooden walls' as wooden ships were proved correct," she concluded.

When the Roman emperor Nero was warned: *Beware of seventy-three*, he chose to interpret the prediction as meaning that he would die at the age of seventy-three. Instead, he was overthrown at age thirty-one by Galba, who was seventy-three. "Some predictions were accurate in only an ambiguous or even a cynical sense," she continued. "For instance, Croesus was told that if he invaded neighboring Cyrus he would destroy a mighty empire. He did: his own."

Hocus-pocus, Indy thought. He doubted that Plato or Socrates gave a damn about the oracle. They gave lip service to the oracle only because it was the religion of the time; to defy that authority would have cost them dearly.

Indy knew from his studies that the powerful priests who interpreted the babblings of Pythía were at the center of the Amphyctionic League, a coalition of Greek city-states, and were therefore well informed about important activities through the region. They simply used the oracle to create an aura of truth to their proclamations. In effect, the old woman called Pythía was simply a ritualistic vehicle of no actual consequence.

He also knew that his father would lash out at him if he ever said such a thing to him. Reducing Apollo's Oracle to a form of political corruption lacking any mystical reality was heresy. But all through his childhood, Indy had watched his father become increasingly mired in mystical musings that had taken over his life, and virtually ruined his own.

He raised his hand. "What exactly were those vapors that Pythía breathed when she made her prophecies?"

Belecamus sounded amused by the question. "Ah, the legendary 'mephitic' gases, as they were called. Who knows? Legend has it that the vapors came from the rotting carcass of Python."

"Fortunately, scientists don't take myths and legends as fact," Indy responded. "That's where religion and science part."

Belecamus stopped in front of him. Indy's eyes were drawn to her strong, tawny legs bare almost to her knees. "So what do you think the vapors were, Mr. Jones?"

He raised his eyes from her legs. For a moment he didn't answer. Her presence so near him nearly overwhelmed him. He cleared his throat and gathered his thoughts. She challenged him, and he would meet her head on. "Most likely they were a mixture of burning incense and bay leaves. Pythía inhaled the mixture and chewed narcotic laurel leaves to enter a trance state. The so-called vapors were just another way for the priests to mystify and ritualize the activities."

Belecamus crossed her arms. "You're very rational, Mr. Jones. That's good. But sometimes we need to spur our imaginations in archaeology. Myths are often a spring-board to truth and understanding."

"They can also baffle and mislead, and too often are taken as the truth themselves," he responded. "Even by intelligent people."

His father, for instance.

Belecamus smiled, and moved back to the podium. "Well said. I hope everyone here understands the double nature of myths."

As the hour neared its end, Belecamus said she wanted to make an announcement. "This lecture on Delphi, as you know, has been scheduled for weeks. But oddly enough it coincides with an urgent matter at Delphi. Just two days ago there was a minor earthquake in the area."

"Was there much damage?" someone asked.

"The quake caused the earth to buckle, and a crevice has opened in Apollo's Temple. But on the bright side, there apparently has also been a new discovery—a stone tablet has been spotted protruding from inside the chasm."

"What's on it?" someone else asked.

"We don't know yet. I'll be leaving Paris shortly to inspect the site. What this means is that my teaching assistant will take over the course for the remainder of the semester."

Indy felt a sudden vacancy in his chest, an absence of vital organs, as though his heart had been suctioned out. "I want to wish you all the best for the semester. You've been a very attentive group. I'll miss you."

Everyone applauded. As a line of students filed past Belecamus, wishing her well, Indy remained at his desk. Finally, as the last few students left, he stood up and approached the podium.

"Mr. Jones, I hope I'm not keeping you from anything. Another class? A girlfriend waiting in the hall, perhaps?"

"No. Not at all."

"Good. I asked you to wait because I wanted to tell you more about my immediate plans."

"You do?"

Her eyes locked on his. Her look was as penetrating and intimate as an embrace and its intensity astonished him. "Would you be interested in accompanying me to Delphi as my assistant?"

"Me?"

"Yes. You are my best student, and I'll need help from someone not associated with the University of Athens. Politics, if you know what I mean."

"Well, I'm not, uh, sure that I can leave right away," he stammered. "I mean, it's the middle of the semester."

She waved a hand. "Don't worry. I'll take care of everything with the university. My emergency leave was approved, and you'll receive credit for field study. Your basic costs will be covered by my research budget. What do you say?"

Indy wasn't quite sure how to respond. On the one hand, he was ecstatic. But on the other, her assumption that he would simply drop everything irritated him. Besides, archaeology wasn't even his field of study.

"It's kind of sudden."

She took a step closer to him, and smiled. "It'll be worth it, Henry."

He wanted to correct her, to tell her to call him Indy, that Henry was his father. But just the fact that she'd addressed him by his first name was a major breakthrough. It was as if some invisible barrier between professor and student had been pierced.

To act familiar was saying that you were equals, and she'd made it clear from the first day of class that she was not their equal. She'd not only been schooled in Greek archaeology since her teens, but she was *of* the Greek culture. It was in her blood. In her class she was the authority, the living source of knowledge, and they were sponges, there to absorb her wisdom.

And now she was giving him what might be the chance of a lifetime. *It will be worth it.* Of course, she'd meant the opportunity to work at Delphi, but hadn't she hinted at more? Or was he just imagining it? "I'd like to think about it, but it sounds ... interesting." Such a weak word, but nothing else came to mind.

"Don't wait too long, Henry." Her voice was low and breathy. "Opportunities like this don't come along every day."

4

DADA AND JAZZ

Indy opened the door of the Jungle, a *boîte* in Montparnasse. It was early and he was relieved to see that the tables the Dada crowd usually claimed near the door were empty. He wasn't in any mood to listen to their banter. They were, for the most part, arrogant cynics who enjoyed insulting virtually anyone who walked in the door.

He looked around, his eyes adjusting to the dim light. The ceiling was layered with copper, the walls were wooden, and the small bar was trimmed with copper. Hanging high overhead were several dim Victorian candelabras, and a balcony with more tables encircled the place. At one end of the nightclub, under a lip of the balcony, was a small wooden stage. A single red light bulb glowed above it, spilling light onto an upright piano and a set of drums.

Only three or four tables were occupied, and at one of them near the bar Indy spotted a lone figure bent over in concentration as he scribbled something on a sheet of paper. Light from a burning candle stuck inside an empty wine bottle streaked the man's red hair. Indy strolled over and pulled out a chair.

"Hey, Jack."

"Indy," Shannon said without looking up. "Kinda early."

"I know."

He eased down in the chair, and noticed how a strand of Shannon's unkempt hair hung dangerously close to the candle's flame. His old college roommate had been living in Paris for the past year, after quitting his job with the trucking company in Chicago. Although he'd kept his bargain with his family and hadn't played in any clubs, he'd practiced nightly in his apartment, collected dozens of new jazz records, and all the while saved his money and planned his escape to Paris.

"I want to talk to you about something."

"Go ahead." Shannon looked up for the first time. "What's on your mind?"

He told Shannon about Belecamus's offer. "I just heard about it today, and I'm still trying to sort everything out."

Shannon set his pencil on the table. "Let me buy you a drink. I think you need one." He raised a hand, caught the eye of the bartender, and ordered two Pernods.

"Tell me more about this woman. This professor of yours."

"Not really much to tell. I don't know her very well." A sly smile altered the shape of his mouth. "Not yet, anyway."

Shannon didn't seem amused. "If I were you, I'd

ask around before I took off with her. I'd find out
what she's all about."

Shannon, the analyst. "Oh, come on. You think
she'd just make this up so she can go home to Greece
in the middle of the semester and take me with her?"

"I don't know. It seems to me that she could be
playing you for a sucker."

"Jack, for chrissake, we're not on the South Side
making some gangster deal."

Shannon stared coldly at him, and Indy realized it
was the wrong thing to say.

"I'm sorry. It's just that if you'd sat in on one of her
classes, you'd know she isn't that type. She's serious,
intelligent."

"And beautiful," Shannon added. "Right?"

"That too."

"Just watch yourself. It sounds sort of suspicious
to me."

"Why?"

"Look, if you were an archaeology student, I
wouldn't think twice about it. But you're not."

Indy shrugged off the remark. "Look, it's an opportunity, a good one, and I don't want to pass it up
on account of some vague suspicion."

Shannon held up his hands. "Hey, I'm not arguing
with you. I'm just telling you what I think."

"You know how ambivalent I've felt about life as a
scholar. Maybe this is what I've been looking for—a
career with some adventure."

"I'm not sure about the career, but I bet your professor's going to be an adventure. Hell, I don't know.
Maybe it's just what you need."

As their drinks arrived, Indy looked around and was

surprised by the number of tables that were now occupied. It was as if a crowd had seeped out of the wall. "To Greece," Shannon toasted. "Hope it works out."

Indy sipped his Pernod, then nodded at the scrap of paper in front of Shannon. "What were you writing?"

"Just a song."

"A song? For the band?"

"Sure."

"Who's going to sing?"

"The band" was Shannon on cornet, a piano player from Brooklyn whose professional experience had been limited to performances at bar mitzvahs, and a Parisian drummer who'd never played jazz until he'd heard Shannon's records. None of them sang as far as Indy knew. Shannon waved the paper in the candlelight.

"I'm looking for a singer. A woman. She's got to be real sultry with a deep voice. No sopranos. If we were in Chicago I could go down to the Gardens or Dreamland and have my choice of ladies fitting the bill."

"I suppose. Not too many of them visiting Paris, though."

"Oh, they'll be here, Indy." He leaned forward, his eyes bright with sudden excitement. "You look at the crowds we get here with this make-do band. They're hungering for jazz in this town. The bands will be coming here. Lots of 'em. Listen and tell me what you think. This is called 'Down in the Quarter.'" Shannon frowned at the paper, then started reciting:

> *"You know I fled Chicago*
> *Late in twenty-one.*

Floated on 'cross the water,
And never did see the sun.
Finally landed in the Quarter,
Left side of the Seine.
But found so many Americans
thought I was back from where I came.

Down in the Quarter;
Down in the Quarter.
Meet you tonight
Down in the Quarter.

Shannon shrugged. "That's all I got so far."

"Why don't you say, *thought I was going insane,* for your last line on the first verse instead of *back from where I came?*"

"Because it's not true. Besides, the number of beats is wrong."

Indy nodded. "I like it. Never knew you wrote songs."

"Well, it's just words on paper now, but I think I've got some real gutsy love songs in me. Gotta find that singer, though."

Indy laughed. "Ha. I think you're looking for more than just a singer."

They both turned as they heard a ruckus near the door. Chairs clattered. People shouted. Indy peered over his shoulder. "What's going on?"

"Looks like they're arguing about the table."

"The Dada gang. Should've guessed," Indy said dryly.

They had taken over two tables on either side of the door, and now one of the men was rapping on the

table and chanting what sounded like *czar* ... *czar* ...
czar.... The other chimed in: *arf* ... *arf* ... *arf* ....

"What are they saying?"

"Tzara and Arp. Tristan Tzara is a poet. Jean Arp
is an artist. I heard they were going to be here tonight."

"So it's going to be a Dada sort of evening," Indy
said unenthusiastically.

Shannon knocked back the rest of his drink.
"They're really not a bad bunch. Just sort of abrasive
sometimes toward anyone they see as standing for traditional ways."

"Toward anyone who walks in the door," Indy remarked. "They rub me the wrong way."

"They're making a break, Indy. We need people
like that to wake us up sometimes."

"I agree, but they're as dependent on traditions as
anyone. Maybe more so."

"How can you say that?"

"Where would they be without tradition, Jack? If
there were no traditions, there would be no basis for
nontraditional art."

Shannon grinned, shook his head. "Yeah, I guess
so. But like I said, we need people who show us a way
of breaking the old molds. If we don't do something
different soon, we'll blow ourselves up in another
war."

"You're making a break, Jack, but I bet you don't
spit on priests and nuns. How's that sort of behavior
going to stop us from making wars?"

"Indy, they spat on their own friends. It was an
event, you know. They were just dressed like nuns

and priests." Shannon stood up. "So you staying around?"

"Just for the first set."

"Listen, you serious about Greece?"

"I don't know, Jack. I've gotta think about it."

He punched Indy on the shoulder. "I've got the feeling you're going."

The club was crowded by the time the band was midway through the set. Indy emptied his second glass of Pernod just as a solo by Shannon came to a close. The green, licorice-tasting drink was taking its effect, and he felt like walking. He debated whether he'd go over to the bar for one more drink or leave right away.

He pulled on his leather jacket, and looked for his hat. He peered under the table and on the other chairs. Finally, he reached up and felt it on his head. Yeah, it was definitely time to leave. He stood up and looked toward the stage. Shannon was pattering about the next song.

"I first heard this tune in a place called Dreamland in the Windy City," he said as Indy threaded his way through the tables. "The song's by Freddie Keppard's band. Kep doesn't record his music. Says he's afraid people will steal his tunes. He's right because I remembered this one. It goes something like this."

As the song began and Indy headed toward the door, the dadaists looked him over. "Hey, where'd you get that jacket?" one of them called out. "You going on a bombing mission?"

Everyone at the two tables started chanting: *Arp, Arp, Arp, Arp*. Like a pack of seals, Indy thought. A real swell bunch.

"You got something against our German brothers?" another shouted in Indy's face.

"Save it for an old lady or a nun," he snapped, and moved on. As he reached for the door, something hit him in the back; alcohol splattered his neck. He stopped and turned.

"That's for the Red Baron's mother, ace," a bespectacled man yelled from the table on his left.

"*Tzara, Tzara, Tzara, Tzara,*" the crowd shouted in cadence.

Indy stepped over to the man, jerked the chair out from under him, then grabbed the edge of the table and stood it on end. Drinks crashed to the floor. The wine bottle with the candle in it shattered. The flame hissed for a moment, then went out.

Suddenly, the music stopped and everyone in the club turned to see what was going on. No one moved or said a word for a long moment, then a voice boomed from the stage.

"That's my friend, Indiana Jones, all the way from Chicago," Shannon said. "He turned over a table on the South Side one night, but that was his own table. I think he was looking for his hat."

"What an asshole," someone said.

"Hey, do our table, man."

Indy started backing toward the door, but Shannon wasn't finished. "Then another time, this is a true story, he hung George Washington, the first president of the United States, and three of his friends from lampposts at the University of Chicago. Imagine that. A real traditional sort of guy. Well, he had his reasons. But watch out for him next Bastille Day."

Indy smiled, tipped his hat toward the stage, and

left the Jungle. As he walked down the street, he felt the dampness on his neck and hair chilling him. But he ignored it. It was his own fault. Why had he let the bastards get the better of him? He could've just ignored them and left. Instead, he'd played their game with them, and they'd got just what they wanted—a reaction.

He wandered aimlessly around the Latin Quarter, his thoughts drifting from dadaists to his impending decision. Maybe it *was* time for him to leave Paris. He needed a change; he needed something.

He passed a theater with a marquee advertising several serials from *The Perils of Pauline*. He slowed, and glanced at the poster in the front window, which showed a blonde hanging by her fingertips from a cliff. He smiled. He'd grown up on that stuff. Pauline never failed to get herself in a bad fix. If she wasn't dangling from an airplane or facing a roaring locomotive, she was trapped in a snake pit, sinking in quicksand, or chained in a dungeon. He looked at another window displaying coming attractions: *The Death Ray, The Poisoned Room,* and *The Blood Crystals.* He would be gone before the serials arrived, he thought. He moved on. Now he knew he was leaving.

He walked for nearly an hour and finally found himself back in Montparnasse and outside a neighborhood dance hall. He knew he'd stopped here because this was Madelaine's favorite *bal musette,* and one of the first to move from the Luxembourg district. Soon, no doubt, they would all be located in the Latin Quarter. Popular trends, it seemed, always followed the artists by a few years, and the bohemian crowd was well ensconced here, just as the Impressionists of the last century had been in the Montmartre district.

Inside, dancers were fox-trotting to an accordion player and a violinist. The crowd was young, and well behaved compared to the Jungle or any of the *boîtes*. Once on the dance floor, the men never even spoke to the women they asked to dance. It was considered uncouth. In some ways, things hadn't changed much since the days of the minuet.

"Indy, I haven't seen you for ages. How are you?" Madelaine said in her high squeaky voice. He turned and she planted a light kiss on his cheek. She was as vibrant and bright-eyed as ever. Her short, bobbed hair curled around her sharply sculptured face, softening it.

"I'm okay. How about you?" He cursed himself for not noticing her first. He hadn't really expected to see her and didn't particularly want to talk to her. But now he didn't have a choice.

"I'm wonderful, and it's a wonderful night." She tilted her head, listening to the music as a new song began. "Do you want to dance? We can do the java to this one." Her hand slid down his arm and gripped his fingers. She took a couple of steps and her body swayed in front of him.

"No thanks. I'm not up to dancing tonight." Madelaine was her usual exuberant self, the life of the party, and acting as if nothing had come between them.

"You're no fun, Indy," she pouted.

"I'm going to Greece," he blurted, as though his pending trip would make him more interesting to her, worthy of her attention.

"What? Greece? How splendid. Can you take me along? I'd love to see Greece."

Short memory, he thought. "I seem to remember your saying you didn't want to see me again because you thought we were getting too serious. You wanted to be free, I think that's the way you put it."

"Well, I am free. We don't have to get married to see Greece, do we?"

"It's an archaeology field trip to Delphi. I'll be working and I can't take anyone with me."

"Oh, so you need to be free!"

Indy grinned. "You got it."

"Madelaine, there you are," a man called out as he approached them. He glanced at Indy. "Jonesy, what a surprise. Give up on the dead languages for the night?" Then he looked at Madelaine again. "We going to dance, love?"

Indy knew the handsome, young British man as Brent, one of Madelaine's acquaintances. Like her, he seemed to do nothing but float from dance hall to dance hall, café to café with the same crowd. There were more like him in the Latin Quarter every day. If given a choice of spending the evening with Brent and his crowd or being abused by the dadaists, Indy would be hard pressed to choose.

"Brent, guess what, Indy's going to Greece, to a place called Delphi, and he won't take me with him." Her voice squeaked to a new high.

Brent shrugged. "I'll take you to Greece any time you want, darling. Paris is getting so dreadfully boring. But let's dance right now. My legs won't stop moving."

With that, Madelaine was swept away onto the

dance floor. She turned once, waved and laughed, then vanished into the crowd.

Indy felt sick. Why hadn't he just left his past alone? Now more than ever he was anxious to move into the future. "Good-bye, Madelaine," he said without regret, and turned away.

5

ENCOUNTERS

It was almost noon as Indy pulled on his sneakers and jacket. Normally on a Saturday he would take a book and walk down to the corner for a lunch at the Deux-Magots. But today he was going to stroll over to Le Dôme, the café where Dorian Belecamus had suggested they meet. She would answer any of his questions, and he would make a decision. It sounded simple. But somehow, he had the feeling that it wasn't going to be simple at all.

He picked his fedora off a hook on the wall. Under it was a coiled bullwhip, the only decorative item in his two-room abode. The apartment was located above a bakery on the rue Bonaparte, a few blocks from the Sorbonne. One room was a tiny kitchen with an icebox, a gas stove, and a cupboard. In the other was a mattress and box spring on the floor, a wooden table with two chairs, and a low bookcase with books strewn on and around it. He had lived in the apartment for two years, and the place looked virtually the same as when he arrived.

He inhaled deeply as he descended the stairs, but the tantalizing smell of fresh bakery goods was faint. Usually, when he left for classes, the smell was so overpowering he stopped for a couple of croissants, which he ate en route to the university. This morning, however, he'd slept late after staying up until three, finishing a new novel called *Ulysses*. After he closed the seven-hundred-thirty-page tome and fell asleep, he dreamed of Madelaine and Belecamus, but both women were in Dublin and, not surprisingly, had the same quirks and concerns as James Joyce's Molly Bloom.

As he headed toward Montparnasse, his thoughts returned to the decision he had to make in the next couple of hours. Last night he thought he had made up his mind, but now he wasn't so sure. Of course Greece was an opportunity. But was it practical? Even though he'd get field-work credit for the archaeology course, he'd still have to retake his other courses. In a sense, he would be penalized.

Besides, what was the purpose? Did he really have an interest in pursuing an archaeology career? Or was he just intrigued by Dorian Belecamus? The fact was he had an interest in both, but he doubted that either was a long-term pursuit for him. He'd already taken two years of graduate school in linguistics. How many more would he need to qualify as an archaeologist? It didn't make sense.

When he arrived at Le Dôme, he looked around the terrace. In spite of the brisk fall weather, a few tables were occupied, probably by tourists who had heard the French always ate on sidewalks. To accommodate them, glowing coals in a large *brasero* warmed the air, at least in one corner. Outdoor cafés were fine with him, but only when the weather was moderate.

He stepped inside the café and scanned the tables. He was a few minutes early and apparently had arrived ahead of Belecamus. His eyes settled on a man in a tweed coat who was seated at a table by himself. There was a book to one side of him, and he held a pencil in his hand above a pad of paper. He looked familiar, and now he was staring intently at Indy.

He met his gaze, glanced away, then looked back at him. The man was rising from the table, moving toward him, threading his way through the crowded tables. Who was he, a writer he had met? Probably looking for a sucker to buy him a drink. He was approaching the wrong guy.

"Henry Jones, my God. How are you?"

Indy stared at him for a moment before his face fell into place. "Professor Conrad. What're you doing here?"

Conrad laughed. "Come over, have a seat. It's a long story."

Indy looked around once more for Belecamus, then followed Conrad to his table. "I'm meeting someone for lunch, but she isn't here yet."

"Wait here until she arrives. Or better yet, why don't you both join me?"

As Indy sat down, the waiter appeared and they ordered cups of café au lait. His old history professor hadn't changed much in two years. His sandy hair was still combed the same way, his blue eyes remained vibrant and alive, and his mustache still drooped over the sides of his lips. But he seemed less formal somehow, looser, more relaxed, as if he'd found something in Paris that had eluded him in the States.

"It's good to see you," Indy said. "Quite a surprise."

"You know, I've thought about you more than once since you graduated."

Considering the situation the last time he'd seen Conrad, he didn't know whether that was a compliment or not. "So why aren't you teaching?"

"Mulhouse refused to give me tenure, and this past summer my contract wasn't renewed."

"Why not? You're a great teacher. Probably the best I had at the university."

"Thanks, Jones." He combed his fingers back through his hair. "Mulhouse never gave me a reason." He shrugged. "He wasn't required to. But the scuttlebutt was that he wanted me out ever since that fiasco over Founding Fathers Day."

No wonder the man had been thinking about him. "I'm sorry. I guess my silly prank had more repercussions than I'd imagined."

"It's not your fault." He smiled and leaned forward. "Ever since then, I made a point of mentioning your particular way of celebrating the day to my classes. I always related the story in a humorous vein, and apparently Mulhouse heard about it."

"So how long have you been here?"

"Just a few days. I'm writing a novel that takes place in Paris during the revolution."

"This is the city for writers. Seems like there's a novelist or two in every café."

"I know. I saw Booth Tarkington the other day. Talked to him for a bit." He tapped the book on the table. "Had to pick up one of his books after that. *Seventeen.* Have you read it?"

"A few years ago." It was about an American boy confronting adolescence; that was all he recalled, except that the kid had a younger sister who ate bread with applesauce. "I've seen James Joyce in here."

"You have?" Conrad looked around as if expecting to see the Irish author. Then his eyes settled on someone approaching the table.

"Henry Jones. There you are." Indy turned and saw Dorian Belecamus strolling up to the table. She wore a blue robe and a white turban. Like Conrad, she'd stepped out of her professorial character. Both men rose to their feet, and Indy introduced the two professors.

"And you can both call me Indy, instead of Henry. That's my father's name."

Belecamus seemed annoyed; she looked about the cafe as if in search of another table.

"It seems the place is full," Conrad said stiffly, reacting to her obvious unease. "You're welcome to join me for lunch."

"Oh, I don't want to intrude," she replied.

"It won't be an intrusion."

Realizing there were no other options, she nodded and took a seat. Indy led the conversation, telling Belecamus about Conrad's history course, and the reason he'd lost his job. At first, Belecamus seemed indifferent, but as Conrad filled in details about the hanging heroes episode her interest peaked. She glanced several times at Indy, and asked a couple of pointed questions about the university's reaction and how he dealt with it.

When the waiter walked over, Indy and Belecamus both ordered fresh oysters and *pommes frites*, and Conrad ordered another café au lait.

"In Greece, there would have been no question about it," Belecamus said when the waiter walked away. "You would go to jail if you hung an effigy of any of our leaders. Weren't you concerned about the possible repercussions?"

"Not when it was happening. Only afterward."

She shook her head. "Then why did you do it?"

"I wanted to make a point."

"But you also got a thrill from it, didn't you?"

He shrugged. "I suppose." He'd never really put it into words, but that was exactly how it had been for him.

She laughed. It was a full, throaty sound, delightful. "You have a reckless streak in you. A bit of a rebel." She sat back in her chair. "Indy." The word seemed to roll off her tongue like music. "I never heard such a name, but I like it. And you can call me Dorian."

Her hand brushed his as she sat forward again, a quick, deliberate touch that he felt all the way to his toes, like a mild electrical shock. It wasn't just the touch itself, but the realization that Lady Ice wasn't quite as impenetrable as he had believed.

Conrad glanced inquisitively between the two of them, but didn't comment. Indy still hadn't said anything about the impending trip to Greece, and Conrad was undoubtedly puzzled about their relationship. He told him about her offer.

"Delphi. Sounds fascinating." He nodded thoughtfully. "So are you taking the professor up on it?"

"I haven't really decided."

"Why not?" Belecamus asked.

"My field is linguistics, not archaeology. I'd be wasting a semester. I don't know. I'm not sure what I want to do."

She averted her eyes and gazed toward the door as though she wished she weren't there anymore. "You Americans," she said with a sigh. "You're a colony here. Writers, artists, students. You're fortunate. You can live in a foreign country and be right at home with your own compatriots. And yet all you do—most of you—is complain. You're just an unhappy bunch, lost in a sea of culture."

There was no rancor in her voice; she was just stating the facts as she saw them.

Indy started to disagree, but the waiter appeared with their meals. They ate in silence for a while, a silence that wasn't entirely comfortable. Finally, Belecamus popped an oyster in her mouth, and pointed her fork at Indy. "You say you're interested in archaeology and have been since you were a boy. So why're you studying linguistics?"

"My father taught me languages early. Languages and myths. Some weeks he would only speak French to me, and other weeks it was Spanish or German. I was studying Latin an hour a day after school when I was nine. I knew the Greek myths by the time I was ten. He always said he was preparing me for a career as a scholar, a linguistics scholar."

She sighed and shook her head. "That was your father. What about you? What do *you* want to do?"

The way she said that bothered him, but only because it mirrored his own feelings. "Something exciting. I guess I just don't like the idea of spending the rest of my life in libraries, poring over manuscripts of dead languages."

"Then why don't you switch to archaeology?" Conrad asked. "You'll get more variety."

"I don't particularly want to be a student my whole life, either."

Belecamus pushed her plate to the side. "Look, Indy, if the tablet that has been discovered at Delphi is important, and I have the feeling it is, you'll be able to use it as the basis for your Ph.D. With your background, I'd say you can have your doctorate easily in two years. One year of intense study, then your thesis, and you'll be an archaeologist. If it doesn't work out, you fall back on linguistics."

That last part didn't appeal to him. If he made a commitment to archaeology, he would stick with it. No falling back. "What if the tablet isn't what you think?"

"Then you choose something else for your thesis," she answered brusquely.

"Don't worry, Indy," Conrad said. "If you really want it, you'll find what you need."

"All right, I'll do it." There. Quick, Simple.

Belecamus smiled. "Good. I thought you would. We're leaving for Athens tomorrow afternoon. Be at my office at one o'clock. Now I must go." She held out a hand to Conrad. "Nice meeting you, and good luck with your writing."

A moment later, the door to the cafe closed behind her. Indy glanced at Conrad. "So what do you think?"

"I think archaeology is something you'll enjoy, and you'll do very well at it."

"What about Professor Belecamus?"

Conrad threaded and unthreaded his fingers. His reply was slow and measured. "I don't know what it is about her, Indy, but I'd be careful. I guess my sense of her is that she is saying one thing, and thinking another."

"You think I should turn down the offer?"

"I didn't say that. It's just that I sense there's more involved than she's telling."

6

ON THE RAILS

The train rumbled along, rolling through the open countryside of southern Italy. Dorian Belecamus gazed out the window toward the shadowy hills that loomed against the plum-colored horizon. The last of the light tipped them in gold, creating a kind of magic about them. But it wasn't the magic of Greece, she thought. Her homeland was a landscape of dramatic contrasts: bleached white houses that dotted the shores of a sea so blue it made her heart ache, mountains the color of ripened grapes, skies burned by the sun.

Soon, she thought. Her self-imposed exile was almost over. By morning they would arrive in Brindisi, where they would take a ship to the port of Piraeus. From there, they would go overland to Athens, and she would be home.

She turned away from the window, reached up, and switched on the reading light on her side of their private compartment. Across from her, Jones was slumped on his left side, his fedora pulled low over his brow.

She smiled as she watched him. No doubt about it, she thought. He was going to prove helpful. He was just what they needed, bright and quick, but not so bright or quick that he would present a danger to them. The quake was a perfect excuse. She and Jones would work at the ruins until the arrangements were made, and the trap set.

She heard a creaking noise; the door had moved. She hadn't closed it tightly, and thought it must be the rush of air down the corridor as someone passed by. But a shadow fell across the crack in the door and she realized someone was standing just outside.

She waited, expecting to hear a tap, and to hear the conductor tell her that dinner was being served. "Who is it?" she demanded when there was no tap.

She took two steps to the door and pulled it open. No one was there. She peered down the aisle and saw a man in a black suit push his way through the doorway to the next car. She glanced back at Jones, saw he was still asleep, then hurried after the man in the suit.

The next car was second class; rows and rows of passengers were reading or resting. No one was in the aisle. He must have sat down. She moved forward, looking at each passenger. She saw a man dressed in black, talking softly to a young girl. A newspaper was spread across his lap and it seemed doubtful that he'd just sat down.

Two rows further, she saw another man dressed in black. He was sleeping. Or did he just look like he was sleeping? He was an elderly man. His breathing was deep and even; his mouth hung open and a spicule of saliva glistened on his lower lip.

She continued down the aisle, where she counted four more men in black. It was useless, and what would she say if she confronted one of them? She would demand to know why he was looking in her compartment; he would deny it, and that would be that.

Then she glimpsed the top of a blond man's head; his face was buried behind an issue of *Punch*. He wore a white shirt and tie. It was Farnsworth, of course. She should have guessed. He must have taken off his black coat, but the fool gave himself away with his English magazine.

She abruptly turned, and retreated from the car. Farnsworth had been following her around campus for the past month. After she'd noticed him and was sure he was watching her, she'd hired an investigator to find out who he was. When she'd found out his name, it was all she needed to know.

Quietly, she slipped back into the compartment. After checking to see that Jones was still asleep, she settled into her seat again and opened a book on her lap. She looked down at it, but she wasn't reading. Her thoughts drifted from Farnsworth to the two most important men in her life, her father and Alex Mandraki.

The things she did for Alex. She didn't love him, but she felt committed to him. She knew, though, that whatever she did for him, she also did for her father. It was he, after all, who had introduced her to Alex, and the middle-aged colonel's future was closely tied to her father's destiny as well as her own. What her father didn't know was that she and Alex were planning on rushing forward into that future. And why not? There was no sense waiting for the inevitable.

But first she had to deal with Farnsworth. He was a trivial matter in the larger scheme, but needed to be handled swiftly and deftly. The train was the ideal place for it. After all, she'd confronted him once and told him to leave her alone. But he'd ignored her warning, and now she could no longer afford the annoyance. If she was going to act, she should do it before she was back in Greece, before Alex found out. It was her problem, after all, not his.

She reached up into the storage compartment above her seat, unstrapped a canvas shoulder bag, and rummaged through her trowels and brushes, the tools of her trade. When her fingers brushed the smooth, cold steel of her favorite hand pick, she smiled. It felt good in hand again. She quickly removed it, and stuffed it in her purse.

Jones was stirring in his sleep as she sat down again. She hooked her foot under his calf, lifted it, let it go. His head jerked. He glanced around, confused, still drugged with sleep, then saw her and smiled.

"Guess I drifted off. What time is it?"

"Almost time for dinner. You've been asleep for more than an hour. Should we go for a cocktail?"

He laid a hand on the stack of books at his side. "I was hoping to work a little more before dinner, but I suppose it can wait."

Indy had brought along a small library on Greek archaeology. His excitement about the prospect of working at Delphi was tempered somewhat by his insecurity about his abilities. It was a quality she intended to use to her own benefit.

When they reached the dining car, they found an empty table. Jones ordered a beer, and Dorian, who normally drank sparingly, asked for a French seventy-five. She would need it for later.

"What kind of drink is that?" Jones asked.

"Champagne and vodka. It's named after a French cannon used in the war."

"Must have quite a kick."

She laughed. "It does at that." She tapped her fingers on the table, scrutinizing him covertly. He seemed nervous, as though he had something to say, but wasn't sure where or how to begin.

"Dr. Belecamus?"

She leaned slightly forward. "Please, don't call me Doctor."

"Dorian." He spoke her name as though testing its sound, savoring its taste. But he didn't say anything more. She sensed he wanted to ask why she had chosen him to accompany her, because he didn't accept her explanation that he was her best student. There were many students in other courses who had far more experience academically and in the field and they both knew it.

"Go ahead. What is it?"

"It's nothing."

"Look, Indy, we're going to be working together for some time, maybe weeks. So it's important for us to be open with each other."

"Open. Yes." He repeated the words with the slow, measured speech of someone who didn't speak the language. "I guess I was wondering what, exactly, you want me to do in Delphi."

Dorian smiled, reached across the table, and touched his hand. "There'll be plenty to do. Don't worry about that. You'll be working and learning. It should be quite an experience."

Though he nodded, he was still uncomfortable. Her gesture had obviously surprised him, as she had known it would. He was definitely going to be easy, she thought. No trouble at all. As compliant as a kitten. Her choice had been an excellent one.

"What I'm trying to say is that I know I don't have experience, but I don't want to do just menial work," he went on. "I mean, I'd like the chance to do something significant."

So that was it. He wanted to be in the center of things. She slowly ran her fingers over the back of his hand. He swallowed and shifted in his chair. His skin flushed. He was staring at her hand. "You'll have that opportunity." *In more ways than you realize.*

Her fingers trailed away from his hand. "In fact, I want you to be the first one to examine the script on the tablet when we bring it up from the crevice. You can put your knowledge of ancient Greek to use."

"Suppose it's not Old Greek, but Linear B?"

Dorian laughed and shook her head. Linear B was the name of the script on tablets found during excavations at Knossos on Crete in 1899. No one yet had been able to crack the code. "You've been reading too much. The chances of a Linear B tablet being found at Delphi are minute. Don't worry about it."

She finished her drink in several swallows, and noted the surprise on Jones's face. She laughed softly.

"What's wrong? Did you think I don't drink, that I never relax or have any fun?"

Jones sipped his beer. "Sometimes, I'm not quite sure what to think of you."

She smiled at him and gazed into his eyes. "Well, I will tell you what I think about you. You not only have intelligence and potential, but you are a very handsome man. I'll admit that if you were an ugly brute I probably wouldn't have asked you along."

The perplexity in his expression amused her. *He's probably never heard a woman speak so bluntly before,* she thought. "So what do you think of me?" She slipped her foot out of her shoe and poked Indy's leg with her toe. "And be honest."

He seemed flustered. "I've never really met a woman like you. I guess you're part of the new women's revolution."

"No. I'm an exception to it."

He looked more perplexed than ever. He no doubt had expected her to agree with him and say that they were in the twenties now. Women were changing, and were no longer willing to be cinctured in dress or spirit. But she had her own ideas about revolution.

"Women are rebelling, Indy, but only in superficial ways—smoking cigarettes in public, getting their hair bobbed. That's not a revolution."

"Well, it's a start."

"The problem with most women, especially the ones your age, is that they refuse to deal with men openly and intellectually. Instead, they prefer subterfuge, intrigue, and sex."

"I guess I never really thought of it that way."

"Well, I have, and I understand it. Most men aren't

ready to deal with women on equal terms. Men don't have to use either subterfuge or intrigue to get their way with women." She reached out and pinched his chest. "They do it right out in the open."

"Most women ask for it. They tease men."

She burst out laughing. "See what I mean? Women ask for it, so anything goes. Women are supposed to be the weaker sex, but let me tell you something. Secretly, most men fear and hate women."

He shook his head, and grinned. "Not me. I'm not afraid of women and I definitely don't hate them. That's the problem... I love women."

By the time their dinner arrived, Indy was filled with expectations. In spite of her dire comments on men, he was sure Dorian would invite him to her berth tonight and he couldn't help but imagine what it would be like with her. He thought of running his hands through her long dark hair, of touching her face, her shoulders, of reading her entire body like a blind man learning braille. He'd never met anyone like her. Never.

"Would you like some dessert?" she asked as they finished their meals.

"Maybe some Italian ice cream."

"Spumoni, of course. I'll go find the waiter. The service is terribly slow."

"No, that's all right, Dorian," he said, but she was already out of her chair and heading down the aisle.

He turned, glancing after her, and saw her pause and lean toward a table where a man was seated by himself. Their eyes locked momentarily, and something flickered between them, something Indy couldn't decipher. Then the man looked away, his eyes flitting about like insects, shoulders twitching nervously. He was about thirty, fair-haired, and slightly overweight. As Dorian disappeared into the next car, the stranger rose to his feet and followed her.

Indy's gaze trailed after him. What the hell was going on? He was tempted to get up and follow them, but decided against it. It was none of his business.

A couple of minutes later, two dishes of ice cream arrived. Indy stared at the multicolored scoop in the dish in front of him. He waited a while longer until the edges of the ice cream started to melt. He quartered it with his spoon, tasted it. *What's taking her so long? What are they doing?* He glanced over his shoulder, then turned back to his dish. Slowly, spoonful by spoonful, he consumed his serving. When he finished, he laid his spoon aside.

Time to take a look around.

He rose from his chair and walked quickly down the aisle of the dining car. The next one, which was the last car of the train, was a bar. It was crowded, but Dorian was nowhere in sight. Neither was the man who had followed her.

He described Dorian to the bartender and asked if he'd seen her. "No," the bartender said with a shake of his head. "Sorry."

"But I saw her walk in here. Just a few minutes ago, and she hasn't left."

He pointed to the far end of the car. "Maybe she went outside."

Outside? He moved through the crowd to the end

of the car, and opened the door. The sweet evening air rushed around him, a scent of countryside and purple skies. He stepped out onto the iron balcony and saw Dorian standing at the railing, smoking a cigarette. For a moment or two, she seemed unaware of his presence. She was as motionless and lovely as a statue in profile, the wind blowing her hair away from her face, one arm crossed at her waist, the other propped against it, holding a cigarette. Then she turned, saw him, and smiled.

"Did you get your ice cream?"

Cool and possessed, he thought, and for a moment "ice cream" turned to ice queen in his mind. He nodded, then gestured toward her cigarette. "I didn't know you smoked."

She tossed the cigarette over the railing and fixed her hands at his waist. "I probably do a lot of things you don't know about."

Indy touched her face and kissed her, a slow, almost hesitant kiss. Her mouth tasted sweet, of exotic fruit, exotic wine, exotic everything. He ran his hands through her raven hair, loving the thickness, the softness, and then she stepped back from him, her mouth still close to his, and whispered, "My ice cream is melting."

"I bet it is."

As he followed her back through the bar into the dining car, it occurred to him that he hadn't seen the blond man, and now the table where he'd sat was empty. A disappearing act.

Maybe he'd imagined the whole thing. Maybe Dorian had stopped to pull up a stocking, and the man had been embarrassed when she'd caught him looking at her. He hadn't followed her, but had gone to the bathroom. By now he'd returned to his seat in one of the passenger cars.

Of course. That must be it.

7

INTRIGUE IN ATHENS

The sun was low by the time they reached the Acropolis, and the city was hidden in a copper haze. But from where they stood, high above Athens, the slanting rays bronzed the magnificent Doric columns of the Parthenon, and Indy gazed in awe.

"I grew up thinking Greece was a legend."

Dorian laughed. "I think I hear echoes of your father."

"His bedtime stories were about the feats of Zeus, Heracles, Poseidon, Hermes, and all the others. Medusa, the Gorgons, Jason and the Argonauts. I heard about them all."

"Well, that sounds like a wonderful childhood," she said, hooking her arm through his.

Yeah, real swell, he thought, but he didn't disagree with her. Not now. He took in a deep breath, as if the magical air surrounding this bastion could somehow preserve the moment.

"What do you think is the single most amazing thing about the Acropolis?" she asked.

He thought back to her lectures, but drew a blank and shook his head.

"That any of it still exists," she said and explained. The Turks stored ammunition in a building called the Propylaea and one day in 1645 it exploded. Forty-two years later, the Venetians blew up the Parthenon. The only reason it still remained was that early nineteenth-century archaeologists restored it to what they believed had been its appearance in the fifth century B.C.

"Now you sound like the professor again." He smiled as he said it just to show her he didn't mean it as a criticism. "This must be a very special place for you."

"It is, of course, but actually my favorite place in Athens is the Tower of the Winds in the Roman Agora, especially at dawn."

"I'll have to see it sometime." Indy gazed over the city below them in the fading light. "Great place to be an archaeologist. All the best ruins are right in your backyard."

He expected her to laugh. She didn't. "Archaeology grew up around this country just as European civilization did."

They moved from the massive columns of the Parthenon and walked over to the Erechtheum, the only other surviving building. "So why do you teach in Paris? I'd think you'd prefer to be here."

"That's complicated. You have to understand that we Greek archaeologists tend to favor the aesthetic aspects of the science. Rather than dirtying ourselves in pits looking for pottery fragments, most of us prefer to study the great works of ancient sculpture. In fact, the chairman of archaeology in all our major universities is actually the chairman of the history of sculpture."

"Really? Why is that?"

"It's a way of compensating for the fact that we are economically and socially behind the northern countries which drew on our legacy. We've only been independent for ninety years, you know, after four centuries of foreign domination. So by focusing on the aesthetic aspects of archaeology, we ever so slightly elevate our present culture."

"You agree with that approach?"

"No, but I understand it. I teach in Paris because it's easier to take a broader approach to the field."

They stopped in front of the Erechtheum and examined the Caryatids, a series of stone maidens who served as pillars on the building's southern porch. The last rays of the sun danced across the faces of the stone goddesses; behind them, light and shadow eddied across the porch. For an instant, Indy thought he saw someone standing near the base of one of the statues.

"You remind me a bit of another student," she said, speaking in such a soft voice that Indy almost thought she was talking to herself. "He was from England. When he came here, he had no sense of our recent history. He knew that Lord Byron died at Missolonghi. That was it."

She was quiet a moment and Indy waited for her to continue. "We should get going," she finally said.

The first lights winked on in the dusky haze over the city. Indy nodded, but his attention was drawn back to the Erechtheum. He peered, as best he could, into the inner recesses of the porch. The light shifted, the glare vanished, and now he could see the porch clearly. There was someone there. No, two people, two men, and they were peering out at them.

"That's odd."

"What?" Dorian asked.

"There're two guys up by the Caryatids watching us."

Dorian swung around as if he'd stabbed her in the back. "I don't see anyone."

"They moved back now."

Dorian took hold of his arm. "Come on."

He didn't know what the hurry was, but he followed her back toward the Parthenon. Below it was a path leading to the road where horses and buggies waited. In Athens, there was a mix of carriages and automobiles, whereas in Paris autos prevailed and horses were a rarity. It was as if Athens couldn't quite decide whether to join the twentieth century.

Dorian tugged on his arm again. "Indy, they're coming after us."

He glanced back. The two men were moving toward the Parthenon, one a few yards ahead of the other. "Why do you think they're after us? They're probably just a couple of tourists."

"Look again." The men had closed the gap. They weren't quite running, but they weren't bothering to disguise the fact that they were in a hurry.

"Let's wait. They're probably not interested in us at all."

Dorian grabbed him by the arm. "Don't be a fool. Run."

They charged forward, hurrying over the rocky

escarpment. Indy felt foolish; he still doubted the men were chasing them. He stumbled and almost pulled Dorian down on top of him. A white-hot pain shot through his ankle.

"Damn it."

"Hurry," Dorian hissed. He winced as he pushed off the ground and hobbled after her.

The shadows had turned a deep purple, making it more difficult to see. They scraped their arms on the heavy thicket as they descended the path, his ankle throbbed and screamed with every step. He kept glancing back, but couldn't see anyone pursuing them.

The ruins were nearly empty and a lone carriage waited at the bottom of the path for stragglers. Dorian rushed over to it, waving her arms at the driver. The man calmly opened the door for her; Indy reeled across the road, limping as he ran.

"You all right, sir?" the driver asked.

"Fine. Let's go."

As the carriage pulled away, Indy glanced out the window into the dusky night. He glimpsed the men just as they reached the road. They stopped, and stared after the carriage as it pulled away.

"They were probably just after the last carriage, not us," he said.

She didn't answer.

Dorian's house was located on a hill in an old neighborhood called Monastiráki, where at any time of the day you could look up and see the Acropolis hovering in the sky like a temple of gods. The house was quaint in appearance, with pilasters at the corners, a tile roof edged with terra-cotta goddesses, and a small yard protected from the street by a wrought iron fence and an abundance of vegetation.

Not bad, Indy thought as they entered the house and he smelled dinner cooking. She'd come home after two years, and it was as if she'd never left. She had another life here that had continued despite her absence. Not only was dinner being prepared by the housekeeper, but a bubble bath awaited Dorian. While she bathed, Indy sat on the bed soaking his swollen ankle in a pail of cold water.

"Hey, Indy," Dorian called.

He looked at the bathroom door. "Yeah?"

"Bring your pail in here so we can talk."

Good idea, he thought. He did want to talk to her and, hey, why not do it while she bathed? A mischievous smile turned on his lips as he raised his foot from the pail. "How come I didn't think of that?"

He set his pail down next to the bathtub and sat on a chair draped with a towel. On the floor next to the tub was a bottle and a wine glass. Dorian held a half-full glass in her hand. "Help yourself to some retsina," she said as he lowered his foot into the pail.

"Thanks. What is it?"

"A wine made from pine sap."

"Pine sap?" He poured himself a glass, sipped it, and made a face.

Dorian laughed. "It grows on you. Believe me. It's very popular. Some people say too popular. You just have to be careful not to overindulge."

He took another sip; his eyes strayed from her face. The sight of her soaking among the bubbles with one leg stretched languidly over the side reminded him of their recent tryst. He saw them entwined in her berth on the train, their movements synchronized with the rattle of the rails below them. Their lovemaking seemed almost surreal now, not like a real memory at all. He still found it hard to believe how rapidly the Lady Ice of Paris had melted in his arms. Yet, here he was, casually watching as she bathed.

Everything since then seemed like a blur to him. They'd left the train yesterday morning, and spent most of the day on the ferry. When they'd reached the port of Piraeus, they'd taken a taxi to Athens. They'd arrived exhausted, and had slept twelve hours.

Today, while Dorian had busied herself with details for the trip to Delphi, Indy had explored the city on his own. First, he'd dutifully spent the morning at the archaeology museum; later, he'd simply wandered around taking in the sights.

"So what do you think of Athens?" she asked.

"I like it, but I can't stop comparing it to Paris."

"And what have you concluded?" She stretched one of her legs, toes pointed toward the ceiling.

The texture of life was different here, he'd decided. The beauty of Paris was seen through the subtle changes in the quality of light. Here the light was harsher, brighter, a contrast to the craggy landscape.

"Greece is earthy, fertile; France is more intellectual, refined."

"I agree."

Both cities were tied to the past, but the past affected each city in different ways. Paris thrived as a center of artistic culture, a creative offspring of past artistic triumphs. Here, even though the past was everywhere, the culture that had flowered was now dormant. Paris was a sculpture still being defined; Athens was a monument, and its people could only stand by and watch it slowly deteriorate.

Yet, in spite of living in the shadows of their forebears, the Greeks still seemed to excel in spirit. He saw them as a gregarious, talkative people who openly expressed their emotions, whether joy, anger, or sorrow. Most of the men were dark, curly-haired, and handsome. They smoked black tobacco and drank endless cups of coffee while they absently fingered beads made of amber or silver. The women, however, seemed resigned to domestic drudgeries and many wore black dresses, as though they were in permanent mourning.

He tried his best to explain his thoughts, but Dorian no longer seemed interested. "Indy, I want to tell you why I thought those men at the ruins were after us."

"Good. I'd like to hear about it."

"First, I should tell you a bit about my family," she said, arching her back as she washed the base of her neck, and the rosy tips of her breasts pushed through the bubbles.

"Your family?" It was difficult to concentrate on what she was saying.

"Yes. My family. You see, Greek peasant girls don't become archaeologists. My father is a shipbuilder, and a large landholder. We even own a couple of islands."

"Entire islands?"

She laughed. "Not large islands."

"He lives here in Athens?"

"He has an estate here, and houses in Rome and London. He's living in Rome right now, and he can't come home."

"Why not?"

"Politics." She uttered the word like a curse. "After Greece won her independence, there was no more nobility left, so those families who became involved in politics were the ones who became wealthy."

"That sounds pretty typical."

"Anyway, when the king decided to invade Turkey last year, my father took exception. He knew that it would end disastrously. And for speaking the truth, he was exiled." The bitterness in her voice was reflected in the tightness of her features. "And is still in exile."

Indy knew that the results of the war with Turkey were exactly what she said. As he understood it, Greece had invaded its neighbor with the hopes of freeing Greeks living outside of Greece. Now the city was flooded with refugees, who had been forced from their homes in the conflict, and the loss of life had been extraordinary. "I guess the invasion didn't solve anything," he said.

"What happened was a horrible mistake. We sent a hundred thousand men and they're still being butchered."

Indy nodded, unsure of what to say. He sipped his retsina and watched her.

"You'd think we would have learned from the Great War. We suffered terribly in our support of Britain and France. The Greek people are tired of fighting, and now we are at it again."

"But what does this have to do with those two men at the Acropolis?"

She rolled the stem of her glass between her fingers, gathering her thoughts. "My father warned me not to come back until things settled down. He said it would be dangerous."

"So you think they work for the king?"

"Possibly."

"Why don't they just stop you from working at the ruins?" he asked.

"The king could certainly block me from returning to Delphi, but he is not a fool. Delphi is a national treasure, and it would look bad for him if he refused to allow me to go back, especially now after the earthquake."

"So you think they're dealing with you covertly, watching you to see what you're doing?"

She handed Indy her empty glass, motioning for a refill. "If they were only watching me, I would not mind. But I believe the king's men, if not the king himself, would like to hurt my father, and if I were killed, they would succeed."

"What are you going to do?"

"Nothing. We're leaving for Delphi tomorrow morning as planned. I refuse to be intimidated."

Indy tipped the bottle, filling Dorian's glass and his own. He decided the retsina wasn't so bad after all. He held out the glass to her, and watched as she soaped one of her thighs with a round sponge.

"Put the glasses down," she said, and slipped her hand around his neck.

"What are you doing?"

She pulled him to her, and retsina spilled on the

floor and in the tub. "I think you need a bath." Her voice was husky, soft, laced with laughter. She wound her wet arms around his back, and he toppled over the side, splashing into the warm bath as Dorian's soft limbs wrapped around him.

"What about the maid?"

"Don't worry."

"And dinner?"

"It'll keep."

"I'm supposed to be the aggressive one," he sputtered, wiping his arm across his face as she tugged at his sopping clothes.

"You're too slow. Besides, you could use a few lessons."

"Okay, professor." He peeled off his wet shirt. "I guess I'm still your student."

8

JOURNEY TO DELPHI

The room was dark when Dorian rose from her bed. She pushed the curtain aside, and the faint gray light of predawn seeped into the room. It was after five; she had to hurry.

She moved silently across the room, glanced once at the covered form on the bed, then quickly pulled on a plaid skirt, a blouse, and a wool jersey. She was about to leave the bedroom when Jones stirred. She froze, staring at him, willing him to remain asleep. When she was certain he hadn't heard her, she turned and left.

At the side of the house, she lifted a bicycle and wheeled it across the yard. She opened the wrought iron gate, winced when it creaked, then climbed on the bicycle and pedaled off.

Three blocks from her house, Dorian veered left and coasted downhill. The morning air was cool, and she was glad she'd worn the sweater. Ahead of her, a distant, barely perceptible pink glow challenged the sullen grayness of the eastern horizon. She braked when she reached the bottom of the hill, turned right, and rode past Platía Monastirákiou. The square usually bustled with nut vendors, fruit stalls, and shoppers, but at this hour it was quiet. The tenth-century monastery church in the center of it looked gray and desolate, a lonely artifact of simpler times.

She passed the crumbling walls of Hadrian's Library and followed Eolou Street until she reached the Gate of Athena Archegetis, the entrance to the Roman Forum. Engraved on the surface of the pilaster that faced the Acropolis was an edict of Hadrian announcing the rules and taxes for the sale of oil. *If Hadrian could see the place now,* Dorian thought.

She walked her bicycle through the gate and into the ruins, passing ramshackle huts built atop the remains of the ancient public latrine. Thin filaments of smoke curled up from the doorways of a few of the huts, the first sign of the new morning. Throughout the ruins of the marketplace were makeshift homes built by some of the thousands of refugees flooding the city. Another national disaster.

She continued on until she reached an octagonal tower where she laid the bike on its side. She wasn't sure why, but the Tower of the Winds fascinated her. It had been designed in the first century B.C. by a Syrian astronomer named Andronicos of Cyrrhos and served as compass, sundial, weather vane, and water clock powered by a stream. If the clock had still worked, she would have been able to tell that it was five-thirty by reading the level of water in the interior cylinder.

She turned her gaze upward. Each face of the tower

was decorated with a relief of a mythical entity which personified one of the eight winds. Directly above her on the northwest side of the tower was a relief of Skiron, who held a vessel of charcoal. Next to it, Boreas, the North Wind, blew into a conch shell.

"I got your message," a voice said from behind her, and a hand touched her shoulder.

"You're here early." She dropped her gaze, and turned. In the pale light, Alex Mandraki was a dark, brooding figure, as mysterious as the mythical entities on the tower.

"Looking out for my interests." His hand strayed to her face, touching it lightly, as though he were uncertain of his right to do so. "You're a clever strategist, Dorian. You'd make a good man. A better one than most. Must be why I like you."

She brushed a hand against his cheek; his skin felt rough even though he had just shaved. "You only like me? I thought you loved me."

He grasped her hand. His features softened as much as was possible for a man whose very glance caused his men to quaver. "Of course I do, and I've missed you." He pulled her to him, and kissed her with a sudden urgency.

"I've missed you, too," she whispered, and drew back from him. "Was it horrible?"

"A slaughter. Beyond words. And there was nothing I could do to prevent it."

"All the more reason for what we must do."

He studied her for a moment, perhaps trying to read her thoughts by the intensity and sincerity of her eyes, her expression. "I know you have to become close to the American, but I hope you aren't taking your task too seriously."

She smiled at him for the first time. "Are you jealous, Alex?"

"No." He raked his fingers back through his short, kinky hair. "Not yet." He took her hand again. They started to walk. His hawk nose, silhouetted in the pale light, looked like a sharp, deadly beak. "Jealousy is like hatred: an emotion that wastes energy."

"You could say the same about making war."

"In the current situation," he said, referring to the invasion of Turkey, "I agree wholeheartedly. But we must never eliminate our army. We would be a weak, ineffective people. Greeks must never again be held in subjugation."

"You don't have to lecture to me, Alex, especially not at this hour of the morning."

"Something's bothering you. What is it?"

She told him about the trouble she had encountered on the train.

He nodded and spoke in a firm, even voice. "You did the right thing. But I warned you that Farnsworth might be trouble. I should've placed someone on the train with you."

She smiled up at him. "I can handle myself quite well."

"So it seems. Then there is no problem."

"I'm not finished. I think there are two others working with Farnsworth." She told him about the men who had chased them at the Acropolis.

A frown burrowed deep between his dark eyes. He shook his head. "They sound like amateurs."

"Thank God. I was vulnerable. I didn't get a good

look at either of them, but Jones did." She described the men as best she could.

"I'll see what I can find out, and I'll assign a guard to your truck."

"That's not necessary."

"Please, let me decide what is necessary for your protection." He smiled, and took her hand. "Now I want to tell you what I have in mind for Delphi."

When she pushed the bicycle toward the street a few minutes later, peach and pale yellow edged the sky. The quiet of dawn was over, and the ancient forum was waking as people trickled out of the huts. *It's going to be a long day,* she thought.

Indy ran through the Acropolis, arms pumping at his sides, legs blurring beneath him, his breath coming in quick, sharp bursts. He could hear the men behind him, their shoes pounding the pavement, their shouts slapping the air. His head snapped around. They were rapidly closing in on him, but he couldn't run any faster; his legs wouldn't cooperate. Panic clawed at his throat.

One of the men suddenly lurched ahead of the other and slammed a bottle of retsina over his head. He knew it should have hurt, that a white-hot pain should have flashed through his skull. But the only thing he felt was an intense reverberation that echoed in his head and sounded like a horn.

"Wake up, Indy."

He opened his eyes and winced at the bright, cruel light. "Oh, God," he moaned. The blast of a horn outside their window hammered against the inside of his head. "What the hell's going on out there?"

"That's our ride to Delphi. Hurry up and get ready. But drink this first."

He sat up in bed, rubbed his face, and saw that Dorian was already dressed. She handed him a coffee as thick as syrup in a cup not much larger than a thimble.

"No ouzo in it, I hope." At dinner they had finished the retsina and after the meal had sampled another Greek invention, a liqueur that reminded Indy of the Pernod he drank on occasion in Paris. His head now pounded with the after effects of the combination.

"Not a drop. I promise."

He grimaced when the horn sounded again, but a few minutes later he was dressed and ready to leave. He reached under the bed for his bag, but couldn't feel it. He crouched lower, spotted the bag—and something else. He stretched his arm, patting the floor, and pulled out a boot. Its mate was behind it, and they looked like military issue.

"Indy, let's . . ." Dorian stopped in the doorway. "What're you doing?"

"I was just getting my bag." He dropped the boot, and looked at her.

"In case you're wondering, it belongs to my housekeeper's son. He died in Turkey. I'll be waiting outside." She turned away.

Indy kicked the boot under the bed, and grabbed his bag. Funny place to keep a dead soldier's boots, he thought. When he stepped outside, two men with rifles were standing in the back of the truck. As he climbed into the front seat next to Dorian, he asked who they were.

"Guards."

"Expecting trouble?"

"Just being prepared."

Within minutes, they were bouncing over a gravel road as they headed into the hills outside of the city. The springs on the truck were in poor condition, and each bounce jarred Indy's head.

The truck's engine roared whenever they accelerated, making conversation difficult. "This road..." he heard Dorian say, and saw her lips moving, but he couldn't hear anything else.

"What?"

"This road ... of Oedipus."

He frowned, shook his head. What possible connection could there be between the road and Oedipus?

Dorian leaned over and shouted. "This road we are driving on hasn't changed much since the time of Oedipus."

He believed it.

Dorian gave up on conversation and Indy stared out at the gray, stony hills and pines. It seemed that every day since they'd left Paris, the trip had assumed a new dimension. First, his relationship with Dorian had shifted dramatically. Then he'd discovered that she might be persona non grata in her own country. The idea that he could be getting caught up in political machinations that he didn't comprehend disturbed him. She had said they should be open with each other, but she apparently was open only when it was opportune.

Now, he was starting to understand Conrad's suspicions about Dorian. Even Shannon, who hadn't even met her, was right about one thing. Traveling with Dorian *was* an adventure, and he had the feeling he hadn't seen the end of it. Hell, they hadn't even reached Delphi yet.

But he'd wanted a challenge, and maybe even some danger. That was what adventure was about, after all. But he also wanted to stay alive. No doubt about that.

Every so often he glanced back to see if they were being followed. But there were only clouds of dust, spewing from under the wheels of the truck. Dorian finally leaned close to him. "Would you stop worrying? We've got two guards with us. If there's any problem, they'll handle it."

He nodded, slid down in his seat and closed his eyes. Soon the drone of the engine lulled him to sleep. He dozed, was jolted awake, dozed again, a rhythm as predictable as the tick of a clock. By early afternoon, they climbed the lower slopes of Mount Parnassós, and his anticipation increased with the altitude.

"Almost there," Dorian said, gazing through the windshield at the mountain peak.

Indy touched her thigh; she nudged it away. "We have to act professionally while we're at the ruins. Here, you're my student, that is all. Do you understand?"

Her expression was hard, cast in stone. Indy gave a quick, nervous laugh. "Oh, c'mon, you afraid of a scandal because I'm younger than you?"

"This isn't funny, Jones, and age has nothing to do with it. It just doesn't look right for a professor to be sleeping with her student."

Look right to whom? But he didn't ask. He suddenly wanted to tell her that he'd never experienced anything like their lovemaking. It was more than mere sexual passion. It was the fulfillment of his longing for a woman who was different from the others he'd known. Yet, he wanted her more than ever. She was as seductive and enigmatic as the mystery of Delphi itself, and he needed her. But he didn't say anything of this, either. He was afraid she would laugh, that she'd call him her sweet student of love or something equally humiliating.

"There." She pointed. "See it?"

Indy leaned forward and saw a mountain terrace that seemed to literally hang in space, in a pocket between ominous craggy peaks. It looked small and insignificant compared to the mountain.

Dorian told the driver to stop for a minute. They got out and gazed up at Delphi.

"I guess I was expecting it would be larger," he said.

"Its size had nothing to do with its importance. Think of it, Indy. For a thousand years, kings and statesmen, military leaders and merchants, climbed the sides of this mountain, bearing questions for the oracle."

He recalled her saying in class that the predictions were often obscure and ambiguous. If that was so, how could it have lasted so long, and impressed so many?

"Did anyone ever keep track of the accuracy of the predictions?"

"Why do you ask?"

"If I were resting my future on some old lady's bab-blings, I'd want to know how accurate she was."

"You Americans." Dorian laughed. "You think the world is like one of your baseball games. You want everyone to have a batting average. I doubt if anyone kept such records, but of course the tradition of the oracle would never have survived for so long if the predictions were usually wrong."

"I'd bet the successes had more to do with the knowledge of the priests, than the oracle."

She said nothing in response. Her enigmatic smile was her answer.

They climbed back in the truck and ten minutes later rounded the final bend and arrived at Delphi. At eighteen hundred feet the air was a bit cooler here than in Athens. He gazed up at the massive surround-ing peaks which rose to more than eight thousand feet, and then down at the sharp drop of the land-scape to the valley below.

The truck stopped and they stepped out. Most of the buildings were merely foundations and rubble, the result of centuries of earthquakes and man's own de-struction. But just the sight of the tilted Doric col-umns of Apollo's Temple so near the steep face of the mountain sent chills along Indy's spine. Here he was at the most famous religious site of antiquity, a place once considered the center of the world, a place of earth and stone and, he was certain, of secrets still hidden.

"What do you think, Jones?"

It bothered him that she rarely called him Indy any-more, but he let it go. What mattered was that he was here, at Delphi. "It's not just a myth anymore. It's a real place, at least, it was."

"It still is a real place. Don't forget that."

He was about to say that right now it was more real than the Sorbonne when he saw a fat man hurrying toward them. He was trying to run, Indy thought, but his corpulence made his effort nothing more than a waddle. As he neared them, it was obvious he was excited.

"Dr. Belecamus, I'm glad you're finally here," he said, sucking in breathfuls of thin air. "We've been expecting you for a couple of days."

"I told you I would come as fast as I could." Indy heard a trace of annoyance in her voice, and sensed there was animosity between them. "Jones, this is Stephanos Doumas, the current chief of archaeology here."

Indy pegged him to be just a few years older than he was. He extended a hand, but the man just nodded and continued talking to Dorian.

"Something incredible has happened," he exclaimed. "You must come quickly and see for yourself."

"What are you talking about?"

"It's the crevice in the temple." He gestured with his hands. "There are vapors rising from it. Vapors—like those the oracle breathed."

9

THE RETURN

Panos, the stonemason, ambled along the main street of the village, en route to the *platía,* the grassy park at the end of the village. As he passed the restaurant, he nodded to the familiar old men who squatted on a long wooden bench outside the crumbling wall. Except for the amber *komboloi* beads they fingered, they reminded him of cats, purring with contentment in the midmorning sun.

Several feet from where they sat, a pair of rough-hewn wood beams were propped against the wall, where the brick had buckled and bulged and sent a spider web of cracks along the tarnished white stucco. Damage from the recent earthquake, he thought. But life continued on. Earthquakes and tremors were hardly more remarkable here in the village of Delphi than a heavy thunderstorm. A part of life: birth, death, earthquakes.

One of the old men called out and asked him about his mother's health. That was about all the old man ever said to him any more. He was in the village, but no longer of it. He was another visitor, like the people who came to see the ruins. Only the old men knew him; they remembered Panos from another time.

So he talked about his mother's health in terms they could understand: "She feels much better now that her son and grandson are here again." He smiled. "She says she goes up and down."

The old men laughed. It was what everyone in Delphi said when you asked how they were. *We go up and down.* That was life on the mountain. Up the mountain and down the mountain.

The sight of the old men always made him feel good. They were the standard-bearers of the village. It seemed they had always been there by the restaurant, waiting, watching, occasionally talking. He knew, though, that there had been a time when they were active, vital men, working and traveling up and down the mountain. Carpenters, craftsmen, merchants, shepherds.

But that was before the shift, when the village was moved from atop the sacred ruins to its present site. Now the men were like the ruins of Delphi itself, their aged bones no longer able to support an active existence.

He kept walking down the road as the men muttered among themselves. They were probably saying something about the accident so many years ago in which Estelle had died. Or, more likely, they were repeating an old story about what had happened afterwards. Estelle had been walking along a mountain trail carrying her infant son, Grigoris, when a landslide had buried both of them. Panos, who had been several yards ahead, had managed to dig Grigoris from the rubble. Miraculously, he was unhurt. But when Panos reached Estelle, he cried out in agony and grief. Estelle, his beautiful young wife, was dead, her skull crushed by a boulder.

That was the year of the shift. Thirty years ago, he thought. The year the archaeologists arrived. The year everything changed.

But out of Estelle's death rose a new life—his own. He was transformed, changed by her death, by the shift of the village, and by Milos, Estelle's father. As long as he had known him, Milos had been called the Crazy One, and afterwards he became even more crazy. But Panos learned to look beyond Milos's craziness, and slowly he came to realize that he was a seer and a guardian of ancient knowledge.

Panos crossed the *platía* and took a seat on his favorite bench. The square itself was small and unimpressive, but the view of the valley made up for it. After Estelle's death he had spent endless days sitting at this very place and imagining himself soaring like a raven out over the valley. It was there in those days that Milos had approached him and told him that it was time for him to learn the secrets of the Order of Pythía.

Nearby, two men in blue work clothes were whitewashing the base of an old oak tree to protect it from insects. He'd never seen either of the men, which was odd since he knew virtually everyone who lived here. Although he'd resided in Athens for several years, he still returned to Delphi several times a year to visit his mother and to be near the sacred site.

He watched the men until the one closest to him

looked his way. Panos nodded to him, greeted him, and asked how he was doing. The man paused, took off his cap, and wiped his brow with his forearm. He said he was fine, but that he'd never sweated in such cool weather before. "The sun is hot, but the air is cool."

"That's how it is on the mountain. It's not like Athens," Panos said, quickly recognizing the man's speech as that of the capital. "How long have you been here?"

"Since yesterday. The government sent me." He puffed out his chest and spoke in a voice filled with self-importance. He watched Panos to see if he was impressed.

But Panos let him down. He laughed, and shook his head. "So now the government sends men to tend the trees after we have an earthquake. Next thing they will move the village again."

The man's voice turned defensive. "I am here because the king is coming to visit Delphi next week."

"Coming here?" Panos was skeptical.

The man smiled, because he knew something that Panos, the local man, did not. "Yes, of course. He will be coming to inspect the damage at the ruins, and he will stay for two nights." The man put on his cap, and turned back to his work.

Panos stared out over the valley, considering what he'd heard. He knew the king had a mountain retreat a couple of miles away, but he rarely visited it. Now he was certain the prophecy was right. The timing was perfect.

"Papa. There you are."

Panos looked over his shoulder to see Grigoris hurrying across the square towards him. His son, now grown, was almost a duplicate of him: muscular, with slender hips and dark curly hair. No doubt he'd just heard about the king's visit, and was expecting to surprise his father.

"You won't believe it, Papa. It is happening already."

Panos rose from the bench, took his son by the arm, and led him away from the workmen. "I know. Come on."

"How could you know? You've been here. I just talked to Stephanos outside the camp."

Panos stopped, and turned to face Grigoris. "I told you to stay away from the ruins, and it's the first thing you did when I left this morning."

"I didn't go into the ruins. I stayed outside. She didn't see me. Neither did the foreigner. I was very careful."

Panos shook his head; his son tried his patience. Grigoris had made a mistake in Athens when he'd let himself be seen at the Acropolis. Then, before Panos could stop him, he'd complicated matters by chasing the pair.

"I said I was sorry about what happened. How many times do I have to apologize? I'm not a child anymore. Now will you listen to me?"

"What would you have done if they had stopped and waited for you?"

His son rolled his black eyes, exasperated. "I told you I was just trying to scare the outsider. Maybe I would have told him to stay away from here."

Panos stared at Grigoris a moment, silently reprimanding him. "This is no reason to apologize to me. Apologize to yourself." He was about to invoke one of the sacred directives: "Know thyself," but Grigoris interrupted.

"Father, the veil has parted. The vapors are rising again from the temple."

"What?"

"That's what I've been trying to tell you."

"Are you sure?" There was always mist around the Temple of Apollo in the mornings and on many occasions he'd imagined that the vapors were rising again and the prophecy of the Return had been fulfilled.

"I didn't see it myself because you told me not to go into the ruins. But it must be true."

Panos knew that Stephanos thought Grigoris was naive; maybe this was one of his jokes. "We'll see," he said.

"What are we going to do?" the younger man asked anxiously.

"We've waited many years. We can wait a few hours or a few days longer."

Panos thought back to the prophecy. After Estelle's death, Milos had predicted the Return and had given all the clues. At the time, Milos had been the last surviving member of the Order of Pythía, but over the years he had slowly passed the knowledge to Panos. Finally, the time had come for Panos to invoke his authority as the new leader of the Order.

He would talk to Stephanos himself, but he already sensed it was true. It was finally all coming together. There was no longer any reason to fear Dorian

Belecamus because of her power at the sacred site. It was clear now; she was the one.

She would be the new Pythía; he would be the interpreter, and the first prophecy, he was certain, would be for the king himself.

10

ICHOR RISING

A lantern rested on a wooden table, illuminating the interior of a primitive thatched hut. Next to the lantern lay a thick book which was open to a page filled with ancient Greek script. It was the text of a stone tablet, which had been salvaged from Delphi's archives, and its author was Plutarch, who served as a priest at Delphi in the first century A.D.

For the past several minutes, Indy had been slowly translating the inscription on a piece of paper. Although an English version was available on the next page of the book, he wanted to test his abilities. There were only three words that he wasn't certain about, and he'd guessed their meaning from the context. He blew on the paper, drying the ink, and laid the fountain pen on the table.

"Okay, let's see," he mumbled, and held the paper closer to the light. As far as he could tell, the script was a response to a question about why the prophecies of the oracle were often ambiguous. He read his translation in a low voice:

"For it was not just a question of some individual person consulting the oracle about the purchase of a slave or some other private matter, but of very powerful citizens, kings and tyrants with mighty ambitions, seeking the gods' advice on important issues. To anger or annoy such men by harsh truths which conflicted with their desires would have had its disadvantages for the priests of the oracle."

Indy turned the page, and saw that there was more of the text. This time he translated it verbatim without writing the words. Like a child learning to read, he slowly read the text, stumbling over words here and there.

"As for the answers ... given to ordinary people, it was also sometimes advisable that these ... should be concealed from their oppressors or ... hidden from their enemies. Thus these too were wrapped up in ... circumlocution and ... equivocation so that the meaning of the oracle, while hidden from others, could always be grasped ... by those whom it concerned if they applied themselves to unraveling it."

It sounded like a politician explaining why he hadn't carried out his campaign promises, Indy thought as he turned the page. He scanned the accompanying English translation, and smiled. He was pleased with his accuracy, and confident he could translate the tablet that awaited him in the fissure. Now, if Dorian would stop wasting time, he could get on with it.

He pulled out his pocket watch and glanced at it. Without exception, the vapors rose from the crevice for twelve minutes before they dissipated, but the length of the quiet periods was slowly increasing. The first time they'd measured an interval it had lasted three hours and five minutes. The next time the vapors had risen, three hours and eleven minutes had elapsed. It hadn't taken long for them to realize that each interval was lengthening by six minutes. But now, their third day at Delphi, Dorian was still insisting they continue taking the measurements.

Indy had been watching the fissure since 1:00 P.M. The gases had risen at 4:16 P.M., and had been quiet now for four hours and five minutes. If the schedule that had been established continued, the vapors would rise in eighteen minutes, at 8:39 P.M.

Ironic, he thought. He'd left his studies in midsemester for what seemed like the chance of a lifetime. But so far all he'd done was play watchdog for a hole in the ground. He shook his head in disgust. At least he could look forward to dinner. He'd be relieved at nine, then he would head into the village.

He held his hands out over the charcoal brazier which heated the hut. When he was satisfied that he was as warm as he would get, he pulled aside the cloth which covered the door. He reached for his hat, which lay on the table, but his hand hit the lantern and tipped it over. It rolled toward the edge of the table. He lunged for it and caught it just as it was about to roll onto the floor.

He carefully stood it up in the center of the table, eased his hands away. "Now, stay there." He took a step backward, and his heel knocked over the brazier. Hot coals catapulted across the dirt floor, and bounced toward the walls.

He cursed, and scurried about kicking one coal

after another toward the center of the hut, then out the door. He glanced around; he sniffed.

Smoke.

Flames suddenly raced along the base of the wall. Indy slapped at them with his jacket, then finally found the coal and kicked it out the door. He stomped out the sparks, and flapped the cloth door to get out the smoke. But the rush of air ignited a spark he'd missed, and the wall was ablaze again.

"Aw . . ." He yelled, grabbed a gallon jug of water from the floor, and doused the fire. When he was sure every spark was out, he lowered the lantern and examined the damage. Several square feet of the wall were blackened and the hut smelled of smoke, but the structure still seemed sound. The last thing he wanted to do was end his watch by burning down the hut.

But on second thought, Dorian probably wouldn't mind.

The hut, which was made of branches, feathers, and beeswax, was an attempt to recreate the first temple of Delphi. It was part of a plan promoted by Stephanos Doumas to connect the present with the past and make the ruins more accessible and interesting to non-scientific visitors. It had been constructed outside the temple by Doumas and his assistants shortly before the earthquake, and had survived unscathed.

Upon their arrival, as Doumas led them over to the crevice, Dorian had stopped at the hut, looked it over, then asked Doumas what it was. She laughed when he finished his explanation. "So you're becoming a tourist promoter as well as an archaeologist. Is that what I taught you when you were my student?"

"Well, not exactly, but—"

"In fact, what I taught you, Stephanos, is that tourists are a costly nuisance. Tourist promotions take away money that might go for research, and if left to their own devices tourists destroy our work."

Doumas was taken aback by the criticism, but he quickly recovered. "Well, a very important tourist is coming here, Dr. Belecamus. None other than the king, and I'm sure you'll agree it is a good idea to please him."

Dorian had turned away from the hut, and gazed toward the temple for several seconds. Indy was surprised by how well she hid her feelings. She must be thinking that the king's trip to Delphi was related to her family's tenuous political situation, and her return.

When she looked back toward them, she was smiling. "So everything is happening at once. The vapors are rising, and the king is coming."

"And you are here," Doumas added.

"Yes. I am here. Now, tell me more about these vapors."

Doumas said the vapors had risen three times that day, each eruption about two and a half to three hours apart. "Okay, we'll transform the hut into a lookout station, and monitor the vapors," she said.

When Doumas protested that the hut wasn't built for occupation, she reminded him that he had called her about the earthquake damage and requested her assistance. "As long as I have come all the way from Paris for that purpose, let me do my job the way I see fit, Stephanos. Is that understood?" Doumas quickly backed off, and from that moment on there was no question that while Dorian was in Delphi, she was in charge.

Indy put his hat on and stepped outside. Moonlight washed across the ruins, illuminating the columns of Apollo's Temple, the rubble and remains of ancient walls. Beyond the temple, the abrupt rise of the mountain face was hidden in shadow and left a sense of foreboding. He rubbed his hands together, fighting off the chill, and headed toward the temple.

He thought about what he'd read in recent days about Delphi, and tried to imagine what it had been like to visit the sacred shrine at its height of power. The temple had been built in the middle of the fourth century B.C. after an earlier temple was destroyed by an earthquake. In the decades and centuries that followed, a regular routine had been established. Visitors seeking knowledge of the future would first sacrifice a goat or a sheep, and if a reading of the entrails boded well, they were allowed inside the temple. If the person was wealthy, the entrails no doubt read very well, Indy figured.

Upon entering the portal, they first saw walls inscribed with bits of wisdom, such as "Know thyself" and "Everything in moderation." Beyond the portal were statues of Poseidon, Apollo, and the Fates. Other treasures of the interior included a statue of Homer and the iron chair in which Pindar sat when he came to Delphi to sing odes to Apollo.

Below ground level were the central chambers of the shrine. A huge gold statue of Apollo guarded the entrance to the inner sanctuary, known as the adytum. In the inner sanctuary was the tomb of Dionysus and the tripod on which Pythía sat and inhaled the mephitic gases which supposedly rose from a fissure in the earth. Nearby was the Omphalos, a black, cone-shaped stone, which was regarded as the navel of the world, and was always near Pythía when she spoke.

But all that was gone, lost, stolen, or destroyed, he thought as he crossed the Sacred Way, a wide path which wound through the ruins. He stopped where a rope blocked entry to the temple. Until more was known about the vapors, no one was allowed to go beyond this point.

Before the rope had been put in place, Dorian had carefully measured the crevice. It was about nine feet across at the widest point, and about thirty feet long. The ground on either side of the fissure had buckled and thrust upward so that the crevice was bordered by mounds of dirt and rubble. But it was possible to approach the crevice only on the side nearest the temple entrance. A trench about twenty feet deep bordered the opposite side.

A wispy thread of vapor curled upward from the mound. He checked his watch. 8:39. Four hours and twenty-three minutes after the last rising, and right on time. Within seconds, the vapors thickened and billowed above the crevice.

What would it be like to inhale the gas? Most likely it was just water heated to a vapor by the molten earth below and forced up the chasm to the surface. Hell, he was fed up with vapor watching. He'd sample the gas, and prove that it was harmless. If he felt the least bit nauseated, he could just back away and inhale fresh air.

He glanced back across the ruins, then pushed

down on the rope and stretched a leg over. The air around the top of the mound was a violet hue now. His heart beat faster as he raised his other leg. Maybe this was a mistake. Maybe it was a poisonous gas.

Get it over with. Do it.

"Jones, what're you doing there?"

He lowered his leg, straddling the rope, and looked back to see Dorian stepping out from the shadows of the hut. The moonlight fell across her, illuminating one side of her face. Awkwardly, he stepped back over the rope. He rubbed his hands together, and smiled as she approached.

"It started again. Right on time."

"So I see." She moved closer to him. "But you didn't answer my question. What were you going to do?"

He tried to think of an excuse. But there was no point. "I was going to take a closer look."

"I thought I made it clear to you that I don't want you or anyone going in there when the fumes are rising. We don't know anything about the gases."

"Maybe it's ichor, Dorian."

He could see her face clearly now: she wasn't amused. Ichor was the ethereal fluid that flowed through the veins of the gods. "This is no time to be flippant," she snapped. "The pursuit of archaeology requires rational thought and a step-by-step process."

"If you want me to talk rationally, that's fine. The fact is, we won't know anything until someone just goes in there and inhales the gas."

"And you'd like to be that person, I suppose."

"I'm willing to try it, because I think we're wasting our time."

"No," she said firmly. "That's *not* the way we're going to do it." Just then the vapors faded, turned wispy, and vanished. Dorian noted the time. "Where's the clipboard? Aren't you keeping track of the time?"

"I left it in the hut, and I am keeping track." He told her the times the vapors had risen.

Dorian shook her head. "Jones, if you're going to become an archaeologist, you have to learn patience. The age of the treasure-hunting archaeologist-adventurer is over. Archaeology is a slow, painstaking process. We study the most minute details, the fragments, the rubble, the garbage of the ages. That is how we advance our understanding of the past."

"I'm sure that's true. But in this case, we've got to look at the geological point of view. The longer we wait, the greater the chances of losing the tablet to an aftershock or another quake."

"I'm well aware of that." Her voice had gone hard and cold. "Tomorrow morning, I'm going to tie a goat near the fissure and we'll watch its reactions."

"A goat?" He laughed. "That's appropriate." In the legend of the original Delphic Oracle, a goat had first inhaled the fumes of the rotting carcass of Python, and gone crazy. Later, shepherds discovered the fissure and many of them, intoxicated by the fumes, had fallen into the crevice.

"I thought you'd like that."

But Indy wasn't through challenging her. So what if she got angry with him. It would be better than being ignored. Ever since their arrival, she'd been cool toward him. Not only had she ceased being his lover, but she barely acknowledged him. He wondered if there was another man, possibly someone who lived in the village. After all, she'd worked here for years before moving to Paris.

"I bet you're hoping these gases are the real thing, that they cause people to go into trances and see the future."

"Jones, you're insolent and you also underestimate me. I have no preconceived notion about the vapors. I'm not trying to prove anything."

"What if the goat doesn't react?"

"Then we'll get on with our business."

"Which is?"

"I've decided that you should be the one to go down into the crevice. Of course, you don't have to do it if you don't want to. It's up to you, I'm giving you the first opportunity."

"I'll do it," he said without hesitating. "The sooner the better."

"Good. I'm glad to hear it." Her dark eyes sought his, and he felt as if she were staring through him. In a softer voice, she added: "I'm sorry if I've ignored you, but I've been very busy."

"That's understandable. I guess. Do you have many friends in the village?"

"Why do you ask?"

He shrugged. "You said you've been busy."

"Busy working, not socializing. If you haven't noticed, most of the villagers are very aloof from those of us who work at the ruins."

"Why is that?"

"It's a tradition of sorts that goes back to when the village was moved from the ruins to allow us, the archaeologists, to excavate."

She smiled and was about to say something when

he took a step closer to her and reached for her hand. She abruptly drew back, and addressed him in a formal voice. "You can go to dinner now. The moussaka is great tonight. I'll take over the watch until morning."

Still cold, he thought and even though she had warned him how she would act toward him, it still hurt. He watched as she retreated to the hut. He was about to leave, but decided to wait. He knew she wasn't quite through with him for the evening. It didn't take more than a few seconds.

"Jones," she yelled. "Why is it smokey in here?"

He walked over to the hut as she stepped out and told her what had happened.

She nodded, hands on her hips, and walked around the outside of the hut. Then she moved close to him. "You should have let it burn," she whispered. She leaned forward, kissed him lightly on the lips, and the barrier that had risen between them wavered for a moment. "You'd better go."

"All right. Let me get my books just in case the fire starts again."

She laughed, and he felt closer to her than he had since they had arrived. He stuffed the books into his canvas knapsack and paused at the entrance of the hut.

"You anxious about the king coming here?"

"Anxious? Why no, I'm elated."

11

TAVERNA INTRIGUE

As he ate dinner, Indy paged through his books, taking care not to spill any of the spicy casserole onto the pages. Until the tablet was recovered and cleaned, he wanted to spend every spare moment studying old Greek script. He would prove to Dorian that her choice of an assistant was a worthwhile one.

Occasionally, he picked up scraps of conversation from the villagers dining around him. Most of it was about the king's visit, how long it had been since he was last here, and possible reasons why he had waited for an earthquake to return. The villagers, for their part, cast curious glances Indy's way from time to time, but otherwise ignored him.

As he was finishing his dinner, he took out a pencil and made some calculations. If the vapors continued rising at the same intervals, they would appear again at 1:08 A.M., at 5:43 A.M., and then at 10:24 A.M. Dorian had said she would send the goat into the vapors early tomorrow. So 5:43 must be it, and he would be there. Nothing would keep him from it.

It was almost eleven when Indy gathered his books to leave. Despite the hour, several tables were still occupied. Across the street at the taverna, he heard the wail of a wind instrument he didn't recognize. He was tempted to go over for a drink, but he decided against it. Even though he'd spent hours doing very little during his stint in the hut, he was tired and ready for bed. Slinging his knapsack of books over one shoulder, he gazed upward at the twinkling constellations and headed down the road. He imagined himself an ancient Greek scholar en route to wondrous Delphi. And what would the ancient scholar learn from the oracle? That he would create a great work of scholarship, marry the daughter of a king, become a great teacher? But why wouldn't the bright young scholar realize that the oracle was a tool of the priests, that what he was told was nonsense? Probably because he didn't want to know, didn't want to pay the price of knowing.

As Indy was about to enter the Delphi Hotel, the door swung open and a slender but muscular kid of about fifteen stepped out. His hair was short-cropped; his features classical Greek.

"Hello, Nikos."

"Indy, you're not going to your room yet, are you? It's Saturday night. Come to the taverna with me."

"You're a little young, aren't you?"

His dark eyes darted about, taking in everything on the street. "What do you mean?" Nikos asked.

Indy frowned at the kid. Back home it was illegal for anyone to drink. Here, a teenager was heading to the taverna at eleven o'clock. "You like retsina?"

"I don't drink," Nikos answered. "My father

won't let me. But I can still join the music and dancing. Please, come with me. You will see how we enjoy ourselves."

Nikos was a desk clerk at the hotel, which was owned by his father. He had grown up in the tiny village, but had been exposed to numerous foreigners and had learned English, German, and French.

Indy glanced back toward the taverna, hesitating, but Nikos insisted. "Give me those books. I'll put them behind the counter. And you can have some fun, too."

He shrugged. "Okay. But just for a few minutes." He handed the kid the knapsack and watched him disappear back into the hotel.

Indy didn't want to offend Nikos. He was a valuable source of information, and almost the only person who said much of anything to him. Besides, a drink before bed would be fine, but one would be enough. He wanted to be in his room by midnight at the latest.

Nikos spoke English with Indy and asked a lot of questions about America. One time he'd wanted to know if it was true that there were cities with streets filled with automobiles, and if every house had a radio. Another time he'd asked if America was larger than Greece and Turkey together. Indy answered his questions as best he could, and in return Nikos had provided him with some inside information about what was going on in the village and at the ruins.

From Nikos he'd learned that Dorian and Doumas had argued about him. Nikos hadn't heard everything, but had told him that Doumas had complained about his being unqualified to work at the ruins and

that his presence was an offense to all Greek archaeologists. Doumas had been infuriated when Dorian had
held her ground. Now Indy knew the reason for
Doumas's outrage. She must have told him she
wanted Indy to climb into the crevice and get the
tablet.

"Let's go," Nikos said as he came out the door
again. "Tonight you will have some fun. Did you go
to tavernas in Athens?"

Indy shook his head. "Didn't have time."

"The best ones are at the Platía Phlomouson
Hetairae." Nikos strode along beside him, swinging
his arms.

"The square of the music-loving courtesans," Indy
said.

"Yes. Your Greek is very good."

As they neared the taverna, Indy heard the faint but
shrill whine he had heard earlier. "What's that noise?"

"That's not noise, Indy. That's music. It's an askómandra, you know, kind of like a bagpipe. But it's
made from a sheep skin."

"Never heard of it. They play any jazz around here,
kid?"

"Jazz? What is jazz?"

Indy chuckled to himself. "Guess not. Next time
you're in Chicago, I'll take you to Dreamland to see
the jazz bands."

"Dreamland is in America?"

"Some people think so." Indy opened the door, and
they entered the taverna.

"Good. I want to go to America," Nikos yelled
above the cacophony.

In the center of the taverna, men were dancing in a

circle of the thump of traditional Greek music and the wail of the askómandra. Indy glanced around, feeling out of place. But almost instantly a waiter in a white, blouselike shirt and vest appeared and handed him a drink.

"Ouzo," Nikos said when Indy held up the glass and looked at its clear contents.

"I was thinking about a beer."

Nikos gestured with his hand, moving it back and forth as he shook his head. "No beer here. Only ouzo, retsina, *raki,* and *aretsinoto.*"

"Of course," Indy said, and frowned at the drink. "When in Delphi, do as the dolphins."

Several men around them watched Indy. "He's from America," Nikos announced loudly. They nodded, and gestured with their glasses as if showing him how to drink.

When he took a swallow of the anise-flavored drink, two of the men slapped him on the back, as though congratulating him on some rite of passage. Nikos looked on proudly.

One of the men, who was elderly and wore a battered Greek sailor cap, stepped forward and mumbled something to him. Indy shook his head, unable to hear him above the din.

Nikos leaned close to Indy's ear, and spoke loudly. "He's a crazy old man. He talks about the old gods."

"What did he say?"

Nikos shook his head.

But the old man was insistent. He tapped Indy on the chest and spoke again. Indy glanced at Nikos.

"Something about Pythía."

"What about Pythía?"

Nikos spoke to the old man, who glanced at Indy, and mumbled again.

"Well, what is it?" Indy asked when Nikos didn't say anything.

"I told you he is a crazy old man. They call him the Crazy One."

"But what did he say?" Indy demanded.

"He says Pythía has you in her grasp and..."

"And what?"

"...and she will swallow you like a little mouse. That is what he said."

Indy grinned and leaned down to Nikos. "Tell him I haven't met her yet. But when I meet the daughter of a snake, you can bet I'll know it."

Another old Greek moved in front of the Crazy One, clasped Indy on the shoulder, and spoke in a slurred voice. Nikos said: "He invited you to visit his home to sample his homemade retsina."

"Thanks." Indy smiled and nodded at the old man. "The stuff tastes horrible."

The man, who didn't understand a word, nodded in agreement.

Indy and Nikos both laughed. "A friendly bunch here," Indy said, but as soon as the words were out of his mouth, his smile faded. The circle of dancing men broke up and dispersed, and he suddenly had a better view of the other side of the taverna. Seated at a table near the wall was Doumas, and with him was a familiar looking man with curly hair. The sight of the man made Indy feel uneasy, and he tried to recall where he'd seen him. Then he knew. He was one of the men who had chased him and Dorian at the Acropolis. He was sure of it.

"Nikos, who is that talking with Doumas?"

Nikos craned his neck. "His name is Panos. He is from Athens, but he was born here. He comes to visit his mother. He brings his son with him."

"How does Doumas know him?"

"Stephanos knows everyone."

He wanted to see how the man would react to him and suggested they go over and greet Doumas.

Nikos shook his head. "I don't think that is a good idea."

"Why not?"

"Panos is not friendly, especially to people like you, foreigners I mean."

"Well, it's a big world. He'll have to get over that." Indy worked his way through the crowd, but Doumas spotted him and rose to his feet, stepping between him and Panos.

When Indy had first arrived, Doumas had made a point of showing off his knowledge of Delphi, and archaeology in general, at every opportunity. Then, by the second day, when he found out that Indy was not even an archaeology graduate student, he had simply ignored him.

"Evening, Stephanos," he said casually. "Who's your friend? Don't think we've formally met."

"Mind your own business, Jones."

Indy shrugged. "Okay." He started to turn, but instead sidestepped around the rotund archaeologist, and pulled Panos to his feet.

"Hi there."

The man looked surprised. He shook his head.

"No English."

Indy poked him in the chest. "I know you," he said as the music started up again. "We were playing tag at the Acropolis just the other day."

Doumas grabbed Indy by the shoulder. "Jones, what the hell are you doing?" he shouted over the music.

He jabbed an elbow into Doumas's gut, and shrugged out of his grip. "You were chasing me and my friend. Why?" He spoke slowly and loudly, but Panos just shook his head again and tried to wrench his arm free.

"Indy, watch out," Nikos yelled, but it was too late. Indy saw a blur out of the corner of his eye. It wasn't Doumas, but someone else, younger, slender— and in that instant the newcomer's fist slammed solidly into Indy's jaw.

He staggered back, crashing through a new circle of stomping dancers. Someone caught him under the arms; he was turned around and pushed away. Voices shouted in Greek, and the wailing askómandra wrapped around him. Fragments of faces leered. Eyes and noses shifted positions like a cubist portrait. Then he saw the man again, a younger version of Panos. The stranger pulled back his arm for another punch, but this time Indy reacted faster, and crashed his fist into the man's nose.

Nikos suddenly was at his side. "Come, fast, we must go."

Indy was almost out the door when the skin rose on the back of his neck as he heard a commotion behind him. He turned to see the man he'd struck charging toward him, a knife raised above his head. The man slashed as Indy raised his forearm, but his blow fell short as Doumas's meaty arms wrapped around the assailant. He was lifted off his feet, spun around, and pulled away.

Indy looked around, and saw everyone in the taverna staring at him. He smiled weakly. "I think it's past my bedtime." He backed out the door, and felt his jaw.

Nikos hurried to his side as he walked away. "Are you all right, Indy?"

"Think so. Are the tavernas in Athens this much fun, kid?"

"Jones," a deep voice called out. Indy turned and saw Doumas standing at the door of the taverna. His face was red and sweaty, and he was jabbing a finger at him. "You don't belong here. If you want to see Paris again, stay out of Greek business."

Indy unlocked the door of his hotel room, opened it a few inches, and laid his books on the floor. He glanced over his shoulder, making sure Nikos hadn't followed him. Then, instead of going inside, he slammed the door shut, and moved down the hallway to the back stairs. Outside, he walked around the side to the hotel stable and mounted one of the camp's horses.

He had to get to the ruins as quickly as possible. Delphi was a trap. Doumas must be part of the conspiracy against Dorian and her father, and he had to tell her. They had to get away from here, and there was no time to waste.

He couldn't take the road through the village; he

would have to pass by the taverna and Doumas or one of the others might see him. He directed the horse around the back of the stable to a narrow trail that led through the woods. He'd only taken the winding path once, and that had been during the day with Nikos. He knew he would have to rely on the horse's own savvy to find its way back home.

As Indy cantered along, the darkness closed around him like a blindfold. He could see no more than a couple of feet ahead of the horse. The trail rose steeply, then fell, and rose again. He rocked back in the saddle, gripping the reins, and slowed the horse to a trot.

"Easy, boy. Just follow the road."

Suddenly, the trail plunged downward, and the horse skidded sideways and whinnied. "Whoa, whoa," Indy yelled, pulling in the reins.

This was a mistake, a big mistake, he told himself. But he wasn't turning back now. He'd make it. Somehow. As if in response to his thoughts, the horse abruptly stopped. "What's wrong, boy?"

Then Indy saw that the path divided, and the horse was waiting for directions. "Hey, I don't know. Just head for camp. You know, your stable."

The horse blew out its nose, shook its head, and pawed the ground. But it didn't move either way. Just then Indy heard a noise behind him. He turned his head and listened. There it was again. The sound of a horse moving toward them on the trail.

Christ. They were following him. *Move.*

He jerked the head of the horse to the left, touched its sides, and shook the rein. The horse broke into a trot, and climbed the incline. They must have seen him leaving the hotel and realized what he was doing.

This was definitely no place for a confrontation, and it was probably just what they wanted. No witnesses. Real pretty. *Boy, am I a sucker,* he thought as he heard his pursuers closing in on him.

Maybe he should get off the horse, and send it down the trail. They'd chase the horse, and he could get away. Good idea, he told himself, but just as he was about to dismount, the reins slipped from his hands. He fumbled for them in the darkness, but couldn't find them.

"Hell with it," he said aloud, and started to dismount the moving horse. But at that moment, the path rose, and a thick branch caught him squarely across the forehead, knocking him out of the saddle. He tumbled through the darkness and crashed with a thud to the ground.

He gasped for breath; heard hoofbeats. He rolled onto his stomach, then stumbled to his feet. He wobbled one step, another, then dropped to his knees. He tried to rise again, but fell backwards. Far overhead, constellations spun in tight, mad circles. He closed his eyes, shutting it all out, and lost consciousness.

A voice. "Indy, are you all right?"

He blinked his eyes open and saw Nikos. "Where'd they go? They were after me, and—"

"It was me. I was trying to catch up to you. I almost rode right over you."

"I feel like you did."

"Can you walk?"

He sat up and rubbed his head. "Who knows. Don't think I broke anything."

Nikos helped him to his feet. "Why were you going back to the ruins at night?"

"I've got to talk to Dr. Belecamus. Where's the horse?"

"Over here," Nikos said, motioning down the trail. "But you turned the wrong way. You won't get to the ruins on this path."

"Show me the way." Indy brushed himself off and walked over to the horse.

"Indy, I think you should watch out for Dr. Belecamus."

"Watch out for her? Why?"

"Because of who she is. You don't know everything about her."

"You're right, I don't." He recalled what Dorian had said about the villagers' attitude toward her. "Let's talk about it sometime. Right now though I've got to get to the ruins."

He untied the horse from a tree, and slung his leg over the saddle.

"Listen to me." Nikos hurried after him. "It is dangerous for you to be close to her."

Indy turned and stared down at him. "What are you talking about?"

Nikos moved nearer and gripped the reins of Indy's horse. "The Oracle is coming back, and they say Dr. Belecamus is Pythía."

"Who says that?"

"Those men in the taverna. Panos, his son, Grigoris, also Doumas, I think. They are all in the Order."

Indy shook his head. "What order?"

"The Order of Pythía. They are the keepers of the old knowledge."

"And why do they think Belecamus is Pythía?"

"The old man in the taverna, the Crazy One, is the oldest member of the Order, and many years ago he predicted that Pythía would return. He said it would happen after the earth shook and before the king arrived."

"Swell. But that doesn't answer my question. Why is Belecamus the new Pythía?"

"The Crazy One said that Pythía would be a Dorian."

"*A* Dorian? How many are there?"

Then he remembered something he'd recently read. The Dorians were an invading tribe whose name was synonymous with the Greek Dark Ages around 1000 B.C. They had displaced the mother goddess with male deities, and their influence may have been the reason that Apollo had come into power at Delphi. There had been lots of Dorians, and Belecamus had nothing to do with them. Yet, she definitely was a "Dorian."

"For years, no one said much about the prophecy," Nikos explained. "But then after the earthquake, Doumas contacted Dorian Belecamus, and when she said she would return, Panos was sure the prophecy was about to come true."

"Do you believe it?"

Nikos looked up at Indy, surprised. "No one ever asks me about such things. But I thought it was just crazy talk until I heard the king was coming. You see, it fits."

"How do you know so much about what's going on?" he asked suspiciously.

Nikos smiled, and leaned closer. "That is what I

do. I watch, and I listen. There is much to hear and see. Otherwise, it would be very boring here for me."

"That's nice, Nikos. But whether Dorian is Pythía or not, I've got to talk to her. Those men are a threat."

"No. You don't understand. They are not interested in harming her. They want to protect her."

"Protect her? From what?"

"From outsiders. Like you."

12

IN THE MIST

In the first gray light of dawn, a surly little goat climbed the mound of ancient rubble. It hung its head, shaking it from side to side as though it had no control over its neck muscles. As it reached the top, it leaned forward, straining on its fetter. From where Indy and Nikos stood on the Sacred Way a couple of hundred feet from the mound, it was difficult to tell whether the goat wanted to leap across the crevice, or into it. It was 5:40 A.M., and the vapors were due to rise in three minutes. No doubt the aggressive creature would get a good whiff.

Indy glanced toward Dorian and Doumas, who were chatting amicably, as if they were the best of friends. He thought about the trouble he had gone to last night just to reach her, and all for nothing. He had rushed to the hut and told her about the men in the taverna and what he'd found out about the Order of Pythía. Dorian had listened quietly until he was finished, then said she was relieved that the mystery of the two men was solved. Now they could go about their business.

Indy was dumbfounded by her attitude. She wasn't concerned about the organization, and thought it was amusing that they would consider her to be Pythía. She had known about the group for years, she said. It was just part of the village culture and folklore and the men were harmless. She also knew that Doumas had taken an interest in the Order; in fact, she'd encouraged it, since it provided a link between the village and the scientists.

Indy had returned to the hotel feeling like a popped balloon. He was confused, but he realized Nikos was probably right, the Order was more concerned with him, the outsider, than Dorian, the supposed Pythía. As if to show his concern, Nikos had begged Indy to allow him to come along this morning. Reluctantly, he'd asked Dorian for permission, and she'd agreed, stipulating that he be responsible for the boy.

Doumas suddenly shouted and pointed toward the fissure. Indy looked up, expecting to see the vapors. For a moment, he couldn't tell why Doumas was so excited. Then he realized that the goat had pulled its stake loose and was pacing precariously along the edge of the chasm.

"I'll get him," Nikos called out, and climbed over the rope blocking the entrance.

"No, just leave him," Indy shouted. "Stay away from there."

But Nikos had already darted toward the base of the rubble heap. "Goddamn it, Nikos." Indy chased after him, but stopped several paces short of the mound. Nikos was crouched within a couple of feet of the rope.

"Easy boy. Easy," Nikos said, edging closer as the goat stared down into the abyss. He was about to grab the rope when a low rumble erupted, followed by an ethereal, haunted hiss. *Oh, God, another earthquake,* Indy thought, then realized he'd heard something similar, but fainter, last night when the vapors had risen.

The goat lost its footing. It slid forward toward the crevice. Nikos lunged, grabbed the end of the rope, and pulled. The sudden tug knocked the animal off its feet, but an instant later it was up and scrambling to the top of the rubble again. Beyond the goat, the first tendrils of vapors rose skyward.

Indy rushed to Nikos's side and grabbed the rope from him. "Stay down," he ordered.

He was about to yank the animal down from the pile, when he remembered their intentions. He huddled low, covering his nose and mouth. He glanced up once and saw the goat standing motionless, enshrouded in a thick, white mist. Its head was bent down and moving slowly from side to side.

Then, without warning, the goat bucked, and the rope snapped out of Indy's hand. He watched it snake away, and looked up to see the goat performing a strange dance, spinning in circles, contorting its body in odd, unlikely positions. It kicked its hoofs, front, then back. It dropped to its knees, and pounded its horns into the ground.

Nikos suddenly bolted up the mound after the rope. "Get back here," Indy yelled, but it was too late.

The vapors were thickening, and Nikos vanished into the mist with the goat.

The mist flowed over the rubble and wafted toward him. It was almost as if the vapors were sentient and aware of his position. Indy didn't know whether to go after Nikos, or back away. Then, as quickly as he'd disappeared, Nikos emerged out of the mist, and they both fled the temple.

"Are you all right?" Dorian asked, looking between Indy and Nikos.

"Where's the goat?" Doumas demanded.

"The goat was dancing," Nikos said. "I almost got its rope, but it jumped right into the hole."

"Are you sure? Maybe it's made it to the other side," Doumas said.

"Why did you let him go up there?" Dorian glared accusingly at Indy.

"I did it on my own," Nikos said. "It's my fault. I wanted to show you that I could save the goat."

The mist finally dissipated, but the goat was nowhere in sight. They climbed the mound and Indy followed Nikos around to the far side, and peered into the narrow gully. It was empty. Then they were sure. The goat was lost.

Dorian laid a hand on Nikos's shoulder after they crossed back to the other side. "It's all right. Did you breathe the vapors?"

He shook his head. "I don't think so. I held my breath."

"Good." She stared into the abyss. "It's a shame, though, about the goat. Now we won't be able to tell whether its reaction was temporary fright or the actual effects of the vapors."

"I think it was just frightened," Indy said. "Just pulling on the rope the way Nikos did might have caused the goat to react that way."

"Maybe," Dorian said. "But you can't be sure." The doubt in her voice was clear. It seemed to him that Dorian was trying to convince herself that the vapors caused some effect.

"The only way we're going to find out for certain that the vapor is harmless is for one of us to inhale some of it," Indy said.

Dorian nodded. "I agree. Next time the vapors rise, I'll do it myself."

"You will?" Now Indy, who last night had been ready to inhale the vapors, wasn't so sure it was a good idea.

"It's time to end the speculation. Besides, I wouldn't do it if I really thought it was harmful."

She turned and strode down the mound and away from the temple.

Indy looked at Doumas, expecting him to protest. But he simply stared after her. In about four and a half hours, they would know.

Panos's expression was fixed with grim determination as he strode along the unpaved, tree-lined road with Grigoris at his side. The confrontation with the foreigner Jones had unnerved him, but it had also pushed him into making a decision. He knew it was time. Dorian Belecamus must be confronted. She must be told. She must be made to understand.

He squinted against the sun, which at midmorning had risen above the mountain's peak. They passed the turnoff to the stable and workshop, and continued ahead a short distance until they reached a trail where an ancient wall had once surrounded Delphi. The trail would take them above the sacred precinct, and they would make their approach from the steps of the theater, which overlooked Apollo's Temple. It was a longer route, but no one would see their arrival.

"She won't listen, Father," Grigoris said as he hurried alongside Panos. "She is an intellectual. She will laugh at you. She will think you are a silly peasant with superstitious ideas."

"Is that what you think, too?"

Panos was confident that his son was deeply committed to the Order, but nonetheless he tested him from time to time.

Grigoris hesitated before he spoke. "If I had grown up in Athens and attended one of the colleges, I am sure that is what I would think."

Panos gave him a sharp look of rebuke. He had taught his son to answer questions directly, not with obscure comments.

"But I know too much," he quickly continued. "I am not as shortsighted as the intellectuals. I am open to what *they* would find unacceptable."

Panos nodded in agreement. It was the answer he had hoped Grigoris would give; he beamed with pride. Someday his son would lead the Order of Pythía. As the high priest of Delphi, and emissary of Apollo, he would grow into a determined, disciplined man. But first he must learn to understand and control his darker emotions. If he failed to do so, Panos knew that the years he had spent preparing his son for his role would be lost.

Whenever he became concerned about Grigoris's temperament, he thought about the Olympian gods. They behaved at times as poorly as his son. They were a tempestuous lot, who had come to power through a brutal struggle with their predecessors, the Titans. Apollo, in particular, showed the same sort of aggressiveness that Grigoris did. When Apollo was consulted at Delphi about the viability of undertaking a war, more often than not he had recommended invading the enemy.

The trail turned and they emerged just above the bowl of stone benches that formed the old amphitheater. Below, the temple was blanketed in mist, the way it was in early morning. He could barely see the columns. But this was no ordinary fog; it was too late in the morning. It was the mephitic gases—ichor, the vapors of the gods—welcoming him. Somehow, he had known that the vapors would be rising as he arrived. They were another sign the timing was right.

He gazed a moment at the thatched hut outside the temple, between the Sacred Way and the place where the Sanctuary of Poseidon had once stood. Doumas had told him that it was built in such a way that several men could carry it to the edge of the fissure where he and Pythía would hold court for the king and others who requested their service. Later, when Delphi's renaissance was widely recognized, there would be plenty of money available to build a new temple. As far as Panos was concerned, the remains of the old buildings could be cleared away for the new.

More than anything, Panos was anxious to hear Pythía speak. He knew he would instantly recognize what others heard only as babbling. The cryptic language of the gods was the legacy of the Order. It wasn't taught like an ordinary language, but learned at a deeper level. For sixteen hundred years, generation after generation, century after century, the Order had served as the caretaker of the sacred knowledge and the secrets. At times, the Order had fallen to one or two members, but always the knowledge and the secrets had survived.

Panos had no doubt that the gods had watched over the Order, guiding its members, always instilling them with the understanding that the Oracle would return one day to the world. The gods and destiny after all were one, and the return of Pythía was inextricable. Now, at last, after all the centuries of awaiting, the new epoch was about to begin.

At that moment, he saw Dorian Belecamus— Pythía—walking away from the hut. He stopped and watched as she entered the temple and disappeared into the mist. He wanted to shout for joy. He had puzzled over how he would draw her into the vapors to prove to her that she was truly Pythía. But she was doing it on her own, and that made him even more confident that everything was working out just as it was meant.

He hurried down the stone steps, Grigoris just a step behind him, and as they neared the base of the theater two more figures moved into view, trailing after Pythía. "They're going into the temple," Grigoris shouted.

Then, before Panos could tell him to watch and wait, Grigoris called out to Doumas. He and Indy stopped and turned toward the theater.

"You have no sense of caution," Panos snapped,

even though as he said it he knew Grigoris was right. It was time to act, not watch.

"Panos," Doumas yelled. He waved his hands frantically. Grigoris charged ahead, and Panos hurried to keep up with his son. When they reached him, Doumas explained what they already knew. Belecamus was in the mist and there was no sign of her. Jones stood several steps away and watched them with curiosity. If the incident at the taverna had frightened him, he didn't show it.

Grigoris stepped between Jones and the temple. "I'll watch him, Father."

"What's going on?" Jones demanded.

"None of your business," Doumas said. "Do not forget what I told you last night."

Grigoris took a step closer as if to reaffirm that he was the one who had attacked Jones.

Panos turned his attention back to the temple, and asked Doumas the exact location of the fissure. The wide-girthed archaeologist waddled forward and pointed. Just then an eerie shriek pierced the veil of mist. The sound sent shivers up and down Panos's spine.

"Stay here and wait for me," Panos said, and rushed toward the temple. He climbed over a rope and the remains of the wall, and hastened toward a mound of rubble that was partially enveloped in the mist. He knew that the vapors would only affect those who were susceptible to trance states and that as a priest of the Order he was protected. Still, he took a deep breath and held it as he climbed the mound.

He reached the top and glanced around. No sign of her. He expelled his breath, and cautiously sniffed at

the air. There was no odor to the mist, and no immediate effect. He took a step forward and gazed down
into the yawning mouth of the abyss. His heart
plunged in his chest as he realized that the scream he
had heard might have been her last utterance as
Pythía plummeted into the void. There would be no
return. Not in his lifetime. Belecamus was the one; no
one else could replace her now. But how could he
have been so wrong?

He suddenly felt dizzy, the way he would if he
stood quickly after drinking a couple of glasses of
retsina. Dizzy, yet his head was clear. He felt acutely
aware, and sensed that something was about to happen. Cautiously, he took a step back from the chasm;
a hand gripped his elbow. He turned, startled, and
jerked his arm free. It was Belecamus and her hands
were raised as if she were about to shove him into the
hole. Then he saw her face. Her eyes were rolled back,
her mouth hung open, and her tongue lolled to one
side.

He gaped, astonished. "Do you know who you
are?"

Her mouth moved, her head rocked back and
forth, but no words came out.

"You are Pythía. You must understand. The Oracle
is returning, and you are Pythía."

She took a wavering step forward, shook her head
from side to side. Her jaw was working up and down,
but no sound came out. Then, with a wild burst of energy, she whirled in a circle, flailing her arms, and tottered near the edge of the crevice. She was going to
jump.

Panos grasped her firmly around the waist, pulling her back. "You must accept; you must accept."

She rocked back and forth in his arms. Then, from deep within her, a wail rose, a bellow of uncontrollable pain, of a mother giving birth. She shuddered violently and collapsed.

Panos lifted her, and as he did, he realized that the air was clearing. He carried her away, knowing that the transformation was complete. Dorian Belecamus was Pythía, and the next time the vapors rose she would be drawn into the mist again and he would be there, her guide, her interpreter, and her voice to the world.

13

READINGS

Dorian stood beside a bench in the *platía* overlooking the valley. She was wearing a cotton peasant dress instead of the baggy pants she'd worn since they'd arrived. Her hands were braced against her hips. As Indy crossed the park toward her, she reminded him of a Greek statue.

He stopped a few feet away and cleared his throat. "How are you feeling today?"

"Much better." She didn't turn her gaze from the valley.

The intensity in her eyes led Indy to believe she was watching something in particular. But all he could see was scenery. Great scenery, yes, but nothing that he or anyone else would stare at like she was. "What do you see down there?" he asked quietly.

She didn't hesitate. "History...culture...the past." Her voice was soft, distant.

Indy glanced out over the valley. It had been two days since Panos had carried her from the temple. She had slept for eleven hours and when she awakened, a doctor examined her, but found nothing wrong. He'd said she was probably suffering from stress and over-work and needed a rest. However, by noon the fol-lowing day, she'd gone to the workshop, which was near the ruins, and had stayed until nine.

She seemed detached, as if only part of her were present. Was it just exhaustion, or the vapors? He'd been thinking a lot about it. It was both, he'd decided. She must have been fighting off exhaustion for days, and the vapors, or at least Dorian's suspicions about them, had triggered her collapse, a nervous break-down.

"Well, Jones," she said, turning away from the val-ley. "We can't just spend our entire morning in the park. We've got work to do."

"You sure you're up to it?"

She straightened her back. "I'm feeling fine. Make that great. I'm feeling great."

The sudden change in her mood, her energy, sur-prised him. It was as if she'd just awakened from a dream. "What are we going to do?"

She looked at him as if he'd lost his mind. "Don't you know that we have to get the tablet out of the fis-sure as soon as possible? We've wasted too much time as it is. I want the tablet cleaned and on display by the time the king arrives the day after tomorrow."

"Aren't you rushing things a bit? I thought archae-ology was slow and detailed work."

She smiled at him. "It is, but we have an emer-gency. Every hour that tablet remains in the crevice, the danger of losing it increases." Now she was sounding as anxious as he had been before she walked into the vapors.

"Why do you want to show it to the king?" he asked. "Don't you think his trip here might be a way of harassing you for coming back?"

She laughed. "Come on now."

"What's so funny?"

"The king may be petty, but he doesn't change his plans and take emergency trips because of someone like me. I really doubt that he even knows I'm here."

"You don't think there's any danger now from your family's political enemies?"

She shook her head. "No, especially not in Delphi. Don't worry. We're safe, and when the king sees the new find, he'll see that even earthquakes have a good side to them."

Indy shrugged, still perplexed by the sudden urgency to remove the tablet and her benign attitude toward the king. "So what do you want me to do?"

"Everything is being prepared. You'll be making the descent right at noon."

"What about the vapors?" he asked.

She brushed her mane of thick dark hair off her shoulders. "I've taken them into account. This morning they rose at 9:03 A.M., five hours and thirty-five minutes after the last rising, an increase of six minutes in the interval. The same pattern."

He took out his pocket watch, and started to calculate the next rising.

She watched him a moment, then said: "At 2:44. You'll have plenty of time. All you have to do is set the net in place over the tablet, and chip away the earth at the base of it."

"What if the vapors start early?" He was curious

about her reaction, since she'd said little about her experience.

"We have no reason to believe that they won't continue to follow the pattern," she answered, evading the intent of his question.

Indy glanced at his pocket watch again, then put it away. It was 10:35. He wondered what they were going to do until noon. "I suppose I should get some rest before noon. You going back to the hotel?" If she recognized his sly overture, she didn't show it.

"I said we have work to attend to, Jones. Let's go to the workshop. I want to go over the tools with you."

She walked at a quick pace toward the hotel where the horses were hitched. "Coming, Jones?" she called over her shoulder.

He tugged at his fedora, and strode after her.

"Hey, what about Doumas?" Indy asked as they mounted their horses.

She frowned. "What about him?"

"I heard he was against my going down for the tablet."

She waved a hand. "Oh, he's over that now. It was just a matter of wounded pride."

Indy nodded, but he couldn't help thinking about Doumas's connection with the Order of Pythía. As they rode out of town, he wondered if the archaeologist was as interested as Panos and his son in protecting Dorian from outsiders. If so, going into the crevice with him anywhere in the area could be dangerous. But Doumas was also interested in the tablet, he rationalized, and probably would do nothing to endanger its recovery.

They'd ridden almost halfway to the workshop when Indy spotted a lone figure standing on the roadside. As they neared him, he saw it was the old man in the Greek sailor hat who had talked to him in the taverna. The Crazy One. With everything else that had happened since that night, he'd forgotten about him. He tried to recall what the man had said to him. Something about Pythía. She would swallow him. That was it. Now it meant considerably more than it had at the time. Still, it was probably just an old-timer's barroom babble.

The old man stared as they cantered by. "Do you know him?" Indy asked.

She smiled, and it was obvious that she did. "He's no one to be concerned about."

"I've heard he's a member of the Order of Pythía, and that he's made predictions."

She laughed, and shook her head. "Maybe that's why he's known as the village fool. No one takes him seriously." As if to tell him she didn't want to talk about the old man any longer, she prodded the sides of her horse and galloped ahead.

Indy chased her all the way to the stable where they left the horses, then walked to the nearby workshop. It was a wood frame building that looked on the inside like a dusty, poorly lit library. But instead of books, the rows of shelves held artifacts. As far as he could tell, none was the type of ancient handiwork that would interest treasure hunters. No gold, silver, or valuable stones. No sign of a single piece of the vast treasure that Croesus had donated for a single reading: one hundred seventeen bricks of precious metals, a gold lion weighing five hundred seventy pounds, a four-and-a-half foot statue of his pastry cook, and a variety of other treasures. The entire fortune had long ago vanished, claimed by emperors and kings and others. Nero alone had stolen five hundred gold statues from Delphi.

Most of the shelves were stacked with row after row of hand-size tablets on which were inscribed ancient readings. A dozen or so were laid out on the long table where Dorian did most of her work. "Been catching up on your reading?" Indy asked as he ran his fingers over one of the tablets.

"I read a couple of hundred tablets yesterday," she said.

"Why?"

"I haven't read any of them for years. It's good to refresh myself from time to time on the nature of the readings."

Indy picked up one of the tablets, and translated the ancient Greek. It was a mundane reading regarding a merchant's plans to sell six hundred bales of wool to a new customer. The oracle had told him to hold firm on his price, then drop it slightly before sealing the bargain, and he would establish a strong, profitable relationship with the customer that would last years.

He laid the tablet down, wondering what Dorian could gain from reading such material. Maybe it was simply a way of relaxing after her breakdown. He was interested in hearing about her experience, but the only time he'd broached the subject, she had said nothing to reveal her thoughts about the matter.

He watched her as she removed a shoulder bag from a locker, and carried it over to the table. She spread out six picks with heads of different lengths, and explained that all of them originally had been the same size, but were worn by use.

"Many archaeologists prefer to use trowels because they cause less damage to artifacts. But I've found that if you're careful, the pick is a much handier tool. Go ahead and take one."

Indy ran the point of the one he selected over his palm. "You sure I won't damage the tablet?"

"Not unless you hit it. Take your time and work around the base. From what's visible I'd say that about six to eight inches of it is buried. You don't have to go very close to it."

"Why did they use large tablets sometimes, and smaller ones other times?" he asked.

"Most of the readings were recorded on small ones. But important readings that were not for one individual, but for everyone, were sometimes inscribed on larger tablets like the one you'll recover."

Indy pointed to a set of brushes inside her bag, and asked if he would need one. She shook her head. "The tablet will be cleaned after it is out of the hole."

She reached into the bag, and picked up a brush with wiry bristles. "But take this one just in case you hit something unexpected. And before I forget here is a torch holder and a mallet to pound it into the wall."

As Indy placed each of the tools into his knapsack, Dorian looked around as if she were missing something. "Stephanos must have taken the ropes and net already. One rope goes around you, of course, and the other is for the tablet. Cover the tablet with the net as soon as you're down, and then attach the hooks at the opening to the loop at the end of the rope."

"I think I can handle that." The way she was treating him was annoying. Maybe he didn't have experience, but he wasn't an imbecile, and he knew how to attach hooks to a rope.

"Any questions?"

"Don't think so."

She pursed her lips; he couldn't read her expression. "This may seem very elementary to you, but what I've been telling you can make a difference between success and failure. I don't want you to get down there and not know what to do or worse, do it the wrong way."

"How long should it take?"

"You're not going to be able to work comfortably dangling at the end of a rope for very long. We'll pull you up after forty-five minutes. Then, if you're up to it, we'll send you down again after a fifteen-minute rest."

"Maybe I'll finish the first time down."

She grinned. "Don't count on it. Working in that position won't be easy. If you haven't finished by the second period, we'll wait until after the vapors have cleared, and try again around three o'clock."

"So the vapors are dangerous?"

She zipped her shoulder bag shut. "It would be difficult working in the vapors. Don't you think?"

She was hedging, he thought. "Yes, especially if they are dangerous."

She carried the bag over to her locker, and put it away. It was time to press her. "What do you remember?"

She walked back, and stopped in front of him. "Pardon me?"

"In the vapors. What happened?"

Her eyes shifted from him to the row of tablets on the table. "I'm not sure, Indy." Her voice was suddenly weary. "I guess I've been avoiding thinking too much about it."

It was the first time she'd called him Indy since they'd arrived in Delphi. "It might be a good idea to remember."

She nodded, and slowly turned to face him. "I remember entering the mist, inhaling and thinking that there was nothing mephitic at all about it. That it was harmless. In fact, now that I think about it, I felt good, better than I have for a very long time."

"But you passed out."

"I don't remember anything else."

"Maybe you were reacting to your relief that the vapors were harmless," he suggested. "You were tired, you overworked yourself, and that's all it took."

"That's possible, I suppose, but I'm not the fainting sort. The other explanation, of course, is that the vapors were the cause."

Indy made a face. More than ever he suspected Dorian was prone to the same sort of fascination with the mystical that consumed his father. "Think about it. If the vapors were dangerous, then the man who carried you out—Panos—would have suffered a similar reaction. I'm sure he didn't hold his breath like Nikos. He was in there too long."

A floorboard creaked behind them, and they both turned. Doumas was standing inside the doorway. "It's almost noon, Dr. Belecamus."

Dorian straightened, and nodded. "Yes. I think we're ready."

* * *

Dorian watched the top of Jones's fedora vanish into the fissure as Doumas and two of his assistants slowly threaded the rope through their hands. Soon they would have the tablet. It might prove interesting, but was probably nothing of consequence.

The excavation of Delphi, for all practical matters, was over. Anything that was found would probably only reaffirm what was already known. Of course, she hadn't told that to Jones, and in his naïveté he had followed her here thinking that he would be involved in a major discovery. But Jones *would* play an important role, and soon. He had no idea how important.

Alex's ally in the king's office had done his job perfectly. Everything had worked out fine. The king had been persuaded. If anything, she was surprised with the swiftness of the decision.

Yet, she was having a hard time focusing on Alex's mission. Which was exactly it, she thought. Alex's mission, not hers, not really.

The vapors had changed everything. By the time she had walked into the vapors, the mystery of the oracle had dominated her thoughts. That in itself was odd. She had never really thought of the oracle as a mystery. It was a phenomenon of ancient times, of a prescientific era. Yet now she saw it as something more, as a phenomenon with a future as well as a past.

But maybe this was all wrong. Was it really possible that she could be Pythía? She needed to talk to Panos. That was critical. But she had to make sure that no one saw them.

"Can I help?"

Dorian's head jerked around. Standing behind her and to one side was a young Greek she'd seen in the village. "What are you doing here?"

"That's Panos's son," Doumas said. "Come on over here, Grigoris, and help with the rope."

Dorian watched suspiciously. Suddenly, the rope went slack, and Doumas yelled down to Jones.

"He must be there by now," Dorian said.

Doumas shook his head. "No. He hasn't gone far enough yet."

"Then pull it tight," she barked, thinking that Jones must have wedged himself between the walls. "Hurry up." But Doumas didn't react fast enough, and the rope snapped taut with a twang.

Dorian leaned over the crevice, and called down to Jones. He answered after a moment that he was all right, but that he had lost his torch. Another one was quickly fastened to the rope that was intended for the tablet, and sent down. When Jones signaled that he had the torch, Doumas and the others resumed lowering him.

"Be careful with him," Dorian cautioned. It wasn't long before Jones called out that he had spotted the tablet, and they slowly lowered him the rest of the way.

Dorian paced back and forth along the crevice. If Jones was lucky, he might be able to complete the job and return to the surface within half an hour. A lot depended on how difficult he found the work. If her primary concern had been the tablet, she would never have let him go after it. Although he had a good mind and was surprisingly well informed about archaeology, he lacked experience. Of course Doumas had been right about him; he was unqualified. She'd chosen him for the task, though, because she realized that she had to create a challenge for him, or his interest would fade and he might return to Paris in disgust.

She couldn't let that happen. Not now. He was too much a part of her plan.

She was near the far end of the chasm when she heard an excited exchange of words between Doumas and the others. Jones couldn't have loosened the tablet already. Not that fast. Not unless it was cracked and had broken. When she reached the men, Doumas was holding one of the ropes in his hand as it dangled loosely above the hole.

"What happened?" she yelled.

"Dr. Belecamus. The rope broke. I don't know how it happened."

"Which rope?" she demanded.

"The one Jones was on," Doumas answered.

"What? No!"

She dropped to her knees and peered into the chasm, but she could see only blackness. She grabbed the rope from Doumas and quickly pulled it to the surface. It looked as if it had been cut partway through, then rubbed in the dirt to look as if it were frayed. She stood up and held out the rope accusingly. The bastard Grigoris was smirking. She swore he was, though his expression was blank. And Doumas? He rocked from side to side as though he would tumble over if he didn't keep adjusting his balance.

Then she suddenly remembered the other rope. Maybe Jones had grabbed it when the first one snapped. She scanned the ground, but it wasn't there. "Where is the other one, the other rope?"

Doumas glanced at Grigoris. "He lost it. In the excitement."

Just then she heard a sound, a sound she couldn't believe, coming from the crevice. She dropped to her knees, and cupped her hands at her mouth. "Indy, can you hear me?"

His voice sounded distant, strained. "Yeah. I can hear you."

"Are you all right?"

He didn't answer for a moment. "Not really. Get me a rope. Fast."

"Okay. Where are you?" she yelled.

"Hanging on the tablet, but I don't know how much longer it's going to hold me."

Dorian glanced over her shoulder at Doumas. "Stephanos, hurry. A rope."

Doumas looked around as if he expected to see one lying nearby. "I'll have to go back. There's one in the stable."

"Well, don't stand there, damn it. Get it. Fast."

"Run to the stable, Grigoris," Doumas said. "Quick. Get the rope hanging on the hook by the door."

"I didn't tell you to send him for it," Dorian snapped, but Doumas was already waddling after the villager who had scampered away. Close behind him were his assistants. Neither of them apparently wanted to stay with her. She wondered why not.

Shaking her head, she turned back to the hole. "It's coming, Jones. In a couple of minutes."

She should have gotten the rope herself. She didn't trust any of them.

There was no reply. "Jones. Are you okay?"

Again no reply.

If he had fallen, wouldn't he have yelled?

"Indy, answer me!"

"Yeah," a faint voice responded after a long moment. "Hurry."

14

LAST GRASP

Indy straddled the tablet as if it were a saddle. He pressed his face against it, and wrapped his arms tightly around it. He could feel the etched lettering against his cheek. How much longer would he have to wait?

He tried to take his mind off his precarious situation by going over what had happened. He'd no sooner finished scribbling the translation of the tablet when the rope had started unraveling. He'd desperately pulled himself up the rope, but it had snapped just as he'd grasped the end above the fray. He'd dangled a moment, then felt a jerk from above, and the rope had slipped through his grasp. But his free hand had been reaching up, and as he fell he'd snagged the other rope and slid down it onto the tablet. He'd yelled, and the rope had gone slack and tumbled down, nearly knocking him off his precarious perch.

Indy's thoughts were interrupted by a creaking as the tablet slipped downward under his weight. It tilted at a forty-five degree angle and it was getting difficult to maintain his grasp.

He realized that he was still wearing the knapsack with the tools. Nothing like digging your own grave. He didn't need the weight. He carefully shed the pack, one arm at a time. He was about to let it drop when he realized that the pick might still come in handy. He slipped his hand into the pack, felt its sharp tip, and pulled it out. Then he dropped the pack, and a moment later heard a clatter as it crashed against something. Must have bounced off the wall, he thought. He listened for it to strike bottom. He shook his head when he didn't hear anything.

"No bottom. Swell."

Talking aloud seemed to ease his fear. "Gotta do something. But what?"

He felt the tablet slip another inch. He closed his eyes. He remembered Dorian stressing the use of the pick and how he should attach the rope to the tablet. She should've been more concerned about what was going on at the other end. Hell, she should've inspected the damn rope before he went down. And what about Doumas? But there was little time to ponder what had happened. He was too busy trying to stay alive.

He felt the net beneath his legs, and wondered if he should unhook the rope to lighten the load. No, that would require too much maneuvering. A good jolt now and the tablet might break loose. Besides, he was the excess weight, not the rope.

"That's it. I've got to get off."

If he could carve footholds and handholds with the

pick, he might be able to balance himself on the wall. But for how long?

"Better to die trying to save my ass than doing nothing," he muttered.

The tablet groaned and slipped again. It wouldn't hold much longer. Slowly, he worked his way up the tablet toward the wall. A few more inches, he told himself. Patience. Finally, he was close enough to touch the wall with the pick. "Now, get some leverage."

He stretched his hand above his head and slammed the pick at the wall. But to his surprise, he struck something, and the pick flew from his hand. The tablet groaned, tilted even further, and he slid down several inches before he caught himself.

Christ, he'd hit the torch holder. He'd forgotten about it. It was still there, secured to the wall by four prongs. Now it was his only hope. He had to get back up to the wall, and get a hand on it. If he distributed his weight between the base of the tablet and the holder he might save himself yet.

He imagined himself a feather-light acrobat gliding up the tablet and effortlessly balancing himself. The tablet groaned again, and he forgot about acrobatic maneuvers. He froze, but the tablet was shaking, and he was sliding back. He cursed. He thought of his whip still coiled on the wall in his room back in Paris. If he had it now, he could lash it around the torch holder with an easy snap of his wrist. He swore that if he lived to go on another archaeological dig, the whip was going with him.

He slipped another few inches. The further he slid, the more the tablet pulled away from the wall. The groaning grew louder; the tablet was about to fall. Desperately, he clambered up the tablet and lunged for the wall. His fedora fell off his head and tumbled into the darkness, but his fingers hooked over the torch holder, first one hand, then the other. He tested the strength of the holder. The pick had knocked it slightly askew, and the prongs started to pull away.

"Real nice." Carefully, he stood up on the tablet, using the holder and wall to balance himself.

"Indy... are you all right?" Dorian's voice echoed eerily down the fissure. "Indy?"

"No."

"The rope should be here any moment. Hold on."

"Good advice," he said.

She was calling him Indy again. Lot of good it would do if he fell. *Pythía will swallow you like a mouse.* The old man's words echoed in his head. Maybe he hadn't been talking about Dorian, but about the mythical python, and how he was dangling precariously inside the creature's gullet.

A shiver ran up his spine. "I hate snakes, even mythical ones."

But the morbid thoughts kept coming. Maybe his first professional archaeology experience would be his last. A short career. "Good joke, Indy. Keep 'em up."

He looked up toward the spot of light high overhead. "Hurry with that rope."

Another stray thought pushed against his mind like an annoying burr. What if no one was getting a rope? If Dorian had dispatched Doumas, he might not return at all. The bastard had probably cut the rope, and when he found out Indy had managed to save himself on the other one, he let it go. What else could it be, an accident? He doubted it.

Someone, probably Doumas, had already been down here and cleaned the tablet. That was why Doumas hadn't wanted him sent down here in the first place. Then he'd changed his mind when he realized he could protect Pythía by getting rid of him.

That made him angry. He'd show Doumas. Somehow he was going to get out of here alive. "I'm going to make it," he said between clenched teeth. "I'm not going to fall."

Hell, he might even be able to salvage the tablet yet. When the rope got here—and it would get here—and he was firmly attached to it, he'd grab the rope that was still knotted to the tablet. He was sure that a tug from the top would loosen it. But he'd wait until he was out of this damn hole before he'd try it.

"Indy?"

"You got it?" he yelled hopefully.

"No. I'm going to go see what's taking them so long. I should have gotten it myself. Doumas is useless."

Great. More waiting.

He tried to relax by adjusting his feet. A mistake—but he realized it too late. The shifting of his weight had been all that was needed to jar the tablet free. With a loud snap, it broke and tumbled away.

His legs kicked out, then scraped against the wall. He heard a crash as the tablet struck something. His feet searched for a foothold, but the wall was nearly smooth. The torch holder bent downward, the prongs slowly working their way free.

"Oh, shit."

This was it. He gritted his teeth; his heart pounded in his ears as the prongs pulled out of the wall.

He fell. Again.

He was moving through a tunnel, toward a light. It was growing brighter and brighter. *This is death.*

Indy. Indy.

The sound echoed around him.

He blinked his eyes against the light. So bright. Like a ball of flames. So close now. What would happen when he reached the light? Where would he go?

His eyes slid sideways and in the light he saw his fedora and the pack he'd dropped, and pieces of the shattered tablet. It all came back to him. He'd fallen into the abyss. His thighs had jammed against his chest. He'd felt searing pain.

Then nothing.

Now his ribs ached. His right hand throbbed; it was wet with blood. His throat was choked with dust, and one thigh felt as if it had been struck by a hammer. Was death this painful? Did you wake up feeling all the pain you missed when you lost consciousness? He tried to lift himself up, but couldn't. He was still moving toward the flaming light; it hurt his eyes.

Then he realized it was a torch. It was attached to a rope, and coming toward him. He was alive and still in the goddamn hole.

He cringed as he sat up. Why was he still alive?

The torch was swinging several feet above him now and he could see that he was on an overhang that loomed from the wall. He squinted up into the light. He couldn't tell where the tablet had been, but he was sure now that he hadn't fallen far. Maybe only fifteen, twenty feet. He felt bits of rubble from the shattered tablet underneath him. If he hadn't been wearing his leather jacket, he would have been hurt much worse.

He watched as the torch continued down past him, and the brightness faded until it was just a glimmer below him. *I'm supposed to stop it. But I didn't.*

"Indy. Can you hear me?"

"Dorian, we've gone well past the depth of the tablet," another voice said. "He's gone. Face it." The voice wasn't as loud as Dorian's, but the chasm was like a megaphone and it carried easily to him. Doumas. The bastard was giving up on him.

It was getting bright again. The torch was rising. He understood exactly what was happening. He was being abandoned. But he was in a stupor, and couldn't coordinate his thoughts with actions. He had to do something.

He cleared his throat. With an effort, he yelled: "Dorian."

But it came out as a whisper. His throat was dry and felt like it was caked with dirt. He tried again. Louder this time, a gravely sound. But not loud enough.

The torch swung at his knees, his waist, his chest. He reached out; snared it. He felt a tug, and pulled back. Then the rope slackened, and wriggled like a snake.

"It must have caught on something," Doumas said. The snake rose until he felt the torch being pulled from his hand. He jerked on it.

For a moment there was no reaction, then he felt

another tug on the rope, and he was pulled to his feet. He felt as if he were fishing, only he was the fish.

"What is it?" Dorian asked.

"I don't know."

"Give it to me. Indy . . . Indy."

He bent over to pick up his hat, and realized he was standing a half step from the brink of the prominence.

"Indy. Please answer."

He edged backward. He saw a cone-shaped rock protruding from the wall and grabbed hold of it. He pulled on the rope, and tugged again, and a third time.

"It's him. I felt it. He's down there. Indy, pull again if you can hear me."

He did. Quickly, they worked out a simplistic way of communicating. One tug, yes. Two, no. Was he badly hurt? No. Could he tie the rope around himself? Yes. Did he need more rope? Yes.

Another several feet coiled in front of him. He sat down to figure out the best way of attaching the rope. He didn't want it around his waist or his chest. He had at least one cracked or bruised rib on each side. Maybe more. He fumbled with the rope; his hand throbbed. He pressed his bloody palm against his stomach, trying to stop the bleeding. Finally, he tied a loop, threaded the rope through it, then stepped inside the large loop. He would sit in it like a swing.

He was about to signal Dorian that he was ready when he took another look at the rock he'd been grasping. It was black, shaped like a cone, and still partially buried in the wall. He held the torchlight over it. Its surface was thatched as if it had once been encased in a rope sheath and the strands had petrified.

"What is this?" he whispered hoarsely.

He grabbed the pack and took out the hard-bristle brush. He scraped away some of the dirt encrusted on it and ran his fingertips over the rough surface. He lowered the torch until it was almost touching the cone. It looked like obsidian, or iron, and the thatching, he was convinced, was not natural, but man-made.

"Indy, are you all right?" Dorian called down to him.

He glanced up, then tugged once on the rope.

"Ready?" Dorian called.

This time he jerked twice. "Not quite." He'd lost the tablet, but maybe he could salvage the cone. He didn't know why, but he sensed it was something important, something he shouldn't leave behind.

He wrapped his arms around the cone to see if he could loosen it. He pulled, and he thought it moved. He took in a deep breath and pulled again. There. It moved. He was sure of it. He laid his chest against the cone to catch his breath. He was exhausted, dizzy.

Then he saw the eagle.

It was winging skyward. He watched it.

The eagle. His eagle.

Here to help.

The eagle. His guardian, his protector.

But where have you been? I needed you. Indy heard his thoughts as if he were talking, but he was sure his lips weren't moving. The eagle continued soaring higher and higher. His skin tingled. He was neither asleep nor awake.

His thoughts drifted back to when he was fourteen and had met an old Navajo named Changing Man while on a desert hike with his father. The Indian had taken a liking to young Indy, and said he would see him again. It hardly seemed likely, because a few months later Indy had moved to Chicago. The summer after he graduated from high school he returned to the Southwest to work on his uncle's ranch, but by then his encounter with the old Indian was only a distant memory.

However, one day he stopped at a trading post to buy supplies, and there was Changing Man. He not only remembered Indy, but acted as though he'd been expecting him. Was he ready for his vision quest? he asked. Indy didn't know what he meant, but he was curious about the old Indian and his ways and said yes, he was ready. The following day, he met Changing Man at daybreak outside the trading post and they hiked up a mesa. By nightfall Indy found himself alone and without food on the windswept surface. Changing Man had told him he must wait there until an animal approached him, and from that time on it would be his protector and spiritual guide.

After two days he was delirious from hunger and his canteen was nearly empty. It was a mistake, a big mistake. Maybe vision quests worked for Indians, but no animals were interested in him, unless it was to pick at his bones after he was dead. He walked away from the stone shelter he'd built, hoping he had enough strength for the trek down. He would find water and food, go back to the ranch, and in another few weeks he would be home in Chicago again where he would start college. As he reached the edge of the mesa, he heard a voice behind him. The voice of Changing Man. *Where are you going?* Startled, he turned around. No one was there. He was hallucinating. But he hesitated. The trail was too steep. The sun was low. Feeling defeated, he headed back to the shelter for the night. He would wait until morning.

Suddenly, an eagle swooped low over the mesa and landed on the top of the wall of his shelter. He stopped and stared, and again heard the voice of Changing Man. *He will always guide you.* In spite of everything, or maybe because of it, he had found his protector.

He recalled all of it as he watched the eagle soaring above him. He could see it turn its head as if it were looking for prey. Or maybe back at him. It made a noise. What was it saying? The eagle faded, but the sound continued.

"Indy, Indy."

It was Dorian. She sounded frantic. "Answer me."

He tugged on the rope.

"There's not much time. The vapors."

Vapors. Christ. He'd forgotten all about that. Had he been down here that long? He pulled his pocket watch from inside his jacket. It had survived his fall and was still working. It was 2:44. He stood up and tightened the loop of rope. He wasn't convinced the vapors were dangerous, but there was no reason to take any chances.

No time now for the cone. He must have drifted off for a minute. But he'd come back for it, he told himself. He tugged once.

A moment later, he felt himself rising and swinging out from the debris-strewn overhang. His eyes focused on the black object frozen in the wall. Then it was blanketed in darkness, lost in a lightless abyss.

He held the torch out and watched for the spot where the tablet had been. Ten, fifteen, twenty feet. He continued rising. It was hazy from the torch smoke, but then he saw it. A dark hole, and above it a smaller indention where the torch holder had been yanked from the wall. God, he was lucky. People fell three feet and broke bones. He'd tumbled two stories through pitch darkness and survived with cuts, bruises, probably a couple of cracked ribs.

He heard a deep rumble from somewhere below. It was followed by the same hissing that preceded the rising of the vapors, and he knew he would not escape them. The slow, easy swing of the ascent continued, and there was nothing he could do to speed it up. He swung the torch in front of him, noticing a haze. There was too much of it to be torch smoke.

He squeezed the rope tighter and sucked in a deep breath. It hurt his ribs, and he expelled some of it. He wondered how much longer it would take to reach the surface. A minute passed. Slowly, he released the rest of the air. Tainted air. No use holding his breath if he was already breathing the vapors.

He sniffed at the air. It didn't seem to have any effect, except he was feeling drowsy. He was exhausted from the fall and his injuries. He pressed his forehead against the rope and closed his eyes. Within seconds, he felt himself drifting, half asleep, half awake.

His head jerked up, and he grabbed the rope. He must have dozed. Then he saw the vapors rising around him. How long had he been breathing them? He forced himself to concentrate on the rope and keep his balance.

Just hold on. Stay awake. Try not to breathe. God, he ached.

Another minute passed, an elastic minute that felt like hours, but finally he popped through the lip of the hole, and drank in the cool air. The mound was covered in mist, and he couldn't see anyone. He climbed to his feet, wincing in pain, and felt himself being pulled down the mound.

"Indy, down here."

He stumbled forward, picking up momentum. He raised his arms to block his fall. Then suddenly hands were grabbing him. The rope was pulled over his chest, shoulder, arms. He crumpled to his knees, fell onto his stomach. Someone rolled him over.

"We've got to get him to the doctor." Dorian's voice. "Carry him to the wagon. Fast."

He saw movement around him, shapes, blurs. He felt himself being lifted again. He closed his eyes.

"What happened down there, Indy?" Dorian asked. "How did you survive?"

"I found a stone, a black stone," he mumbled.

"What kind of stone?" It was Doumas's voice.

"Shaped like a cone, thatching on it."

"Can you find it again?" Doumas asked.

But Indy never answered. His eyes closed and he was out.

15

MANEUVERS

Dorian looked up from a stack of stone tablets on the workshop table as she heard a tapping sound. It was so faint that she thought it might be the wind. Then she heard it again, louder this time. "Come in."

The door creaked slowly open; she saw a shadow in the doorway, then recognized Panos. "Well, I've been waiting for you."

Panos hesitated, looked down at his hands. "Not as long as I've waited." The words were forced, a confession. Then he stepped inside and peered at the rows of stone tablets. "Soon, a new, modern house of records will be built." His voice was stronger, and the words were spoken like a challenge. He watched her closely.

"I know," she answered.

"Do you?" Again, he shifted his eyes as she met his gaze, and she realized that he was feeling self-conscious, maybe overwhelmed.

"It will be needed," she added.

"Tell me who you are," he demanded, but his eyes still shifted about uneasily.

She smiled and answered without hesitating. "Pythía, of course."

He nodded, glancing up at her. "The veil is receding. I knew it would."

She picked up one of the stone tablets and ran her fingers over it. "I understand now that the oracle never left us. The last Pythía merely put it to bed, and now it is reawakening."

"Well said."

"It's very strange, but I understand now that my life's work has been only a prelude to the Return. A week ago I would have laughed at such an idea. Now, I know it for a fact."

Panos paced in front of the long table covered with stone tablets. He picked one of them up, examined it briefly, then laid it back down. There was something defiant in the act, as if he were making claim to the workshop and everything it represented and daring her to challenge him. "My son, Grigoris, told me that Jones found something in the crevice. What was it?"

"I'm not sure. He said something about a black stone."

Panos spun on his heels and faced her. "The stone is important, and Doumas must not ever touch it." He spoke sharply; his eyes flared. "It is ours, and we must have it."

Dorian was baffled. She was surprised by his outburst. She didn't know what he was talking about.

"Don't you understand? He has found the Omphalos. We must claim it."

The Omphalos was a mysterious aspect of the Oracle of Delphi that Dorian had never clearly grasped. In legend, it was sometimes described as a stone that was as large as a room, other times as one that was small and portable, cone-shaped, like Jones had described. Sometimes, even Delphi itself was called the Omphalos, the navel of the world. She'd always viewed it as more symbolic than real, more of a definition of Delphi than a relic that could be recovered.

"How do you know it's the Omphalos?"

"The Oracle could not return without the Omphalos," he answered.

"Why is that, Panos?"

He frowned at her. "You still have much to remember. Pythía should know the great secret of Delphi."

She smiled at him. "I am Pythía, but I am also Dorian Belecamus, and I do not know everything that Pythía knows. Tell me about the Omphalos."

Panos paused a moment; she had the distinct impression that he wasn't sure he should say anything. Then he made up his mind, and spoke. "The secret is simple. The vapors only enhance what the Omphalos creates. The Omphalos is the power of Delphi."

"Yes. Simple." She made it sound like an interesting fact. Nothing more. But in all her years of study and her work at Delphi, she had never heard such a thing. The Omphalos had always been nebulous, symbolic, never *the* power itself.

"Does that mean the authority of Pythía can be taken beyond Delphi if we have the Omphalos?"

"The navel of the world is wherever the Omphalos is."

Dorian crossed her arms, and leaned against the table. "Panos, I have so much to remember. Tell me more about the Omphalos. Where did it come from?"

He pointed his index finger skyward. "It was a gift from Apollo himself."

She raised her eyes as if the gods inhabited the rafters. "You mean the Omphalos fell from the sky and landed here at Delphi?"

He stared at the stone tablets on the table for well over a minute before answering. "That is another secret."

She waited expectantly for him to continue. "I would like to answer yes, but the truth is that it fell elsewhere, and a messenger of Apollo brought it here, to the sacred place where the gases were rising from the ground."

Probably a meteorite, Dorian thought. It made sense that such a stone would be worshiped, and the fact that it had not fallen right where the vapors were rising made it even more believable. She smiled confidently. "We will get the Omphalos. But now the king is coming."

"Yes. And you must speak to him. He needs to understand who you are. He must accept it."

She nodded solemnly.

"I know you will sway him." His words were gentle, soothing, but he was still uncomfortable in her presence, and stared at the table as he spoke.

"Yes, and I already sense what Pythía will say."

He slowly shifted his gaze. His eyes gave him away. He was hoping she would give him a hint.

"I'll tell you what I already know," she began. "Soon the world will recognize that the Oracle of Delphi is alive. All the world will look to the Oracle for hope, and the power of Greece will be magnified a hundredfold."

Panos smiled broadly. "And Pythía will tell this to the king."

Her eyes blinked rapidly. "Yes, and more."

She took the stonemason by the arm and led him to the door, all the while whispering, telling him far more than he had expected to hear.

Panos sipped his retsina, and listened to Doumas. It was early afternoon and only a couple of other tables in the taverna were occupied. They were seated in the same booth where they had been when Jones swaggered over to them the other night, and now the foreigner was on his mind again. The man was a problem, potentially a serious one.

Doumas, unfortunately, didn't see it that way. A fat intellectual, all paunch and jowls, he was more committed to ideas than action. "I don't know what Grigoris was thinking, but you've got to control him. He almost killed Jones. What's worse is that Belecamus suspects it was no accident."

Doumas's double chin was shaking as he spoke; he reminded Panos of an overweight turkey. He wanted to tell him that he was spineless, that he'd failed to deal with Jones, but instead he acted surprised. "How do you know that?"

"Because she found me arguing with Grigoris in the stable. He actually pulled a knife on me so I wouldn't take her another rope."

Panos poured himself another glass of retsina from the bottle on the table. "Did she see the knife or hear anything that was said?"

"I don't think so. She was in a hurry. But she knew we were arguing."

Panos cast a look of annoyance at the occupants of one of the other tables. They were foreigners, three men and a woman. They were talking loudly, and spoke English. The woman, in particular, had an abrasive voice. He wished they would leave. They shouldn't be here, not in the taverna, not in Delphi. Not now.

"There is something I don't understand. If the rope broke, why is Jones still alive?"

Doumas looked exasperated. "He got lucky."

Panos thought a moment. He knew he should tell Doumas that he would control Grigoris, but the truth was he was out of control. "I will talk to my son. He should not have threatened you. He will apologize. I promise."

Doumas didn't look satisfied. Too bad. "Now, tell me something. What is the connection between Jones and Belecamus?"

Doumas smiled, a sly smile that said he should know what it was. "She likes younger foreign men. What else can I say?"

So that was it. Now Panos was more certain than ever that Jones must be quickly eliminated. He could only be trouble; he could slow the transformation. It was time to put Doumas to the test. "One way or another Jones must be taken care of. Immediately. We can't chance him interfering with our work."

"He won't interfere. He's confined to a bed in his hotel room. I'm sure he won't be going anywhere until after the king has come and gone. Besides, you are sure to anger Belecamus if anything happens to him."

"How can we be certain he stays in bed? I don't trust him. He doesn't understand what Delphi is about."

"You worry too much, Panos. You know what the tablet in the crevice said. Nothing can stop the Return now. Not Jones, not anyone. It will happen as sure as the king is rich."

Panos glowered at him. "The tablet was confirmation of the blueprint. But we must still do what is necessary to fulfill it."

Doumas emptied his glass, then set it on the table. "You have to understand my position. I am a scientist, an archaeologist. I have a reputation."

Panos laughed. "What is your reputation, Stephanos? Caretaker of old stones. Stop wavering. Your rubble will still be there no matter what you do."

"What do you want of me, Panos? I got Belecamus here. I went down that hole and interpreted the tablet. I could have been killed. What more do you want?"

"You wanted to know about the Order of Pythía. You wanted to know everything. Now you must fulfill your responsibilities."

"I'm not a killer. That's Grigoris's work."

Panos bolted out of his chair, and grabbed Doumas by the collar. "Don't talk that way about my son," he growled between clenched teeth. "Do you understand? I don't want to hear that."

As he lowered himself back into the chair he saw the group of foreigners looking their way. He ignored them.

Doumas glared back at him. "Don't ask me to kill Jones, or anyone. I won't do it. But I will tell you something that you don't know. Something valuable."

Panos stared sullenly at him. "What is it?"

Doumas leaned over the table. "I know precisely when the vapors will rise. There's a pattern, and unless things change I can predict the time of the risings tomorrow, next month, and for years."

Panos considered what he'd said. He was surprised that Doumas would know such a thing and made an effort to control his astonishment. "Go ahead. Tell me."

As Doumas spoke, Panos gazed over the archaeologist's shoulder at two uniformed men who had entered the taverna. They looked around, and took a table. The taller of the two looked familiar.

Panos concentrated on what Doumas was saying. "That's good to know. Six minutes is the key."

His gaze shifted to the other table again. Now he remembered where he'd seen the man. Belecamus had met him the morning he'd followed her from her house to the Roman Agora. From the way they'd acted he was sure they were close to each other. He remembered thinking that the officer was potential trouble, and now he knew he was right.

"We have another problem." He tilted his head toward the table.

Doumas followed his glance. "Military men. Probably related to the king's trip."

Panos could tell by Doumas's expression that he knew something more. "Who is he, Stephanos? I've seen the one with her."

Doumas looked back again, as if he hadn't recognized the man. He leaned over the table again. "Colonel Alexander Mandraki. Belecamus has been seeing him off and on for years. Lovers."

Panos frowned. "What could she see in him? He's ugly."

Doumas grinned. "Power, of course. You should know that."

A tight smile curled on Panos's lips as he sat back in his chair. A plan was taking form. "We must turn him against Jones so that he does our work for us."

Doumas glanced warily over his shoulder, making certain that Mandraki wasn't listening to them. "That's a possibility."

"Then, Belecamus will be angry with him, which will also be to our advantage."

"But her allegiance is with Mandraki," Doumas said. "She won't turn against him."

"Maybe not for long. But the shock of finding out who has killed her young lover-student will surely alienate her, at least temporarily, and all we need is a few hours."

Doumas threaded his fingers, and cracked his knuckles. "Two birds, one stone. You're clever, Panos. You should have been a politician."

Panos looked over at the foreigners, who were getting up from their table. When the transformation was complete he would be a politician of sorts, a power broker for the world's leaders who would come to him seeking access to Pythía, Oracle of Delphi.

"Let's not waste any more time, Stephanos."

"All right, I'll go tell him about Jones."

"No, I'll do it myself. You intellectuals have a hard time dealing with emotional matters. I want to make sure it gets done right. I want him angry so he acts."

Panos pushed his chair away from the table, and moved away without another word.

Doumas watched as Panos leaned over Mandraki's table and said something to him. This should be interesting, he thought, and refilled his glass. The colonel nodded, and turned to the other man at the table. The soldier abruptly stood, and walked over to the bar. Mandraki motioned Panos to sit down, and listened as the little man rested an elbow on the table and raised a hand to his mouth in a gesture of confidentiality.

Doumas looked away as two of the foreigners from the other table left the taverna. He knew exactly what Panos thought about him. To rugged, earthy people like the stonemason, excessive weight was a sign of weakness. Panos saw him as a bumbling, overeducated guardian of the ruins. But that was fine. Just what he wanted.

He knew that Panos envisioned himself as the new high priest of the oracle, but he was a fool to think that Dorian Belecamus would let him manipulate her. Belecamus had her own agenda. Even if the vapors affected her as Panos said, she would not always be under their influence.

Panos didn't know Belecamus; he only knew *of* her. He didn't know the stories about her, which anyone in the archaeology faculties could tell him. Even the Crazy One, who supposedly knew so much, didn't know anything of her private life. Doumas knew Belecamus; he knew the stories, and knew they were true.

Mandraki's face darkened and clouded over. The corners of his lips turned down. He rubbed his chin and nodded, then with a flick of his hand dismissed Panos as if he were chasing away a fly. Panos literally leaped to his feet, and knocked over his chair.

The colonel sneered and pointed to the door; Doumas clearly heard Mandraki's angry voice. "Get out of my sight, *maláka*."

Panos quickly retreated. The colonel's companion moved back to the table and picked up the fallen chair. Mandraki waved a hand, as if to say it was nothing, then motioned for the soldier to sit down. "*Maláka*," Mandraki repeated loudly.

Doumas laughed to himself. It felt good to see the leader of the Order of Pythía, who thought so much of himself and so little of him, called an asshole and dismissed like a servant who performed his duties poorly.

If Belecamus was a normal woman, she would act as Panos expected. She would shun her Colonel Alex if he killed Jones. But to Belecamus, Jones was already a dead man. He was sure of it.

Now everything was in his hands, Doumas thought. The colonel would never let Panos near Belecamus long enough for him to lead her to the crevice and if Panos failed, the blueprint would no longer be viable. The opportunity would be missed. Panos, his lifework destroyed, would go back to Athens and his masonry work, and Dorian Belecamus, the failed Pythía, would return to Paris and her teaching.

But that wouldn't be the end of it. After all, the message he'd uncovered on the tablet before

Belecamus arrived had convinced him that Panos was on the right track. However, the inscription clearly had left open the matter of who would assume the duties of the new Pythía. Even the Crazy One's old prophecy, which had mentioned the return of *a Dorian,* did not specify that she was the oracle.

In spite of what had happened at the crevice, he was certain she was not Pythía. She was ruthless and cunning, and those were definitely *not* traits of a good Pythía. Maybe the high priest was cunning, but Pythía was an innocent, an immaculate peasant woman transformed to a divination tool.

When everyone left and he was alone and in charge of Delphi, he would quietly recover the black stone—the Omphalos. Then he would test the young village girls, and maybe among them he would find the true Pythía. More and more, he was feeling that it was his destiny, not Panos's, to nurture the new Pythía. He would be the interpreter, the priest, and the one who would present her to the world.

The power would be his.

16

ROYAL RECEPTION

His eyes blinked open, but Indy didn't move, barely breathed. He felt something in the air that shouldn't have been there, a presence. Someone was in here with him. His limbs tensed instinctively. Slowly, he turned his head, scanning the room.

Then he saw a figure standing in front of the window, silhouetted by the afternoon sunshine. "Ah, Christ, Nikos," he said as he recognized the aquiline nose and classical Greek features. "What are you doing now?"

The kid was getting to be a pest. He'd been looking in on him every few hours for the past two days, and Indy had just talked to him before he'd fallen asleep.

"Sorry. I was just leaving, and didn't want to wake you up. I got the knapsack. I put it under the bed."

"That was fast."

"You slept almost four hours."

"I did?" Indy grimaced as he sat up, and touched his side. The last time they'd talked he'd asked Nikos if he would discreetly pick up his knapsack from the workshop. He rubbed the sleep from his eyes. "Did anyone see you?"

Nikos shook his head. "No one was there. I got in through a window."

Indy's gaze strayed to the bedstand. He squinted, trying to make sense of what he saw. A ceramic bowl rested on the bedstand, and inside it were three heads of garlic twisted together. "What's this?"

Nikos's dark eyes moved from the bowl to Indy. "Moly. It will help you."

Indy looked at it again. "Moly. God, I haven't heard anyone call garlic by that name since I was a kid."

Nikos took a couple of steps closer to him. "I didn't know there was moly in America. What did you use it for when you were a kid?"

"It's a long story."

"Tell me," he said, sitting at the foot of the bed.

Indy clasped his hands behind his head, and recalled the incident, one of those he would never forget.

"Get me the moly," his father had said one day, and when Indy admitted he didn't know what he was talking about he was forced to eat a clove of garlic a day until he knew why it was called moly. The question mystified Indy for nearly two weeks, long enough for him to lose a couple of friends who thought he smelled. As a result, he spent more time reading Homer, another task required by his father.

Finally, while struggling through a scene in *The Odyssey,* he discovered moly. It was a species of garlic which supposedly possessed magical power. Hermes gave it to Odysseus for protection against the

enchantments of Circe. After that his father never required him to either eat garlic, or call it moly.

"You think I need protection, Nikos?"

"Yes, I do."

"Why?"

"There are strange things going on."

"Like what?" he asked. He'd bet it had something
to do with the Order of Pythía, and expected Nikos to
tell him that Panos and Doumas had conspired to kill
him. But he was wrong.

"After I got back from the workshop, two
Americans came to the hotel. They were very friendly.
They told me they knew you, and wanted to see you."

"What?"

"Yes, but before I could bring them up here, three
soldiers came and took them away."

"Took them where?"

Nikos shook his head.

Indy was baffled. "Did you get their names?"

"They didn't say, but there is something else I must
also tell you."

"Oh, what else?" Now he'd hear about the Order.
Again, he was wrong.

"It's Dr. Belecamus. I didn't think it mattered, but
now I am not so sure."

Three sharp raps at the door cut Nikos off. He
jumped off the bed as if he'd just been shocked by a
jolt of electricity.

"Go ahead, open it," Indy told him.

It was Dorian. She was dressed in a white gown,
and looked as if she were on her way to a ball. Her
black hair shone in the late afternoon light filtering
through the window, and her beauty was startling.

She glanced from Nikos to Indy. "An I interrupting anything?"

"No. Come on in."

"I have to go now," Nikos said. He gave Indy a furtive look, and disappeared out of the door.

Dorian moved over to the bed. "How are you feeling today?"

Indy shrugged. "Better. Nice to see you." His voice was tinged with sarcasm. It was only her second visit since his accident, and the first time she'd stayed just a couple of minutes. She'd apologized for the accident, but when he'd asked how it had happened, she'd said she had no idea. He didn't believe her. He was sure she'd been hiding something, probably her suspicions about Doumas.

"I've been busy, but I've been thinking about you. I hear Nikos has been keeping you company." Her smile indicated she thought the boy's interest in Indy was humorous. "That's nice, but what do you two talk about?"

"Lots of things. Just now, for instance, he was telling me about two Americans. He said they came to the hotel and were asking for me."

"Did you see them?" she asked brightly.

"No, Nikos said that soldiers came and took them away."

"That was their escort," she said. "I met them at the taverna earlier, and invited them to the royal reception this evening. A charming couple. I came up to ask if you'd come, too."

"But who are they? I don't know anyone in Greece."

Dorian gave him a wicked smile. "I found out a little bit about your past. It was your old girlfriend you left in Paris."

"Madelaine?" Indy was baffled.

"That's the one. She was with a British man named Brent. Friendly chap. They were in Athens when they heard that the king was going to be here, and they came straight away."

"I can't believe it. Why did you invite *them* to the reception?"

"Well, actually they were hinting around for an invitation. They were delighted when I made the offer."

"I can imagine. They're very good guests. They've got lots of experience at parties."

Dorian sat on the bed and patted his thigh. "You sound a bit jealous."

He laughed nervously. "No, not jealous. Just amazed."

"Please come with me? I'm sure they would like to see you."

"Think I'd like to see them myself."

"Good. Then you must be feeling better."

"Guess so. I know I don't like laying in bed day and night."

"Now you'll get a chance to meet the king. I understand he's heard what happened to you, and I'm sure he'll want to see you. You can tell him all about your adventure into the heart of Delphi."

"I was hoping you'd be interested yourself. You haven't even asked about the tablet."

She looked baffled. "Why should I ask about the tablet? It was lost, wasn't it?"

"Someone was down there before me and cleaned it off."

"What?" Her expression turned incredulous. "Are you sure?"

"I even had time to translate it."

"You did? What did it say?"

"I'll read it to you." Indy swung his legs over the side of the bed, and straightened his nightshirt. He reached under the bed, and gritted his teeth as he felt a stab of pain in his side. Then his hand touched the knapsack, and he pulled it out.

"How did you get that?" Dorian asked, suspiciously.

"Oh, I sent for it," he said evasively.

He reached into the side pocket, and found the notebook. He could barely make out his handwriting. Considering he'd scribbled it while suspended in near darkness, it wasn't surprising. Slowly, he read his translation. The legend began with a question, and was followed by a response.

" 'We must know. Will Pythía always be?

*This question is asked by each generation
and the answer is always the same.
Wide is the power of Apollo's Oracle
but only as long as belief exists.
Indeed, the day will come when the last
Pythía departs sacred Delphi.
Only then will fade the great power of
    Apollo
and crumble to dust the works of his
    followers.' "*

He looked up from the notebook at Dorian who remained quiet, pensive. "There's more." He turned the page to where he had written the second question and response.

" 'O Pythía! We pray thee reverence these
boughs of supplication which we bear in our
hands, and deliver to us something more
comforting concerning the future of the oracle.
Else we will not leave thy sanctuary, but will
stay here till we die.

> *True it is what has been said.*
> *Only when the Oracle*
> *is a distant memory,*
> *will there be hope.*
> *Now lift thy hearts*
> *and journey happily home*
> *for upon the restoration*
> *the oracle will return*
> *and its great secret will be revealed.' "*

Dorian put a hand to her throat. "Interesting, very interesting," she murmured. She stood up and ran her hands down her gown, pressing out the wrinkles. She smiled weakly. "Too bad we weren't able to recover it. Well, you'd better get ready. It's getting late. I'll have a carriage in front of the hotel in twenty minutes."

"Twenty minutes? Gee, thanks for the advance notice." But she didn't respond; she was already out the door.

He winced as he shrugged on his shirt, then carefully slipped into his pants. He didn't have many clothes with him so his khaki pants, white cotton shirt and a tie would have to do for the reception. When he was dressed, he pulled on his leather coat and hat. He looked around the room, and saw the moly. He picked it up off the table and turned it over in his hand. He didn't consider himself superstitious. Moly was garlic, and garlic was just that—garlic. But then again, it couldn't hurt having it with him, he thought, and stuck it in his jacket pocket.

The lobby of the Delphi Hotel was anything but grandiose. It was a shabby parlor with a worn rug, a couch that had seen better days, and a couple of straight-backed chairs. On one side was the check-in desk, and to the rear of it beneath the staircase was a cot where Nikos was lying on his side. When he saw Indy, he bolted to his feet.

"What are you doing out of bed?"

"I'm going to the king's reception."

"But—"

The door to the street opened, and Dorian peered in. "There you are. Come on. The carriage is waiting."

"Okay." He glanced at Nikos and shrugged. "Talk to you later."

As they headed out of the village and up the mountain to the clip-clop of hoofs, Indy tried to get comfortable. But he was jostled from side to side, and his ribs ached. He wished he'd stayed in bed, and almost told Dorian he wanted to turn back. "When are they going to get automobiles around here, anyhow?"

"You're not in Chicago, Indy. Besides, a buggy ride is as smooth as a Model T on this road."

"You're probably right," he said. "By the way, why

are you going to this reception? I'm surprised you were invited, or even wanted to attend."

"Come now, Indy. We are not barbarians." She laid a hand on his arm, but only for a moment. "It is the 1920s, after all. We have protocol like any civilized people. The king will show respect toward me, and I will do likewise toward him. My political opinions won't be discussed."

He was tempted to rest a hand on her thigh, and test her reaction, but he thought better of it. Sure, he wanted things to be as they were before they arrived in Delphi, but then again, if she did change her attitude, he wasn't in any condition to do anything about it. At least, not this evening.

"Tomorrow morning, Indy, I'd like you to join the king's entourage when he visits the ruins."

"Why?"

"Why not? I was thinking it would be a good time for you to tell him about the tablet. He'll be very busy this evening."

A few minutes later, the king's retreat came into view high above the road. The massive structure was made of stone and seemed almost to grow from the mountain itself. Both mansion and mountain were painted shades of red and orange by the last rays of sunlight. As they turned off the main road, he noticed groups of tiny figures on the veranda, then the mansion vanished from sight.

They stopped at a security post, and a guard consulted a list when Dorian gave their names. Then they were waved through. The carriage brought them to the front door. As they climbed the steps, another guard manning the entrance looked them over. He frowned at Indy's outfit, then reluctantly waved them through. Dorian ignored him, but Indy appraised him with the same stern demeanor. "Straighten your tie, fellow."

Then they were inside. The room was crowded with guests and waiters in white coats carrying drinks and hor d'oeuvres. There were at least a half dozen fireplaces in the room, fires blazing in each of them. "You ever been here before?" Indy asked.

"Just once. It's a lovely place."

"Big, I bet."

"Thirty-four rooms, including fifteen bedrooms. Just average for a king, I'd say."

"Lots of places to lie down at least. Maybe we could borrow one. It's the 1920s, after all."

She tipped her head toward him, and spoke tersely. "Don't be silly, or flirtatious, and whatever you do, don't say anything foolish to the king."

"I think I can handle myself."

Indy spotted Doumas moving through the crowd toward them—just the person he didn't care to see. The roly-poly archaeologist either was incompetent or had intentionally allowed him to be lowered on a frayed rope. "Look who's coming," he said to Dorian. "I don't feel so well."

"Jones, on your feet already? Remarkable recovery. I'm amazed at your resilience."

Suddenly, they were good friends. Wonderful. "So am I."

"Now what's this you were saying about a black stone?" He busily munched on a plateful of hors d'oeuvres as he spoke.

Indy frowned. "I don't remember saying anything about it."

"Well, whether you remember or not, you did," Doumas said. "When we pulled you out of the hole you mumbled that you had found a cone-shaped stone and you wanted to go back and get it."

"Did I say that?"

"You were out of your head," Doumas said. "But what exactly was it you saw?"

Indy glanced at Dorian. She watched him intently. "Just what I said. It had something covering it like rope that had been petrified. And I would like to go back for it."

"Why?" Dorian asked.

Indy didn't know, but he'd been thinking a lot about the stone. In fact, he couldn't get it out of his head. "I just think it's worth going after, especially since we lost the tablet."

"You're not really in any condition to do it," Doumas said. "Don't you agree, Dr. Belecamus?"

Dorian spoke sharply. "I'm not sure that you are, either, and I don't want *anyone* going into the crevice without asking me. Is that understood, Stephanos?"

"Of course, but—"

Dorian walked away without another word, and disappeared into the crowd.

"She's angry with me," Doumas said. "Because of the rope." He picked a slice of sweetbread off his plate and bit away half of it.

A beat passed as Indy considered the man's audacity. "I'm the one who should be angry. What the hell happened, anyhow?"

"The rope was rotten. Then in the confusion, we

lost the other one. Sorry. I was going to apologize earlier, but I didn't want to disturb you."

Indy was about to accuse him of going into the hole himself and cleaning the tablet when Doumas leaned close and spoke in his ear. "If I were you, Jones, I'd be careful around Dr. Belecamus tonight. Her boyfriend is here, you know. That's him over there, the man in the colonel's uniform. He's jealous, I understand."

Indy almost gagged from the putrid odor emanating from Doumas. He stepped back. The man Doumas nodded toward had a ruddy face and a prominent hooked nose. He looked to be in his early fifties, maybe twenty years older than Dorian.

"Thanks. I'll remember that," Indy said. One day Doumas was trying to kill him, the next he was warning him of danger. It didn't make sense.

And what about the way Dorian had reacted in his room to his comments about the tablet? She'd seemed shaken, not by the fact that someone had cleaned the tablet, but by what it said. Particularly, the last lines which were about the Oracle returning, and some great secret being revealed.

The number of coincidences connected with the old man's predictions were growing, he thought. The earthquake had happened. A Dorian had shown up. The king had arrived. Now the tablet seemed to confirm what the old man had said. Hell, no wonder she'd blanched. She was probably starting to wonder if she actually *was* Pythía. But coincidences happened all the time. They were only mysterious if you were looking for mystery.

"Indy, there you are."

He turned at the sound of the squeaky voice.

"Madelaine." She looked as if nothing had changed and she was just at another *bal musette*. "I heard you'd be here, but I hardly believed it."

"Isn't this just splendid. I just love Greece, don't you?"

"It grows on you."

"Your friend, Dorian, said you had an accident. But you look fine to me."

Indy was about to tell her what had happened when she said something that stopped him cold. "Isn't your buddy, Jack Shannon, going to be here?"

"What are you talking about? Shannon's in Paris."

"No, he's here. I saw him earlier today in the little taverna. He was with someone else who said he knew you, too."

"You saw him here?"

"That's what I just said."

"Who was the other man?"

"I don't remember. Jack introduced him, but there was so much going on. Tom, Terry, maybe Larry. He was older."

"How much older?"

"He was maybe thirty-five, forty. You know, old. He had a beard. He was a Canadian, I think. I don't know."

Who did he know who had a beard and would travel to Greece with Shannon? He couldn't think of anyone, no one who was older, no one he knew.

"Are you sure about this? Did you talk to Shannon?"

"Of course. We had a glass of ouzo together. He said they were looking for you. He seemed worried."

She glanced around. "Now where did Brent go with my drink?"

"How did Jack know I was hurt?"

"Don't think he did. They'd just gotten here, about an hour before us."

"You met Dorian. Did she talk to them?"

"I don't know." She was getting annoyed by the questions. She craned her neck, and stood on her toes, looking about the room.

But Indy persisted. "Did you and Brent come to the hotel to see me after you heard I was hurt?"

She smiled awkwardly. "Well, we really didn't get a chance yet." She squeezed his arm. "But now you're here, and everything is okay."

"Yeah. First rate."

Just then the king was announced and a tall graying man entered the room. He shook hands with one person after another as he moved through the crowd, walking with a slight limp. Madelaine slipped away, either for a closer glimpse of the king or in search of Brent and her drink.

Indy spotted Dorian standing with the colonel. He was sure that they'd both been looking his way. He wanted more than anything to ask her about Shannon and the other man, but he hesitated, remembering that Nikos had said it was soldiers who had taken the pair away. What reason would Dorian give this time, and where the hell had they taken them?

He couldn't hold himself back any longer. He wanted answers. He headed across the room, but suddenly he found himself face to face with the king, who extended his hand. Indy quickly introduced himself as they shook hands.

"Oh, yes. You must be the one I heard about who fell into the hole."

Indy nodded, uncomfortable at the royal attention. "It won't happen again."

The king laughed, and clasped him on the shoulder. "Let's hope not. Tomorrow morning I'm going to visit the ruins. Will you be there?"

Indy had other things on his mind right now, but what could he say? "Yes. Of course."

"Good. Then maybe you can tell me all about what happened. See you then."

Indy stepped back as the king turned and began talking with someone else. He didn't see Dorian or the colonel now. He wandered about the room, and out onto the veranda. She was nowhere in sight.

"You look lost, Indy," Doumas said from behind him.

"Have you seen Dr. Belecamus?"

"She's gone. She left with Colonel Mandraki a few minutes ago."

17

AROUND THE FIRE

Indy quietly slipped out of the mansion, and walked to the rear where the drivers waited near their carriages. He asked after Doumas's carriage, and was directed to the driver. "Mr. Doumas said you should take me back to the hotel."

The driver looked dubiously at him. "Are you sure? He told me to wait for him."

"He's staying the night." Indy leaned forward. "Too much ouzo."

"Already?"

"Already," Indy said gravely.

The man nodded, and climbed into his seat as Indy slid into the carriage. None of what he'd said was true, but he didn't feel guilty about stranding Doumas.

When he arrived at the hotel, Nikos was lying on his cot intently reading a book. "Have you seen Dorian?"

"No. She hasn't returned," the boy said, rising to his feet. He ran a hand over his short-cropped hair. "You are back early."

"Maybe not early enough. Who is this Colonel Mandraki?"

"That's what I was going to tell you about when she came into the room. He is Alex, her boyfriend."

No wonder she'd turned cool toward him since they'd arrived in Delphi.

"He is a very dangerous man, and I think Dr. Belecamus is the same when he is around. That is why I brought you the moly. For your protection."

"Thanks. Now tell me more about the Americans who came to see me."

"One was tall and thin with red hair and a little beard on his chin." Nikos rubbed his chin, indicating the sparse beard. "The other one was shorter and had a big beard. And look. I have something for you." He reached under the counter, and held out a coiled whip. "Your tall friend wanted me to give this to you before you saw him. He said you would know about it. Then he was going to walk into your room. But the soldiers came."

Indy took the whip and ran his hands over it. That confirmed it. Shannon was here, but he still didn't know the identity of the other man.

"Indy, I have another question about America."

He wasn't in the mood for small talk. "It's not a very good time, but go ahead."

"Is it true that Americans put applesauce on their bread?"

Indy stared at him. "What are you talking about?"

He held up the book he'd been reading. "In here the girl eats bread like that." It was a ragged-looking copy of *Seventeen*.

"Where did you get that book?"

"One of the Americans gave it to me. The shorter one with the beard."

Indy remembered that day in Le Dôme in Paris when Ted Conrad had talked about meeting Booth Tarkington and showed him his used copy. He took the book, and opened the cover. It was signed by Tarkington and inscribed, "To Ted—best of luck in your writing."

But what in the world was Conrad, his old history professor, doing here, and why with Shannon? They didn't know each other. And why did Mandraki want to keep them away from him?

"Look, I found this in the book," Nikos said. "Do you know him?"

He handed Indy a picture of a handsome, smiling man who looked about Indy's age. He was standing beside what looked like a Greek statue and behind him were the stone steps of an amphitheatre.

"Never seen him in my life," Indy said. He tapped the edge of the photograph against the counter and frowned. "You said my friends were taken by soldiers. Were they asked nicely to go with them, like an escort?"

He shook his head. "Nothing nice about it. They were taken like criminals, and Colonel Mandraki was the one who was in charge."

"Where would they take them?"

"I don't know, but they left in the direction of the ruins."

"That's a start. I'm going to look for them. Can I keep this?" He held up the photograph.

"If you let me go with you."

Indy hesitated. "I don't want you to get in trouble, Nikos."

"I can help you find them. I know good hideouts near the ruins. We can look there."

Indy slipped the photograph inside his jacket pocket, and hooked the whip on his belt. "Okay, but just remember that we're not playing hide-and-seek with these soldiers. This is serious business."

"I know. Do you have the moly?"

Indy forced a smile. "Yeah."

A few minutes later, they mounted horses. Indy touched a hand to his sore ribs, then nudged the sides of his horse and they rode off at a gallop. As they neared the ruins, Indy gestured toward the workshop and they turned off the road. The place appeared quiet and deserted, but he wanted to check anyhow. They dismounted near the stables, and walked cautiously toward the workshop. He tried the door, and was surprised to find it unlocked. Slowly, he pushed it open. A kerosene lamp was burning on the long table.

He moved along the rows of shelves stacked with stone tablets, looking down each aisle. There was no sign of Dorian or anyone else. He was heading back toward the door when he noticed something white and filamentous protruding from one of the lockers. He dropped to one knee, and felt the material. He was almost sure he knew what it was. He opened the door. He was right. It was Dorian's dress, the one she'd worn this evening to the reception. She'd been here, and changed. The fact that she hadn't gone back to the hotel meant she and Mandraki were in a hurry.

He was about to close the door when he noticed a sheet of paper taped to the back wall of the locker. On it were three columns of numbers. The first two sets of numbers read across the page as:

1   4:23 P.M.   (3:05)

1   7:28 P.M.   (3:11)

It didn't take long to figure out what it was. The number on the left represented days, and day one, he was certain, was the day they arrived and had started monitoring the vapors. In the center column were the times of the risings and the numbers on the right represented the length of time between risings.

He ran his finger down the page and realized that it was not only a record of previous risings, but a schedule of future ones for the next several days. One set of numbers was underlined. It read:

9   11:41 A.M.   (6:53)

Indy counted the days since they had arrived. Today was the eighth. Tomorrow morning the king would visit the ruins and the vapors would rise at 11:41. That could be useful. He quickly memorized the times of the risings for the next couple of days.

"There's nobody here," Nikos said.

"I know. They were here and left, and wherever they went, Dorian didn't want to wear her dress."

"Maybe she didn't want to get it dirty."

Indy nodded. "Could be. Know of any dirty hiding places where they might have taken my friends?"

Nikos thought a moment. "There's a cave above the ruins."

"Do you think Dorian knows about it?"

"I know she does."

"How do you know?" Indy persisted.

Nikos suddenly looked uneasy. His dark eyes darted about. He scuffed his shoes on the floorboards. "You see, one day when I was twelve, I did something bad."

"Go on."

"I followed Dr. Belecamus and a boyfriend up there. I snuck in the cave after them, and watched them do it."

"This boyfriend. You mean the colonel?"

Nikos shook his head. "No. Someone else. A helper. Someone like you. A student."

So she made a habit of getting involved with her graduate students, Indy thought. Real nice. He didn't know why, but he felt jealous, betrayed.

"Come on. Let's go take a look."

They followed a trail to the ruins, and ascended to the old stadium which was beyond the theater. From there Nikos led the way to a wooded path. He pointed toward the dark mountainside above them. "It's right about there."

Indy didn't see anything but the silhouette of trees against the moonlit sky. It didn't look promising, but they didn't have much choice. The path was steep and twisted around boulders. With almost every step, shoots of pain flashed through his sore ribs and thigh. But he kept going, impelled by the dark cloud of Dorian's betrayal. Finally, Nikos stopped and pointed. The moonlight revealed a ledge about three feet wide. "It's just a little farther," he whispered.

The ledge curved around an outcropping of rock. It narrowed; Indy's feet were only inches from the edge. He was suddenly grateful that the darkness obscured the view below. It didn't seem so dangerous when he couldn't see how far he would fall if he slipped.

"Stop," Nikos whispered. He was pressed up against the wall, his face in shadows.

He was about to ask what was wrong when he heard the clatter of footsteps ahead on the ledge. Someone was moving along just ahead of them; the rocks hid whoever it was. There was no time to do anything but try to melt into the boulders. He pressed himself against the wall, and recoiled in pain as a jagged stone poked him in the side.

The footsteps grew louder. He saw movement in the dark. Whoever it was stopped, probably sensing their presence. They were trapped.

A weird, pathetic bleating cut through the silence and Nikos laughed. "It's just a goat with three little ones behind her."

"What are they doing here?"

"They live up here. They're wild."

Nikos softly called the goat, but the animal obdurately held its ground. "Is there any other way we can go?" Indy asked.

"No."

Indy looked around, and spotted a thick branch hanging over the trail. He unhitched his whip, and with a smooth snap of his wrist snared the branch. Then he swung out from the ledge and around the goats, landing on the far side of them.

"Move it," he hissed, and the goat and its little ones hurried ahead.

"How did you do that?" Nikos asked, amazed.

"Lucky, I guess. Let's go."

They cautiously worked their way around the

rocks until they could see the mouth of the cave. Light flickered from the interior. Someone was there.

Indy patted Nikos on the shoulder. "Good going. You were right."

They edged closer.

A tree grew from somewhere above the ledge and its branches shrouded the cave's entrance. No wonder they hadn't seen the light from the fire when Nikos had first pointed out its location. As they moved within a few feet of the opening, Indy heard the murmur of voices. Behind him, Nikos cleared his throat. Indy turned to him, touched a finger to his mouth. But he tripped over a loose rock, sending it tumbling into the ravine.

"There, did you hear that?" It was Dorian's voice. "Alex, go out and take a look."

Indy held his breath. Oh, God. If that eagle was his protector, he needed its help now.

"I was just out there," Mandraki barked. "I told you it's goats. Stupid little goats."

"Sorry. I guess I'm nervous," Dorian answered.

Indy wiped his brow. He thanked God. He thanked the eagle. He thanked whoever else might be responsible for keeping Mandraki in the cave. He carefully moved forward until he reached the corner of the opening. He dropped to one knee, and peered into the cave. A fire burned in the center of the cavern, its smoke disappearing through an unseen chimney in the roof. Several figures were seated around the blaze. Dorian's back was to him, and next to her was Mandraki. Across from them, he could see two soldiers with rifles.

His eyes adjusted to the flickering light, and now he

could see two bodies lying prone beyond the fire. They were on their stomachs, hands tied behind them. Beyond them were three long, shallow holes and a shovel lying on the ground. Was this an excavation site that he didn't know about? He doubted it. The holes looked more like graves. New ones. Three of them.

"Alex?"

"What?"

"This was a big mistake," Dorian said. "We should have left them alone."

"No. It wasn't a mistake. If I'd allowed them to talk to Jones, he'd be gone, and we need him tomorrow."

"By now he knows something is going on. He won't show up at the ruins. He'll be looking for his friends."

"We can control that situation," Mandraki assured her.

Indy motioned Nikos to move back. Cautiously, they edged away from the cave entrance until they were out of hearing range. "Listen, Nikos, I want you to go back to the hotel. If anyone asks for me, say I came back early and went to bed."

"What are you going to do?"

"Find a safe place to keep watch. Sooner or later, Dorian and Mandraki will leave. That's when I make my move."

While Nikos headed down toward the ruins, Indy worked his way above the ledge until he found a spot with a view that would allow him to see anyone leaving the cave. That is, if he could stay awake. He gathered together leaves for a cushion and sat down, propping his back against a tree. He rubbed his sore thigh, and adjusted the band covering his ribs. He tried to relax, and puzzled again over what Dorian and Mandraki would want with Shannon and Conrad, and why the two men had come here. But the more he thought about it the more baffled he became.

He closed his eyes, started to doze, and jerked awake. He stood up and paced to stay alert. Just as he settled down again, he heard a noise, not from below but from the rise above him. He turned his head and listened. Must be the goats.

Below him he saw a dancing shadow. He leaned forward, and watched. Then he realized it was light from the fire in the cave. They'd probably just stoked it with more wood. He readjusted his position, hunkering lower against the trunk as he tried to get comfortable. He hugged himself, rubbing his arms. It was chilly and damp. If the four in the cave were taking turns watching their captives, it was going to be a long night.

His eyelids felt heavy again. He blinked, rubbed his cheeks, and stared ahead. He imagined Dorian and Mandraki huddled by the fire staying warm, then the image slid away and shifted. He and Dorian were in a berth on the train snuggled together. Warm, safe. But then he sensed something ominous. It was near, but he couldn't see it. It was a man, a blond-haired man staring down at him, the same man who had followed Dorian after she'd spoken to him, the man who had disappeared on the train. The man pointed, and his mouth moved. What was he saying? A warning about something, but Indy couldn't hear him clearly.

Indy jerked awake, shaking his head. *Just a dream.*

Stay awake. He rubbed his arms. But a few minutes later he drifted off again. Voices.

Someone was disturbing his sleep. He should know who it was. He should do something, but the voices blended with a dream in which he was back in Chicago. Dorian's voice.

Dorian didn't belong in Chicago. He blinked his eyes open, and took his bearings. *I'm on the mountain. Waiting. But for what?* Then it all came back.

The moon was dipping behind the mountain, but there was still enough light to see the ledge. No one was there. But a man's voice issued from the cave. Then Dorian's voice. They were arguing.

How long had he slept? He pulled out his watch. He'd been here more than two hours.

"I'm leaving," Dorian said.

"All right. I'm coming with you," the man answered. He spoke in a lower voice to someone else, then Dorian emerged from the cave.

Indy peered down at the ledge as Mandraki followed her. He watched them until they were out of sight. He waited, listened. The sound of their footsteps receded, then vanished. He stood up again, a hand resting on his coiled whip. Now he was ready.

He worked his way along the ridge above the ledge, looking for the way down. The scent of the air was rich, cold, almost sweet, and made him want to close his eyes again, sleep again. Somewhere along there the underbrush opened enough to climb down, he thought. Okay, this was it. He was about to descend when the snap of a twig brought him up short.

He spun around.

At first he didn't see anything. Then he glimpsed a

shadow, an arm upraised, a blade stabbing the air, rushing toward him. He blocked the blow with his forearm, grabbed the man by the wrist and elbow and smashed his arm against his knee. The knife flew from his hand into the darkness.

The attacker tried to escape, but Indy snagged his collar, and pulled him back. Then he saw who it was. "You. You bastard."

Indy landed a solid punch to Grigoris's jaw and sent him reeling. He crashed against a tree trunk, and slumped to the ground. He walked over to him and crouched. Grigoris's hand slithered along the ground toward the knife, serpentine, silent. Just as he reached it, Indy snapped it up.

He held the blade beneath the man's chin. "I don't like you very much. You make a sound, I'll remove your tonsils. Got that?"

He checked the man's pockets and found a handkerchief. He gagged him with it. "That was good of you. Didn't have to use my own. Now unlace your boots."

Grigoris stared at him until Indy pressed the point of the knife against his neck. "Do it." When he was done, Indy took the laces from him and knotted them together. Then he bound Grigoris's wrists behind his back and around a tree. It wouldn't hold him long, but it should slow him down. He'd think twice about trying anything again. Or so Indy hoped.

He stood up. "If I see you again tonight, I'm going to throw you off the mountain. Got that?"

Indy made his way down to the ledge, and then to the entrance of the cave. The fire was burning low.

Shannon and Conrad was still lying on the floor where he'd seen them earlier. Nearby sat a guard.

One guard. Where the hell was the other one?

A branch creaked overhead. He looked up, and as he did the other guard dropped to the ledge. He swung the butt of his rifle at Indy's head. Indy ducked, then drove his head into the soldier's gut. The two of them barreled into the mouth of the cave as Indy wrestled for the rifle. Then suddenly he felt cold metal jammed behind his ear. It was the other guard.

"Don't move, *maláka,* or you're dead."

18

UNDER GUARD

The approach of dawn was already washing away the dark texture of the night sky as they were marched along the ledge. Shannon, all arms and legs and wild red hair and goatee, lurched and bobbed as he followed one of the guards. Indy was behind him, then came Conrad, his wool sport coat rumpled and soiled, his face and beard gritty from the damp earth of the cave. Even though Indy had been lying next to them for several hours, it was the first time he'd actually seen them. All three had been gagged and blindfolded.

"*Siga, siga,*" ordered the other guard from behind them, over and over. "*Siga, siga.*" Keep moving, but not too fast.

Indy was groggy from lack of sleep; his body felt battered. But he knew that they weren't going to be killed. Not yet, at least. Fortunately, the guards hadn't realized that Indy could understand them, and they'd talked freely while he'd listened. The one at the rear, who had a slightly higher rank than his companion, had said they must wait for Mandraki to return, as he'd ordered. The other guard, however, the one who had jumped him, was convinced that Indy was someone important and that he should take him immediately to Mandraki. Then the first man said that *he* should be the one to take Jones because of his rank. They had argued off and on for hours, and had finally agreed that if Mandraki had not returned by dawn, they would both take all three captives to the stables and from there the guard with the higher rank would get the colonel.

When they reached the end of the ledge, Indy finally had a chance to exchange looks with Shannon and Conrad. He couldn't tell what they were thinking, but he saw fear in both men's eyes. He didn't blame them. He probably had the same look in his own eyes.

As they descended the path to the valley, the sky beyond the mountain pass to the east slowly turned from sullen gray to a deep rose. Below them, the ruins were still in shadow, and blanketed by fog. All Indy could see of the temple were the pillars, and they looked ghostly, as if they would vanish with the fog. If the vapors were rising now, they would be indistinguishable from the fog. Maybe that was why Dorian wanted the schedule. But if she were Pythía, what did that have to do with what was happening now? Maybe nothing. Maybe everything.

By the time they were near the ruins, Indy's body didn't seem to know whether it should be hot or cold. His forehead was damp with perspiration and his fingers were numb from the cold. They emerged from the path, headed past the stadium, then went around the rear of the crumbling stone theater. The fog was lifting and Indy hoped someone would see them. Certainly, three men bound and gagged would be an unusual sight, and the word would go out. Someone surely would investigate, especially today, the day the king was expected to visit the ruins.

As if in answer to his thoughts, Indy saw a shadowy figure moving through the woods along the path between the stables and the ruins. *Please, be someone with the king,* he pleaded silently. Then he saw it was a woman. It was Dorian, and his hopes plummeted.

As she walked up to them, she quickly assessed the situation. "Good work. We were looking for him," she said, nodding toward Indy as if he were a sheep or cow that had strayed out of its fence.

When the guards told her where they were planning to take them, she shook her head. "There're too many people who might see them. Take them over there to the hut, and remove their gags. Then get them some food."

She smiled at Indy. "We don't want you to starve before you see the king." She looked him over and shook her head. "We'll have to get you some fresh clothes, too, and you must try to get some rest."

She was crazy, she had to be, he thought as they were rushed to the thatched hut. Why the hell would she still want him to see the king? If he hadn't inhaled the vapors himself, he'd be ready to believe that they'd warped her thinking.

Outside the hut, the guards untied their gags, and warned them with gestures not to talk. One after the other they were shoved through the doorway. The light was dim inside, but they could still see each other. No one said a word; not for a minute or two.

Indy rubbed his jaw, and looked around. The table and chairs had been removed, but otherwise the hut was the same as when he'd last seen it. He lowered himself to the floor and leaned his back against the wall. Underneath the cloth that covered the doorway, he could see the guard's black boots.

Conrad slumped down next to him. "I'd say good to see you, Indy, but under the circumstances..."

Shannon paced across the hut. "I don't like this. In fact, I hate it. I mean I'm definitely out of my environment. I can't go on like this. I want to play my cornet. I want to hear some jazz, any jazz, even counterfeit jazz, and I want a drink, even that god-awful pine sap shit they drink here. Anything."

"Jack, shut up," Indy hissed. "Or they'll gag us again."

"No one's ever going to gag me again. We've got to get out of here."

"We will get out, Shannon. We'll figure a way," Conrad said. "But Indy's right, keep it down."

Indy looked between the two men. "One of you mind telling me what the hell you're doing here?"

Neither spoke for a moment. "Come on, you're not wearing gags," he whispered. "And don't tell me you just decided to go off on a Greek vacation together. Hell, I didn't think you two even knew each other."

The two guards were arguing, probably about who was going to get the food for them. Conrad took advantage of the distraction. "Let me start by going back to that day at Le Dôme when you introduced me to Belecamus. After you both left the restaurant, I was approached by an English gentleman named Gerald Farnsworth, who had a lot of disturbing things to say about Belecamus. I got worried and told him that you were leaving for Greece with her the following day, but that I didn't know where you lived or how to contact you. He said he would catch the train, and tell you himself."

Farnsworth promised to send him a telegraph in a day or two, he continued. When he didn't hear from him, he contacted the police, and found out that his body had been found on a railroad bed. He'd been stabbed with a pointed object, like an ice pick.

Indy felt a knot in his stomach as he realized that the man who had followed Dorian from the dining car of the train must have been Farnsworth. He glanced toward the doorway again. The boots were no longer visible, and the arguing was more distant now. He listened as Conrad continued.

That night, Conrad had gone to the Jungle and started drinking. He'd just ordered his third scotch when Shannon recognized him as a professor from his alma mater. It didn't take long for Conrad to discover that Shannon had been Indy's college roommate, and that he also had talked to Indy before he'd left for Greece.

"When I told Jack what I'd found out, he knew you were in trouble, and he wanted to help."

Indy couldn't contain himself any longer. "What did Farnsworth tell you?"

Conrad frowned. "I had a photograph with me when I arrived. I must have misplaced it. Anyhow, it's—"

"Wait a minute." Indy reached into his jacket pocket and pulled out the photo Nikos had given him.

It was crumpled now, and he did his best to flatten it out. "You mean this one?"

"That's it," Conrad said excitedly.

"Keep it down." Now Shannon was taking charge of the noise level.

They all glanced anxiously toward the doorway, and listened. The guards were still talking, but in more restrained tones.

Indy held up the photo. "So who is he?"

"His name is Richard Farnsworth, Gerald's younger brother and a former archaeology graduate student at the University of Athens where Belecamus used to teach. He disappeared two years ago. No trace of him was ever found.

"So Gerald Farnsworth started searching for his brother," Conrad continued. "He found out that Richard and Dorian Belecamus had been lovers, but that she also was involved with Mandraki. It just so happened that the weekend Richard disappeared the colonel was seen with Belecamus."

A chill ran through Indy. Although Conrad was still talking, the words sounded as though they were being spoken underwater. Long vowels, short consonants, like a voice played on seventy-eight rpm. He rubbed his ear against his shoulder and tried to clear his head.

"Gerald Farnsworth also found out about another graduate student of hers who was found shot to death in his apartment just a year earlier. He had also been her lover, and there were suspicions about her, but no one was ever charged in the murder. Then, shortly after Farnsworth disappeared, she resigned from the university. Supposedly, she was about to face charges of unprofessional and inappropriate behavior with students."

"Damn inappropriate," Shannon put in.

"That's when she left Greece for Paris."

"She gave me quite a different story about why she left Greece," Indy said. His anger and resentment were building. "I guess she's got an appetite for graduate students, and I was just one in a line. But how come Nikos, the kid at the hotel, didn't know who Farnsworth was? He gave me the photograph."

"Because Farnsworth never came here to Delphi. Her affair with him was in Athens. She's been careful to avoid romances here where it would be too difficult to hide."

She must have had at least one, Indy thought, recalling Nikos's story. The frigid feeling had passed; in its place was a huge, heavy lump in his gut.

"And when she's done with her boys she feeds them to her killer boyfriend," Shannon added. "But that's not all, old buddy."

Indy couldn't imagine what else they could tell him after the Farnsworth story.

"My family has a few contacts in this neighborhood of the world," Shannon began. "You know what I'm talking about. People with connections. Political connections. Inside information."

Mob contacts, Indy thought, but Shannon was being as cagey as ever. "What did you find out?"

"First of all, your archaeology prof had more than an old stone tablet in mind when she took this trip. Do you know her father is a Greek dissident and he's living in Italy?"

"She told me all about that. Her old man has a gripe against the king. A difference of opinion."

"It's more than a difference of opinion. Her friend, Mandraki, is close to her father. I hear that he's up to something, maybe planning a coup, and that Dorian Belecamus is involved."

"A coup?"

"Right. So someone I know broke into her office at the university, and discovered a letter from Mandraki that verified it."

Shannon was probably that someone, Indy thought. "But if what you say is true, why would Dorian bring me along?"

"They're going to use you somehow," Shannon said. "It must have something to do with your seeing the king today. My guess is that they're going to kill him and you're supposed to take the fall. These guys are just like Chicago gangsters. Maybe smarter."

"Did Mandraki threaten to kill you?"

"Didn't you see those graves in the cave before they blindfolded you?" Shannon asked. "They're planning on killing all of us today."

Just then the cloth door of the hut was pushed aside and one of the guards stepped into the hut. He gestured angrily for them to stop talking. His partner brought in three plates, each containing a piece of hard bread, boiled potatoes, and a slice of feta cheese.

As they ate in silence, Indy decided that Dorian was capable of doing what Shannon had suggested. He didn't know how she planned to do it, but somehow he had to warn the king.

Indy moved over next to Shannon as he finished eating. "Sorry you guys got involved."

"We got ourselves involved."

Conrad laid down his fork. "I didn't realize how quickly we would be singled out once we got here. But Belecamus remembered me, of course."

"By the way," Shannon said, "what the hell is your squeaky-voiced friend Madelaine doing here?" He laughed for the first time. "That really threw me. We'd just gotten here, and the last person I expected to see walks up to me in the street."

Just then the two guards burst into the hut and pulled Shannon and Conrad to their feet. "What's going on?" Indy yelled.

He leaped up, but was shoved to the ground and kicked in the stomach. By the time he uncurled himself, Shannon and Conrad were gone, and he was gagged again.

"Bastards," he muttered into the gag.

He rolled over and peered toward the door. He could still see a pair of boot heels. He wondered if he would ever see Shannon or Conrad again. He thought of Shannon and their college antics, and how upset he'd been that Conrad had turned him in to the dean. All of that seemed distant and petty compared to the trouble they now faced.

His attraction to Dorian Belecamus had gotten the better of him. That was what it amounted to. Angrily, he kicked at the wall, and to his surprise his foot broke through. He realized that the spot he'd kicked had been burned in the fire he'd accidentally started the day he was in here timing the vapors. He pulled his foot back, and looked at the heels in the doorway. They hadn't moved.

Cautiously, he jabbed his foot at the burned thatch-work around the hole. Piece by piece he knocked off chunks of the wall until he'd made a hole that looked wide enough for him to squeeze through. He crept forward feet first, wriggling his way through on his stomach. But his thighs were too large, and he wedged tightly against the wall.

He pressed his legs together, and tried again, gritting his teeth as the thigh he'd bruised in his fall scraped against the wall. This time he made it, and now he was half out of and half in the hut. He worked his knees against the ground and edged further out.

Not much more to go now, he thought, and then his shoulders stuck firmly. He twisted right and left, pulled and pushed, but nothing worked. If anything, he was caught even tighter. He expelled the air from his lungs and buckled his knees, pulling as hard as he could. The hut shook, but he was still trapped. He looked up at the doorway. The boot heels were no longer visible.

Oh, shit. Now what?

It didn't take long for an answer. He felt hands grip his ankles and pull. He grunted as his shoulders scraped sharply against the thatch, and then he was through the hole.

He turned his head and saw a pair of black shoes. He looked up. But it wasn't the guard. It was Nikos.

The kid quickly loosened the rope on his wrists and removed the gag. "The guard," Indy whispered.

"Don't worry. I took care of him," Nikos said, holding up a club.

Indy rose to his feet, and grinned as he brushed himself off. "How did you know I was here?"

"I didn't until I saw the soldier at the door. I came looking for you because I saw Colonel Mandraki taking your friends into the back door of the hotel and up the stairs. There's a soldier guarding them in one of the rooms."

Just then Indy heard the click of a gun being cocked. He looked up to see Mandraki's rugged face glaring at him, a sneer curled on his lips. He was aiming a revolver at him. "You going somewhere, Jones?"

Indy kept his eyes on the gun, and remained silent. The last thing he wanted to do was antagonize this man, who no doubt would pull the trigger without a second thought.

Mandraki looked over at Nikos. "Get back to that hotel and stay there," he said through gritted teeth. "If you say a word to anyone, I'll kill him. Then I'll come after you."

Nikos glanced once at Indy, then hurried away.

"I don't like killing children, Jones, but I will if I have to. It's up to you, you know."

"I don't know what you mean."

Mandraki's smile was sinister. "You're going to do what I say or the kid and your two friends die."

"What do you want me to do?"

"There's going to be an accident. The king is going to fall into the crevice after the vapors rise. You're going to give him some help with a little push."

Like hell I am, Indy thought. "What if he doesn't want to walk into the vapors?"

"He will, because you're going to tell him how the vapors cured your injuries, and that you believe it will help any ailments he might have. He has a bad hip.

He's gone to doctors all over the world, but he's still in pain. He'll want to try the vapors. I guarantee it."

Indy didn't know what to say. He had to find a way to stop Mandraki.

"If you attempt to warn the king, I will kill you instantly. Remember that. But if you cooperate in this accident, you and your friends will be allowed to leave the country right away. Do you understand?"

Indy didn't believe him. Not for a second. Mandraki tossed a cloth bag to Indy. "Get in the hut and change your clothes. We want you to look presentable for the king."

And then he smiled broadly and laughed.

A stray thought crossed Indy's mind at that moment. If the eagle was his protector, he wasn't doing a very good job.

19

ENTRANCING TALES

From his position on a jut of rock at the base of the mountain slope beyond Apollo's Temple, Panos gazed across the ruins toward a cluster of people gathered on the roadway near the entrance. The king had not arrived, but he would at any time. It was after eleven and the vapors would rise at 11:41.

"Let's go," Grigoris said. "We can get closer."

Panos shook his head. "Plenty of time."

As always, Grigoris was in a rush. But this morning he was also in a sudden, dark mood. When Panos arrived here half an hour ago, Grigoris had spilled his tale of woe from last night. He had listened, glanced at his son's laceless boots, and shrugged. It didn't matter, he told him. What he meant was that Jones didn't matter. Not any more. He'd seen two of Mandraki's soldiers march the three outsiders down from the mountain. They were not going to present any more problems.

"Look there." Grigoris's finger jabbed toward the road just as Panos saw a large motorcar stop near the entrance. The king had arrived. He watched as a man in a suit stepped out of the front seat of the car and opened the back door. A moment later, a tall, gray-haired man was helped from the back seat of the car. He wore a safari outfit like so many of the foreigners who came to Delphi, and for a moment Panos didn't recognize him. But there was no doubt from the show of deference by the others that he was the king. Just the sight of the man who ruled his country left Panos feeling awed.

He recalled now what Belecamus had told him as she escorted him out of the workshop. He was still puzzled by it. The king was in danger, and the danger was nearby, she'd said. Had that been Pythía speaking, or Belecamus, or both? It was confusing.

He motioned to Grigoris, and they moved down the trail until they were just outside the ruins. They waited behind a hummock of trees less than fifty yards from the pillars. They'd gone as far as they dared, and now they watched as the group neared the temple.

Panos focused his attention on the king. He felt his heart pounding. He knew a monumental event was about to happen. History. For once it wasn't in the past. It was happening right here and now, an important historical event that affected the world. He was seeing it; he would be part of it.

Belecamus was on one side of the king, Mandraki on the other. He didn't like the way the colonel seemed to lead the procession, as if he were in charge. And why was Doumas hanging back like a fool? Then Panos drew in a sharp breath as he realized Jones was among the group. What was he doing there? It didn't make sense.

Even from this distance, he sensed the danger, a dark presence that chilled him. It must be Jones. But if Jones were free, Mandraki had allowed it. Suddenly, he knew the colonel was the true source of danger. He was going to assassinate the king, and somehow use Jones to do it.

He couldn't let it take place. Not today of all days. Not here in Delphi. So much was at stake. He glanced at Grigoris and saw the hate in his eyes and knew that he too had recognized Jones. "Father, do you see—"

"Yes, now listen closely to me. Don't do anything until I tell you. The timing must be right."

Grigoris stared at Jones and slowly nodded. When he spoke, it was without conviction. "I understand. We are here, and that will be enough."

Grigoris was repeating Panos's own words. But now Panos wasn't so sure they were true.

Doumas followed the king's entourage through the ruins as Belecamus alternated between gloating about her days as Delphi's chief archaeologist and pointing out the damages created by the earthquake. Maybe no one else thought she was gloating, but her hubris was obvious to him. He was well aware of the extent of her work, and the limits of it. Nothing would please him more than seeing her leave Delphi and never return, at least not while he was in charge of the ruins.

This would definitely not be the way *he* would present Delphi to the king. What the hell did Mandraki know? There was no reason for him to be at the king's side. Then there was Jones. Probably the only reason he was still alive was that the king had requested his attendance, and Belecamus didn't want anyone asking questions.

But he looked like a lunatic. The pants he wore were too short, and the shirt too baggy. His shoes were covered with mud. If it had been any other place than the ruins, he wouldn't be allowed near the king. And it wasn't only his clothes. He dragged along as if he hadn't slept for days. What the hell had he been doing since he'd run off with Doumas's carriage?

As they approached the temple, Belecamus was talking about the crevice. She was making much of the fact that the vapors were similar to the historical accounts of the mephitic vapors of Apollo's Oracle. She even tossed in a mythological reference calling the vapors ichor, the life-force of the gods. Doumas almost laughed. He'd never heard her speak of Delphi in such romantic terms. *Must be Jones's influence,* he thought.

"And what effects do these vapors have on someone who inhales them?" the king inquired as he limped ahead.

"All we can say for certain is that they don't seem to cause any ill effects. There may be a feeling of well-being, but that could just be psychological. However, I should say that Mr. Jones has other ideas, which he can tell you about later, if you're interested. He seems to think they have a healing effect."

Very clever, Doumas thought. She was overlooking what had happened to her, probably because she thought it would sound too unprofessional to say that she had been overcome by the vapors and had acted oddly for a couple of days. She hadn't even admitted that she had inhaled them herself. But what was this about Jones?

One thing seemed certain now: she wasn't about to say she was Pythía. So Panos had lost. She wasn't going to cooperate as he'd hoped. Why would she? The stonemason had been a fool to think she would.

"When do these vapors rise?" the king asked.

"They seem to come and go irregularly. Wouldn't you say, Stephanos?"

Now why had she said that, and placed him in the position of agreeing with a lie? He cleared his throat. "Well, they seem to come less and less often with each succeeding day."

The next one was due any time; she must know it. But maybe in all the distraction with the king's visit, she'd forgotten. He wondered if he should mention it. But what if he was wrong? The king would think he was a fool. He might even lose his position here if the king decided to wait for the vapors and nothing happened. No, he couldn't take any chances.

Doumas moved closer to Belecamus as she led the way past the tilting columns of the temple. When he got a chance, he'd mention the timing of the vapors, and let her handle it. But she seemed anxious to keep moving and told the king that he could see the crevice from atop the mound.

"Mr. Jones, why don't you tell his Highness about your experience?" Belecamus said as she took the king's arm, and guided him up the mound. "You know more about it than anyone else."

Incredible, Doumas thought. First, the colonel guiding the way, now Jones, who wasn't any more qualified, was going to take over. He didn't want any part of it. Reluctantly, he trailed after the others, stopping about halfway up the mound near the king's two aides.

As the king peered into the crevice, Jones talked about his fall. He described the tablet, and to Doumas's surprise gave an accurate account of what it had said. The king, however, didn't seem very interested. He listened as Jones described his fall onto a ledge, then interrupted and asked how the vapors had affected him.

"I think the vapors have a healing effect," Indy said, but he didn't sound very convinced himself. "You see, I was injured in my fall, but I recovered very rapidly."

"And no ill effects?"

Jones shook his head.

He didn't look much better, Doumas thought.

"I would like to test these vapors myself sometime," the king said.

Not if they caused you to act like Belecamus, Doumas thought. He took a couple of steps forward, suddenly realizing that Belecamus was setting something up. The king was going to see the vapors, and maybe inhale them.

Now Belecamus was talking about the tablet and the return of the oracle. "In fact, some villagers say there's an old prophecy about Pythía returning after an earthquake and around the time the king arrives."

The king smiled. "Is that so?"

Doumas sucked in his breath as he realized he'd been mistaken. She was going to do it.

Just then, as if their speaking of the vapors had

called them up, Doumas heard the telltale rumble and hissing. The gases started rising. She'd planned it this way. Maybe she was Pythía. But then she stepped down off the top of the mound as the vapors covered their ankles. Mandraki moved ahead of her, and blocked the two aides from reaching the king.

"Let them be," he ordered.

"Your Highness," one of the aides called out as the vapors billowed around the king's chest and shoulders. But the king ignored him. Belecamus abruptly turned away from Mandraki and disappeared into the vapors with the king and Jones as the gases completely engulfed them. It was all happening so fast that Doumas hardly noticed that Panos and Grigoris were among them.

Suddenly, chaos reigned in the temple. Panos charged up the mound toward them, but Mandraki shoved him back down. The two aides were frantic, clawing their way toward the king. Mandraki struggled to contain them, but just then Grigoris barreled into the colonel.

Again, Panos charged up the mound and this time vanished into the vapors. Mandraki had his hands full with Grigoris and the aides and didn't see what was happening. Doumas watched in stunned disbelief until a scream that was more animal than human pierced the air. Shivers radiated up his spine. He knew that Belecamus was transforming into Pythía. It was happening, and just the way Panos had planned it. He heard Panos's voice proclaiming Pythía's presence.

No. He had to stop them. He was the one who must have the power, not Panos. He struggled up the mound, stumbled, and slipped backwards. He could hear Dorian babbling, and the king's voice. He crawled ahead, climbed to his feet, and hurled himself into the vapors at the spot where Panos had disappeared.

The cloud of vapors shut out the others. The commotion beyond the vapors seemed distant, unimportant. Even the king, who stood within Indy's reach, appeared ghostlike, a dim silhouette. But he could hear him filling his lungs with great breathfuls of the vapors.

"Sir. Your Highness." Was that how he should address him? The king ignored him. "Excuse me, Your Highness." He had to tell him about the danger. But how was he going to save Shannon and Conrad, and himself? Their lives were in danger no matter what happened to the king.

"My hip is already healing." Jubilance riddled the king's voice. "This place is a miracle."

Before Indy could say anything further, another figure swirled through the vapors. It was Dorian. Her hair was standing on end as she tossed her head spasmodically from side to side. Spittle ran down her jaw. Her eyes threatened to burst from their sockets. She screamed.

"What's wrong with you?" the king gasped.

Then Panos was moving behind her. "Your Highness, Pythía has returned," he boomed. "What is it you wish to ask?"

The king stared. Pythía moved closer to him and leered at him, her tongue hanging from her mouth. "Get away; get away from me."

Suddenly, she was babbling. The words gushed from her mouth, but made no sense. Indy detected a familiar word here, a phrase there. Latin. French. Greek. English. But it was gibberish.

"Pythía is addressing you, Your Highness," Panos said. "She says you are the one who should get away. You are in danger. Someone very near wants to kill you. Flee this place; flee now for your life. But go with the knowledge that Delphi will soon rise in fame again, and the fortunes of our country will change."

"Who are you to tell me this?" the king demanded.

"It is not I; it is Pythía who speaks."

The king looked skeptically at Dorian. Her head hung to the side, her eyes were closed, and she was rocking back and forth. "She is Pythía?"

Indy jerked his head as the hulking figure of Doumas appeared. His arms were outstretched; he lunged for Panos and grabbed him around the waist. Dorian was knocked off her feet; her head bounced hard against the ground. Indy lurched toward her, but Doumas and Panos rammed into him.

Indy stumbled back, trying to recover his balance, but his feet slipped over the edge of the crevice. He slid down, clawing at the earth until he clutched a partially buried rock at the very brink of the hole. But the rock was loose.

Oh God, no. I don't want to die. Not here. Not with these guys.

He pulled as hard as he could, raising his chest over the edge of the hole just as the rock broke free. His legs dangled; he inched forward, threw a leg over the top, then rolled over on his back.

He looked up just in time to see a foot about to

stomp on his face. He grabbed it at the last instant
and shoved it back. Then he saw that the foot be-
longed to Grigoris, who was coming at him again. But
Doumas collared him. He held father and son by their
necks and spun them in circles dangerously close to
the edge. At any moment they could tumble over, and
take Indy with them.

Indy tried to roll further away from the crevice, but
as he did several feet tripped over him and bodies
tumbled toward the crevice. Someone yelled, and Indy
saw hands grappling for purchase. He reached out
and grabbed a wrist. Whoever it was hung precariously in midair, stretching Indy's arm to its limit.

He heard a prolonged scream as one of the men—
he couldn't tell who—plunged into the abyss. His
yells echoed down the chasm, and finally trailed off
into deadly silence. To his left, Panos was hanging
half over the ledge, and Grigoris struggled to pull
him up.

Who had fallen—Doumas? Then who was hanging
onto his hand? With an effort that took all of his
strength, he pulled, digging his feet into the loose
earth. He saw an arm, a shoulder, then the neck and
head of the king. With the help of the king's free hand,
Indy pulled him the rest of the way out of the hole.

They got to their feet at the same time, and the king
stared at Indy for a long moment. "I'll remember
this," he said. "You saved my life."

As suddenly as the vapors had arrived, they dispersed, like fog burned off by the sun. It was as if
Doumas had been eaten alive by the power below
Delphi and now the enigmatic force was retracting its
ethereal tendrils.

Suddenly, the king's aides were attending to him, hustling him away from the ruined temple. "He wanted to kill me," the king said.

"Who did?" one of his aides asked.

"The obese one, the archaeologist. But I was warned by Pythía. That woman is Pythía."

Mandraki, meanwhile, scooped up Dorian, and Grigoris was helping his father to his feet.

"Good time to get out of here," Indy muttered, and hurried away. He cut behind the theater to the path leading to the stables. He ran as best he could, his bruised thigh throbbing with every step. The vapors hadn't done a damn thing for his thigh, or his ribs, for that matter. The path ended at the workshop, and he dashed across the grassy yard to the stables.

He walked along the stalls and picked out a horse, one that Dorian had said was the strongest and fastest. He threw the saddle over its back, but as he did, the horse reared up, knocking the saddle off and nearly trampling Indy.

He quickly abandoned the stall. "Try you some other day, fellow."

The next stall was empty, but in the one after it was the horse that Indy had been riding. He quickly saddled the steed, and was about to mount him when he spotted Mandraki headed his way carrying Dorian in his arms. He could ride past them, but Mandraki was probably armed.

He cursed under his breath and turned the horse back into the stall, removed the saddle, and ducked low. A few seconds later, Mandraki lumbered into the stable. Stay away from this stall, Indy ordered in his mind. He closed his eyes as he heard the creaking of a door. It was the next stall, the empty one. Mandraki placed Dorian on the hay-covered floor.

"Dorian, wake up. We've got to get going."

Indy heard a sharp slap, then another. "Damn it, Dorian. What's wrong with you?"

Dorian blinked her eyes as she felt a hard slap across one cheek, then the other. She didn't know where she was. Then she saw Alex's face looming over her. She looked around. "What am I doing in this stable? Oh, my head." She gingerly touched a lump near her temple.

"Everything went wrong. What were you doing in the vapors? You were supposed to leave with me."

"I did, but then I don't know what happened."

"Well, the king got away, and he knows there was an attempt on his life," Mandraki said. "Did Jones try to push him?"

"I don't know," Dorian answered. "I couldn't see. I was just trying to find my way out of there without falling into the hole. Are we in trouble?"

Mandraki shook his head. "No. He thinks it was Doumas who tried to kill him, and he's dead. He fell."

"So we're safe."

"Not until we clean up after ourselves," Mandraki said. "We've got to act fast."

"What do you mean?"

Mandraki frowned at her, confused by her sudden denseness. "We've got to get rid of Jones and his friends. Then when we're done with them, I'm going to personally handle those two village idiots, the father and son. Any idea what they were doing there?"

She turned her head aside. "I don't know."

"The other day the older one told me that Jones was pursuing you. Why would he take an interest in my affairs? Or should I say yours?"

Mandraki had always tolerated her flings with younger men, unless he thought they were lasting too long. Then he ended them, his way. Jones would be no exception, she knew. But she wanted him alive. Somehow, she had to stall Mandraki. She had her own plans for Jones.

"You go on, Alex. I'm going to lie here awhile and rest."

"You sure?"

Just then she heard a wheezing noise.

"What was that?" Mandraki said. He stood up, and shoved the stall door open.

The straw and dust tickled the inside of Indy's nostrils. His nose twitched; he held his breath. He tried his best to hold off the sneeze that was building up. Mandraki was only a few feet away, and would surely hear him. In spite of himself, his head jerked spasmodically and he let out a choking, muffled sneeze.

"Damn it," he hissed under his breath. The door of the next stall creaked open. Indy waited, frozen in place. A hand slid into his field of vision; it patted the nose of the horse above him. If Mandraki opened the gate, he'd see him. No doubt about it.

"What's wrong, boy, got a cold?"

Thank God. He thought it was the horse.

"You don't look so good." Mandraki backed out of the stall, and moved on.

Indy's relief was short-lived; almost immediately, another sneeze started to build. *Hurry, get out of here,* he silently told Mandraki as the colonel saddled a horse in another stall. Finally, after one of the longest minutes in his life, Indy heard Mandraki leading the horse out of the stall.

"Are you sure you're okay?" the colonel asked Dorian.

"Yes. I'll be coming along in a few minutes."

As soon as Mandraki galloped off, Indy let out a loud sneeze that ended in a hoot. It felt so good he smiled. But a moment later the smile faded.

"Who is there?"

The danger of Mandraki had been so great that he'd forgotten about Dorian.

"No one."

"Jones! Is that you?"

As he stood up, he touched his belt and wished the guards hadn't taken his whip. Dorian definitely was someone to approach with caution. He opened her stall and stared at her; he felt as if he were watching a poisonous spider. She was lying on her side, propping her head up with an elbow. He didn't see any weapons on her, but he wasn't about to let down his guard, either.

She sat up, threaded her hand through her hair. Bits of straw fell over her shoulders. "Come in here," she said in a low, throaty voice. A few days ago, that same voice had been seductive. Now it was viperous.

He didn't move, didn't say a word. Her eyes beckoned him.

"Did you hear what I told the king when we were in the vapors?" she asked.

"I heard the translation."

"What did I say?" She opened her dark eyes and stared intently at him.

He wasn't sure whether she actually didn't know or was simply testing him. He repeated what Panos had said to the king.

"I warned him of a threat against his life," Dorian said. "You see, I defied Alex."

"Did you?"

"I saved the king's life, Indy. You were going to kill him."

"That was what your boyfriend wanted me to do," Indy countered. "Now he wants to kill me, and my friends."

"I can help you."

He shook his head. "I don't trust you, Dorian. I know too much about you."

Her dark eyes seemed to burrow inside him. "What are you talking about?"

"Your old boyfriend, Farnsworth. You killed him, and his brother. And who knows how many more."

"I did not."

"I'm going." He backed out of the stall, and moved to the adjoining one. But as he saddled the horse, Dorian blocked the doorway.

"I haven't always done the right thing, Indy," she said in a soft voice. "I've let Alex manipulate me. But that's over. I swear. I can help you get your friends away from him. I'll prove to you that I'm not what you think."

"Thanks, but I'll work on it myself."

"If you go to the hotel, you will be killed." She said it matter-of-factly. "That is exactly what Alex expects you to do. He won't kill them until he has you. They are his bait. If you want to live, hide until morning. I'll bring your friends to the temple at eight-thirty."

He thought about it. She was probably right about the hotel. He had little chance of getting Shannon and Conrad away from Mandraki without at least one of them getting killed. "Make it earlier."

"No. Eight-thirty. Be on time. No later."

Indy knew from the schedule in Dorian's locker that the vapors would rise at 8:38. What the hell did she have in mind now? But then what choices did he have?

It came down to this: Dorian was the least trust-worthy person he knew, but at the moment her help seemed his only option.

"I'll be there."

20

NEW RISING

Fog covered the ruins like piles of freshly cut wool. Panos could see only a vague outline of the thatched hut where he had spent the night, and turned away from it in disgust. Despite the fog, he was confident that Belecamus—Pythía—would be here within minutes. She would be drawn to the vapors just as the rich and powerful would soon be attracted to Delphi like ants swarming over spilt honey. Soon, Delphi would flourish in a renaissance of the ancient ways. The Oracle's coffers would weigh heavy, and a new temple would be built on the ruins of the old. There would be no place for thatched huts at Delphi. He would make sure of that.

The hut had been Doumas's way of connecting the past with the present, but it had been a feeble link in comparison to the potent strength of the Return. But Doumas had been a contradiction. He had ponderously sought to understand the Order of Pythía in the same way that he had studied old crumbling buildings. Although he was never actually inducted into the

Order, he had become privy to many of its secrets. But in the end he must have been jealous of the power the oracle priest would amass. He'd foolishly tried to change the tide of history and erase the inevitable return of Pythía.

No, that wasn't quite right, Panos realized. Doumas had wanted the power himself. That was why he had attacked him, instead of Pythía. But of course he was unsuccessful, and his life had abruptly ended in failure. Thanks to Grigoris, Panos had escaped a similar end.

In the two hours since he'd gotten up, Panos had eaten nothing, and he would continue fasting until after the rising. This morning he would ask Pythía how the king would respond to what had happened yesterday, and how long it would take before her power was widely recognized. The more specifics he knew, the better he could plan.

He'd spent more than an hour this morning seated on the dirt floor of the hut figuring out how long the spans between risings would be in a week, a month, a year, and longer. At first, he had been worried about how rapidly the span between risings was increasing. Soon there would be only one rising a day, then one every two days. But he realized that as the quiet periods became longer, the speed of change slowed down. By the time there was a week between risings, it would take ten weeks before the quiet time expanded by another hour, and two hundred forty weeks or almost five years before the breaks would increase to eight days. After that, the increases would be even slower. Decades would pass before the breaks were two weeks long.

He heard footsteps approaching from behind the hut. She was here. He knew it. But then Grigoris emerged from the fog. "What are you doing here? I told you to stay away this morning."

"They are coming, Father. I saw Pythía leave the hotel."

"I knew she would," Panos snapped, then forced a smile. "Thanks for telling me." He had a hard time staying angry with Grigoris, especially so soon after his son had saved him from tumbling into the crevice. Grigoris always tried to do what he thought was right, just as Panos had taught him. But he'd also taught him to obey his commands, and that lesson was the one Grigoris had the most difficulty following.

"But I thought you would want to know that she is not alone."

Indy had slept in what he had hoped would be the least likely place that Mandraki would look for him. The fact that he was still alive told him that the cave above the ruins had been a good choice.

Now, he slowly worked his way along the ledge. He couldn't even see his feet through the fog. It was much thicker than yesterday, making the walk particularly treacherous. One step in the wrong place and he would plunge down the mountainside. The walk was nothing less than a metaphor of what his life had become. One wrong move and he was dead.

As he carefully worked his way around the boulders, he thought back to those first days here when he had spent hours waiting and watching as he timed the risings of the vapors. He'd been terribly bored and restless. Now he was neither. The struggle for survival had honed his senses, making him keenly aware and interested in what was going on around him.

Finally, he reached the end of the ledge and moved along the path. By quarter after eight he was still on the mountainside a couple of hundred feet above the ruins. But when he gazed down at ancient Delphi all he saw was a harsh white haze that looked like a fresh blanket of snow.

He climbed down the rest of the way, not bothering to hide; he was already hidden, but so was everyone else, if indeed there was anyone. He stopped as he reached the Sacred Way and peered through the fog. He couldn't see more than ten feet in front of him. He moved forward, looking from side to side with each step.

Then he heard voices. He listened. Yes, voices like the distant gurgling of water. He couldn't tell which direction they were coming from, or how far away they were. He moved ahead again, stopping every few feet to listen. Had he imagined the voices? Maybe they were the collective babble of all the Pythías drawn back to wander in the fog looking for their sacred Delphi, or to greet the new Pythía. Then again, maybe he hadn't heard anything at all.

Suddenly, the pillars at the entrance of the temple loomed in front of him. He pulled out his watch. It was 8:33. The vapors would rise in five minutes. He looked around, wondering what to do.

"Jones, where are you?" It was Dorian's voice and it echoed through the temple. So she *was* here.

He peered past the tilting columns toward the crevice. "Right here," he shouted.

"Come up here. Right now," Dorian commanded. "I have your friends."

He hesitated.

"Quickly. I've kept my side of the bargain."

He walked into the temple, and approached the mound. "How do I know?"

"Tell him," Dorian said.

"We're here with her. No one else," Shannon said. But Indy thought he detected a sharp edge to his voice.

"Get up here, Jones."

He stopped at the bottom of the mound. "Why up there?"

"The vapors, of course. I want you here to see what happens."

He was halfway up the mound before he saw three silhouettes shrouded in mist. "What's the point?"

"You'll see."

He kept climbing, and now he could make out more details. Shannon and Conrad stood to one side of Dorian. Neither was handcuffed. Why hadn't they tried to get away? Then he saw the reason. Dorian raised a revolver, and aimed it at him.

"Sorry, Indy," Shannon said. "She was holding it on my head."

He heard a sound behind him, and realized what he had feared all along; it was a trap.

Panos didn't like the fact that the two outsiders were with her, or that Jones was climbing the mound to join them. She must have known they were danger-ous, though; that was why she was armed. But why had she brought them here, why now?

He climbed the mound, Grigoris at his side, knowing there was nothing he could do about them right now. They were here; so be it. But in a matter of seconds Belecamus would catapult into trance, and then he would take charge.

The moment he accepted the outsiders, their presence suddenly made surprising sense. He knew why they were here, and what Pythía would tell them. He was in tune with her. He knew her words even before they were spoken. That was the way of the oracle priest.

Jones looked startled when he saw them, but he sounded almost relieved. "You guys! Dorian, what are they doing here?"

"What do you think? The vapors are rising," Pythía responded.

It was time, and Pythía dropped down onto one knee. It was impossible to distinguish fog from vapors, but Pythía inhaled deeply. Her head was bent low, and her hair had fallen over her face. Then the haze thickened and she was no longer visible.

Panos waded into the vapors, Grigoris at his heels. Pythía stood up, rocked from side to side. He looked at her hands and saw that she no longer held the gun. Her head lolled forward, then she raised it up. Her eyes, which had bulged when the king stood here, were now mere slits. There was something different about her. It was as if she were concealing something. She looked at him, then cocked her head, peering at the other men. Finally, her gaze settled on Jones. She smiled, an odd, crooked smile, then stepped forward and embraced him.

Jones didn't return the embrace. His body was

rigid. She muttered something under her breath which Panos couldn't hear. It didn't matter; he knew what she was saying.

"Pythía says you are to leave today for your homelands and tell all those you know about the return of Pythía. Many wonders will soon be taking place here, and the world must know about it."

Pythía laughed, a disturbing cackling sound, and stepped back from Jones.

"Like what?" Jones asked. "What sort of wonders?"

"Guidance concerning the future. Those who know what to expect will be far stronger than those who do not."

"Nobody believes in that stuff anymore," the tall, red-haired man said.

"You are a fool if you don't believe," Grigoris said, and stepped forward as if to challenge him.

"What wonderful things does Pythía foresee?" Jones challenged as he stared intently at her. "Tell me something."

"It is a great gift she offers the world, which must be used wisely," Panos said. "Not for your entertainment."

Pythía giggled again, and grinned.

Jones looked doubtful, and Panos was about to admonish him when he heard a voice from outside the vapors. "Dorian, where are you?"

It was Mandraki. "Ignore him," Panos said.

"It's a trick," said one of the outsiders.

"I'll take care of it," Grigoris said.

"Wait!" Panos shouted, but Grigoris ignored him. An instant later, Panos heard the report of a gun, and a cry from his son. "No! No!" He rushed from the vapors; Grigoris was lying on his face halfway down the mound.

Panos stumbled down the slope, and dropped to his knees by Grigoris's side. His son's head was tilted in an odd way. He turned him over. His face was a shattered mass of blood, chips of bone, and brain.

Panos jerked his head back in horror. "You... you!"

He stared into the icy eyes of Colonel Mandraki, who stood at the bottom of the mound amid the clearing fog, a rifle in his hand and an ammunition belt strapped from shoulder to waist.

"You killed my son."

A shell clicked into the firing chamber. *"Maláka,"* Mandraki cursed, and aimed at Panos's head.

He pulled the trigger.

At the sound of the first shot, Indy ducked to the ground. Conrad and Shannon did the same. But Dorian remained standing.

Why hadn't they run from the mound while they had a chance? Dorian's gun had disappeared from her hand, and she was cackling like an old witch. What the hell was this effect the vapors had on her? But they'd stood there and watched and listened to Panos's prattle, and now Mandraki was here.

Another gunshot exploded. Christ. What was going on out there? Indy didn't really want to know. He wanted to be as far from here as possible. But now they were trapped between Mandraki and the crevice. Either direction was certain death.

"Dorian, come out of there," Mandraki bellowed.

Shannon was at his side. "We've had it, Indy. Soon as the vapors are gone, it's over."

"Dorian," Mandraki called again.

Their only other option was to walk around the crevice and drop into the gully, but that was no good either. They'd be trapped, as good as dead.

Dorian took a step forward. The vapors were starting to thin, and Indy could vaguely make out Mandraki's form.

"Dorian, where are you?" Mandraki demanded. "Do you have all three of them?"

She remained silent. Was she still Pythía, or somewhere in between? Then Indy saw her pull the revolver from the folds of a cloth belt. She raised the muzzle to her head. God, she was going to kill herself. "Alex," she shouted. "Watch out!"

Then she lowered the gun, aimed, and fired.

Mandraki took a faltering step back. His rifle clattered to the ground. He rocked on his heels, clutching his chest. Then he crumpled over, joining the carnage.

21

PARISIAN PALS

"I killed him in self-defense," she said quietly. "He was going to kill all of us."

Indy stared at the bodies sprawled across the mound. "Why would he want to kill you?"

"Plenty of reasons. Jealousy mainly. Panos told him about us. But he was angry that the king got away and he blamed me."

He watched her closely. There was no sign of any trance-induced aberrations in her features. She was calm, and actually looked relieved after killing her long-standing lover. The gun dangled loosely in her hand. He hoped she was going to drop it, because he was going to pounce on it when she did.

His eyes slid to Shannon and Conrad who were standing to one side of him. They were as nervous now as when he'd arrived.

Dorian sensed their unease. "Don't look at me like I'm some kind of madwoman. You're all alive because of me."

"What are you going to do now?" Conrad asked, taking a step closer to her.

She smiled amiably. "I know exactly what I'm going to do, and you three are going to help me."

Conrad moved another pace closer, and held out his hand. "That's good, Dorian. I'll take the gun. You don't need it anymore."

Her body tensed and she pointed the revolver at Conrad. "Don't patronize me, Professor. I know what I'm doing. Sit down, all three of you. I'm going to give you a little history lesson about Delphi. You like history, don't you, Professor?"

She grinned at him, and for an instant Indy recognized the expression he'd seen on her face when she was Pythía. He wondered about that, and sat down with the others as she'd ordered.

"In ancient times, Delphi was like a magnet that drew people from around the Mediterranean," she began.

This was madness. Three bodies were lying behind her, and she was lecturing as if she were in class at the Sorbonne. Indy was tempted to tell her to shut up, but he was certain she could shoot him with as much ease as she had killed Mandraki.

"It was not only the mephitic gases that were involved in Pythía's power, but also the Omphalos, a mysterious black cone-shaped stone." Dorian looked over her audience. "It's down there in the crevice within our reach. Indy found it, and I want it."

"How are we going to get it?" Shannon asked, playing the role of interested student.

"You and the professor are going to lower your friend on a rope. He's going to get a chance to improve his archaeological skills, and recover one of the most valuable artifacts of all time."

She turned to Indy. "Do you agree to do it?"

As if he had a choice, he thought. "I don't see any rope."

"You're going to get it. Go to the workshop. You'll find a rope and my excavating tools on the table. And hurry." Then her voice toughened. "But if you're not back in fifteen minutes, your friends will be joining the others. Do you understand?"

"You don't have to threaten me, Dorian."

She smiled and her features softened. "I like you, Indy. I'm sorry I have to do it this way. But I have no choice. Without the gun, I couldn't count on your co-operation."

Indy quickly descended the mound, passing the bodies of Panos, Grigoris, and Mandraki. He rushed across the ruins to the wooded trail that led to the workshop. He had to tell someone what had happened, but he didn't have time to go to the village or anywhere else. As it was, he had to hurry in order to retrieve the equipment and get back in time.

He found the same rope that had been used to pull him from the hole neatly coiled on the table. Next to it was Dorian's knapsack and her excavating tools. From the way they were laid out, he wondered if she had planned the whole thing. If that were the case, she must also have planned to kill Mandraki. The woman was truly the Ice Queen, after all—a cold-blooded, cold-hearted killer.

He glanced around the workshop. Everything else looked the same as when he'd last seen it. He walked over to Dorian's locker, and found the schedule of

risings still taped to the back wall. The next one was
due at 3:49 P.M. There should be plenty of time to get
the Omphalos, or whatever it was, out of the hole.
But the vapors were more of an annoyance than anything else to Indy. He'd breathed the so-called
mephitic gases a couple of times now and had never
experienced anything unusual. It was like walking in
fog, nothing more.

The king had wanted to believe so badly in their
healing properties that the pain in his hip probably
did subside for a while. Indy would be surprised if the
pain wasn't back. So why was Dorian's reaction to the
vapors so dramatically different from his own and
everyone else's? What made her Pythía, but not anyone else?

He was about to close the locker door when he
spotted something familiar on the top shelf. He
reached up and grabbed his whip. Maybe she considered it a memento from another graduate-student
lover. But this graduate student had a big advantage.
He knew about the others, and of their demise.

He hitched the whip on his belt and as he left the
workshop, he slung the pack over one shoulder and
the rope over the other. He'd taken only a step out the
door when he saw two men approaching on horseback. He was in luck. He'd tell them to get help. As
they moved closer, though, his hope faded as rapidly
as light at the end of the day. Soldiers.

He lowered his head, pulled his hat down low, and
walked quickly away. But just as he reached the beginning of the trail to the ruins one of the men called
out to him. "You there. Have you seen Colonel
Mandraki?"

He shook his head, and kept walking.

"Let's check the ruins," the soldier said, and Indy recognized his voice. The same bastard who had jumped him outside the cave.

"Hey, wait a minute. Isn't that the guy we were guarding?" the other said.

Indy kept moving, hoping the soldiers would start another argument. As the trail curved and he moved out of sight, he broke into a run. But he'd gone only a dozen yards before he heard the thunder of horses behind him.

He leaped off the trail, dropped the rope and knapsack and unhitched his whip. As the first rider neared him, he snapped it with a swift, smooth swing. The whip uncoiled in an elliptical arc, and snared the soldier by the neck. With a quick jerk, he yanked him to the ground. The second horse reared to avoid the soldier in its path, and threw its rider.

Indy snatched up a rifle that had fallen at his feet, and aimed it at the soldiers. "On your feet. Get against that tree." They did as he said, but as he leaned over to pick up the coil of rope, one of the men lunged at him. Indy swung the butt of the rifle around and cracked it against the side of his head. The soldier took two stuttering steps, tottered, then dropped to his knees, and fell over.

The other soldier, meanwhile, slipped a hand into his boot and pulled a knife. With a smooth motion, he hurled it from ankle level. Indy ducked and the knife stuck into the trunk of a tree barely an inch from his head. He glanced at the blade, then back at the soldier. The man stared at him, uncertain what to do.

Then, deciding that retreat was the best idea, he turned and ran.

But Indy was ready for him. He'd gone only a couple of steps before the whip unfurled and caught him around the ankles. He reeled him in like a fish, but his "catch" turned on him. He leaped up, threw a punch that glanced off Indy's shoulder. Indy landed one of his own solidly against the man's jaw. The soldier fell backwards, struck his head against a tree trunk, and was out cold.

Indy found a length of rope in the saddlebag of one of the horses. He tied the rope around the chest of one of the soldiers, looped it over a thick branch, then pulled the man to his feet as he tied the other end around his partner. When he was finished both men were seated back to back, and held up by the rope and branch. "I'd stick around and chat, fellows, but I'm short on time."

With that he hooked his whip back on his belt, grabbed the knapsack, rope, and rifle, and mounted one of the horses. But he was loaded down with too much gear, and tumbled out of the saddle. He glared at the groggy soldiers as he dusted himself off.

"Don't say a word."

This time he slipped the rope and knapsack in a saddle bag. He mounted the horse again, and galloped off. Not much time left, and he didn't want to test Dorian. But now things were going to be different. He was armed and all he had to do was catch her off guard.

He reined in the horse as he reached the outskirts of the ruins. The fog had lifted, but the columns of the temple obscured the view of the mound, and he couldn't see any of them. He dismounted, grabbed the gear, and walked as fast as he could toward the temple, holding the rifle parallel with his legs. As the mound came into view, he stopped short. No one was on it or anywhere nearby. The temple looked empty. And the bodies were gone.

"What the hell."

He wasn't sure what to do. Check the hut. He hurried over to it, and stopped outside the door. On the far side of it were two horses. He heard voices coming from inside.

"You think these bone diggers do it in here on the floor, Brent?"

"Mm. Probably with the bones."

"I don't believe it," Indy muttered. He threw open the cloth door. "What are you two doing here?"

"Indy! Hiya, kiddo." Madelaine was wearing riding pants, high boots, and a felt hat with a pheasant feather.

"Jonesy, look at you." Brent stepped out of the hut after her and stroked his thin mustache. "All decked out for archaeology—rope, knapsack, even a rifle, and dirty, too. Real authentic."

"Can you keep it down?" Indy glanced toward the mound, but nothing had changed. No one was in sight.

"We're leaving for Athens this morning, and decided to ride out and say good-bye," Madelaine said in her squeaky voice. "The king's left, you know, so it's getting boring."

"Boring is not the word for it," Brent chimed in, adjusting the kerchief he wore with his safari outfit.

"Listen, did you see anyone else here?"

"Not a soul," Madelaine said. "Didn't think we'd see you, either. So what exciting things have you been doing? Haven't seen you since the royal reception."

"Nothing much," Indy said dryly.

"Where's Shannon? Haven't seen him since we got here."

"He's around."

He had to do something. He needed them to get help, but they'd probably fetch soldiers, and he doubted he could trust any of them. He jammed a hand in his jacket pocket and felt a head of garlic, and suddenly an idea occurred to him.

"Listen, are you going back to the village before you leave?"

"We're not riding horses to Athens," Brent said. "You can be sure of that."

"Would you mind doing me a favor?"

"I suppose," Madelaine said. "If it doesn't take too long, and if Brent doesn't mind."

"Go to the hotel for me, and tell Nikos, the kid at the desk, that I'm going down into the crevice again and need my moly."

"Your what?" she said.

"He knows what it is."

"Of course. Moly. It's an archaeology thing," Brent said knowingly. "One of those digging tools or something. For boring holes, I think. I'm right, aren't I, Jonesy?"

"That's it. Please hurry. I need it real fast."

"Do you want us to bring it back to you?" Madelaine asked.

"No. Nikos can handle it. I've got to go. Have a good trip."

"See you in Paris, Indy." She kissed him on the cheek, then hooked her arm in Brent's as they walked out of the hut and over to their horses.

Indy picked up the rifle and peered toward the mound. Dorian must have seen Madelaine and Brent, and decided to hide. He moved away from the hut, crossed the Sacred Way, and stopped at one of the pillars.

He set the rifle against it, and stepped out into view. "Dorian, where are you?"

"Right behind you."

Indy jumped at the sound of her voice. When he turned, she was standing by the pillar, one hand aiming her revolver at him, the other gripping the rifle.

"Surprise."

She must have been watching from the other side of the pillar. But he guessed she was too far away to have heard their conversation.

"What did you tell your friends?"

"That I was busy, and wished them a good trip to Athens."

She looked toward the road. "Why are they heading back to the village?"

"To get their bags and a carriage, I suppose. They just rode out to say good-bye."

She nodded, and watched him closely. "You are on my side, aren't you?"

Indy looked at the rifle, then gave Dorian the most sincere look he could manage. "Of course I am. I'd be dead if you hadn't saved us."

"If your charming friends bring back soldiers we're all in trouble, you know."

"They won't. And you don't have to point that gun at me, either."

She jabbed the rifle lightly in his side. "I'm not a fool, Indy. Where did you get this rifle?"

He told her about his encounter with the soldiers. "If I hadn't stopped them, they would be here now looking for Mandraki."

"Well, they wouldn't find him here."

He didn't know what she meant. "Where are Shannon and Conrad?" he asked as they headed toward the mound.

"Jack and Ted?" She glanced toward the crevice. "Let's go find them."

So they were Jack and Ted now. *This better not be a sick joke,* he thought. If they were dead, he would...He didn't know what he would do, but it wouldn't be nice.

"Where are the bodies?"

"Gone," she said blithely.

Gone, he thought, like Richard Farnsworth and who knows how many other old boyfriends. He waited for her to explain as they climbed the mound.

"Did you see Alex anywhere out there?" she asked as she reached the top of the mound.

"What?"

"Alex. Did you see him?"

She was mad, all right. "Dorian. Remember, you killed Alex."

"No, I didn't." She smiled, then turned toward the crevice. "It's okay, fellows. Everyone's gone, and Indy's back."

Oh, Jesus. His stomach knotted. She must have shot them and dumped their bodies in the hole. She was denying everything, even that she'd killed Mandraki. It must be the vapors. Somehow, they had affected her mind, and he couldn't stop himself from telling her exactly what he was thinking.

"What did the vapors do to you, Dorian? I don't understand."

She looked into his eyes, and laughed. "You mean when I was Pythía? You don't know, do you, Indy? You don't know what I felt in the vapors."

"No, I don't."

She took a step closer to him.

Careful. Watch her closely, Indy thought.

"I felt the same as you," she said.

Indy frowned, shook his head. "What do you mean? I don't understand."

"There was no trance," she said, curtly. "I was faking all of it."

"How could you? I mean you were babbling, and Panos was interpreting it."

She shook her head. "Panos wanted to believe so badly that he thought he was interpreting. But he was just following cues I had given him. I told him that the king was in danger the day before I faked the trance. He knew that was what Pythía was supposed to tell him."

God, she was even more devious than he'd given her credit for. "Where are they, Dorian?" He spoke tersely. He wanted to grab her by the shoulders and shake her. "Where is Jack? Where is Ted?"

She motioned Indy to walk around to the other side of the crevice. "Over there."

He moved away from her, sidling around the crevice to avoid turning his back on her. The mound on the other side was more like a pinnacle, narrow on top with steep sides, the crevice on one side, the gully on the other. Indy peered over the far edge and for a second didn't see anything. Then, he spotted the pair twenty feet below, squatting, backs against the dirt wall. "Are you guys okay?"

"Just fine," Shannon said.

"Pull them out with the rope," Dorian ordered. "And hurry, we've got work to do."

He started to say he'd use his whip, but caught himself. So far she hadn't paid it any heed, and he was better keeping it that way.

He pulled Shannon out first as Conrad pushed from below. "You had me worried, Jack," he said as he grabbed him by the arm. "Why didn't you answer?"

He tossed the line back down and Conrad quickly scaled the side of the gully.

"She knew where we were," Shannon said off-handedly. "She made us dump the bodies in the hole, then jump in here."

"Only two of the bodies," Conrad said, brushing off his hands. "Mandraki's still alive. She let him go."

"What?"

"I told you I didn't kill him," Dorian called from across the crevice. "When I saw him stand up so bravely and hobble away, I couldn't do it. I let him go."

"You know what else?" Shannon said. "There was no blood where he'd been lying. Figure that out."

Indy couldn't. But he had an ominous feeling they hadn't seen the last of Colonel Mandraki.

22

OMPHALOS

Indy descended into the darkness clutching a torch in one hand and the rope that was knotted around his waist in the other. In spite of what happened the last time he'd been lowered into this hole, he felt oddly safe. This time he knew he was in good hands. Shannon and Conrad were going to do their best to keep him alive.

They lowered him slowly and steadily, and it wasn't long before he spotted the place where the tablet had ripped away from the wall. Not much farther. He held the torch out, looking for the ledge. A little farther now. Not much more.

He stretched his arm out as far as he could and peered down. The torchlight flickered off the walls. Then he saw it, a rocky plateau jutting from the wall. But there was something else, too. Something he hadn't expected.

"Oh, God."

His feet dropped onto the ledge. The rope went slack. Dorian yelled down to him; her voice echoed eerily off the walls. He tugged twice at the rope to let them know he was here, and all the while kept his eyes on the ghastly sight of Panos's body. It was lying at an angle across the bed of rock with one leg dangling over the edge. His head was face down, and his right arm was curled over the black cone. In death, Panos had found the Omphalos.

Indy moved closer, bent down on one knee. Carefully, he lifted the dead man's wrist off the stone, but as he did the body slid farther over the edge. It hung in midair for a moment, then Indy let go. The body vanished into the bowels of Delphi. An appropriate burial site for the leader of the Order of Pythía, he thought, and he was with his son.

He stared into the blanket of darkness a moment longer. He had no reason to miss either man. They had caused him more grief than most people who crossed his path. Yet, their deaths still affected him, if for no other reason than to remind him that death followed life, and that he was as vulnerable as the next person. Maybe more so. Maybe he *was* the next person.

He shrugged off the disturbing thought, and turned his attention to the Omphalos. He ran a hand over its rough surface, and wondered how much of it was still in the wall. He slipped off the knapsack, picked out a trowel, and began scraping away at the rock and dirt that held it to the wall. After a few minutes, he'd made little progress, and realized that he needed to make a more concerted attack. He put away the trowel in favor of a pick and stabbed at the wall. For the next half hour, he chipped away at rock and dirt, gouging a hole around the stone.

Finally, he took it in both hands and tested how

firmly it was implanted. If he had been dealing with a fragile ceramic piece, he knew what he was doing would have been foolhardy. But this artifact seemed as sturdy as the engine block of a Model T.

The cone moved slightly as he wiggled it back and forth. He pulled harder, but his hands slipped off and he tumbled back onto the ledge. He rolled onto his stomach and his leg slipped over the side. He patted the air as he stared down into the abyss.

"Careful, Indy. Careful," he said to himself. He sidled away from the edge, and went back to work chipping away at the rock.

"Indy. Everything okay?" Dorian shouted.

Sure. Things were great. Couldn't be better. He tugged twice at the rope to let her know that he didn't have it.

He chipped more, pulled and twisted the stone, chipped again, and pulled some more. He was sure that it was almost free. He placed his feet against the wall, grabbed the cone with both hands, and pulled as hard as he could. His hands slipped off, and he sprawled onto his back.

He lifted himself up on his elbows, and stared at the stone in disgust. He kicked it with his heel in anger. It was all that was needed; it broke free. He blinked away the dust, and grinned as he lifted the Omphalos from the rubble. He laid it down on the ledge, and brushed it off. It was about a foot and a half long and about six or seven inches in diameter at the base, and narrowed to a rounded nub. It felt heavy as iron.

Proper procedure, as Dorian had taught him, called for taking out the tape measure and notepad from the knapsack and jotting down its exact dimensions and description and detailing its removal. But considering the conditions he was working under, it seemed a bit ridiculous. He laughed aloud at the irony. The professor was armed and there was a fair chance that after he surfaced with the prize find, she would kill him. That, he knew, was definitely not proper procedure.

He pulled once on the rope. "I've got it," he yelled. "Pull me up."

He dropped the torch on the ledge and pressed the cone against his chest as he gripped the rope. He felt himself being lifted and tried to relax. He didn't want to think about what would happen when he got to the surface. He couldn't do anything about it. Not now at least. Maybe not even then.

The Omphalos felt oddly warm. The sensation spread across his chest until the warmth had imbued him, made him drowsy. He closed his eyes, drifted . . .

It was light as day. He was looking at an eagle, his eagle, and it was perched on the edge of a nest. He could see eggs in the nest. Silver-colored eggs. He was dreaming and awake at the same time. He felt ecstatic, better than he'd ever felt. But what was happening? What was he seeing? The eagle cocked its head as if to get a better look at him, or to see if it had his attention. With a sudden thrust of its beak, the bird broke open one of the eggs.

The bird and nest were gone, and Indy saw himself with the king in a room filled with books. A royal library. The king wore a blue satin robe and slippers. Oddly, he suddenly knew that the king would survive Mandraki's threat to his life, but he also knew that he would soon be exiled. It was as if it had already happened.

He noticed that the king held something in his hands. It was the Omphalos, and he was offering it to Indy. Then as suddenly as the king had appeared, he was gone, and Indy saw the Omphalos in a museum. Standing next to it was the curator, whom Indy recognized as Marcus Brody, an old friend and sometimes substitute father. He was smiling and proud. Then the scene wavered, and Indy's feeling of contentment shifted to shock. The glass case holding the relic was shattered; the Omphalos was gone. He heard Brody's voice: *Stolen. It's been stolen.*

But the outrage he felt was cut short as the eagle again appeared in front of him perched on the nest. It tilted its head as before, then drilled its beak into another egg.

Indy was talking to Dorian. She was excited, telling him he must do something. He had to act fast. But what was he supposed to do? Then Mandraki was facing him. He raised a gun, pointed it at Indy's heart. He fired.

The eagle again. Another egg was shattered, and this time the images came at him fast and hard. He glimpsed a tweedy man with a pipe and mustache in an office crammed with books. He spoke in a tone of voice that inferred authority. "Do not mix mythology and archaeology, or your thesis will be rejected. They are two separate disciplines. If you want Greece as your focal region, take up the challenge of Linear B. You have the perfect background for tackling a language puzzle."

Then the man dissolved. When he solidified again, he was Mandraki. He raised his gun, and fired.

Silver eggs. Two left. The eagle's beak viciously pecked at one of them, and as it shattered Indy saw himself standing in front of a class talking. He couldn't hear the words, but he knew he was giving an archaeology lecture. Suddenly, the classroom faded; he was in the center of a circle of massive stones. Stonehenge. He was embracing a woman. He couldn't see her face, but he knew he was close to her like no other woman.

Then the woman was gone. Mandraki again. Aiming. He fired.

The last egg. The black eye of the eagle watched him. Then it lightly tapped the egg. A crack fissured lengthwise along its shell, and it fell apart. Indy saw himself again, older now, in the prime of his career. He looked savvy, more adventurer than scholar. The vision winked out and was replaced by a collage of images: Jungles. Deserts. Ruins. Lost cities. Relics of power. More ominous now: a pit of snakes, a close-up of an insignia of a black, broken cross. A hand bearing a dagger, but another offering help. A voice overlaid the images: "Adventures beyond imagining, but not without serious danger. Ultimately, a reunion with the father. What he seeks, you will find."

The changing scenes vanished as a harsh light struck him. He heard voices. Hands again. This time they were lifting him from the hole. He squinted his eyes against the bright light. He was on his knees, still gripping the black cone.

"So this is it," Dorian said. "The Omphalos."

Indy felt numb, overwhelmed, unable to speak. He

blinked his watery eyes, and saw Dorian laying down the rifle. Still holding the revolver, she took the Omphalos from his arms. It was heavier than she expected, and she clutched it to her chest.

Indy's head was clearing. The dream, the fantasy, whatever had happened to him, was over. He tried to concentrate on what was real, here, and now. Shannon and Conrad hovered above him. They helped him shed the knapsack.

Suddenly, Dorian sucked in her breath, a look of bewilderment and shock crossing her face. The revolver dangled loosely in her hand inches from Indy's head. She didn't move; her features were frozen in the instant of surprise.

With a quick, deft move, Shannon snapped the revolver from her grip, and Conrad picked up the rifle. Dorian didn't react. Her expression changed to a ghastly stare, then she collapsed, still clinging to the black stone.

"What happened?" Shannon asked.

"I don't know," Indy said, still confused by his experience in the tunnel. "Let's get her to the workshop."

"I'll put the stone in the knapsack," Shannon said. He tried to loosen it from Dorian's grip, but she writhed, grimaced, and screamed.

"Just let her carry it," Conrad said.

Shannon lifted her by the elbows and Indy grabbed her feet. But she kicked and twisted and moaned, and the going was slow. As they left the temple and headed toward the path leading to the workshop, Indy abruptly stopped.

"Wait a minute. I don't think the workshop is a

good idea. She's too hard to carry, and we don't have all day. Besides, I ran into some soldiers earlier." He quickly told them about his encounter. "As soon as someone finds them, we're going to have company."

"You're right," Conrad said. "We've got to get out of here. Maybe we should just leave her."

Indy shook his head. "Let's take her to the hut, then figure out what to do."

They no sooner had made up their minds when a rider on a galloping horse charged into the ruins. "Hurry," Indy hissed.

They hustled Dorian into the hut, and lowered her to the ground. Indy instantly dropped to his hands and knees and looked out the charred hole in the rear. "Take this," Shannon said, and handed him Dorian's revolver.

Indy could see legs. Someone was running toward the hut. "Indy, where are you?"

"Oh, God. It's just Nikos," Indy said, relieved, then yelled to Nikos.

"I got your message. What happened?" the boy said, gasping for breath as he stepped into the hut.

"Plenty," Indy said.

Nikos gaped at the sight of Dorian, who was still twisting about and grimacing. "Pythía!"

"I don't know who she is, Nikos," Indy said. "But Panos and Grigoris are dead." He told him what happened at the crevice.

"What are you going to do? If Colonel Mandraki is still alive he will come for her and all of you."

"We've got to get out of here, and fast," Conrad said.

"You're right about that," Shannon put in. "I'm starting to really miss Paris."

"Nikos, what are the chances of you getting us a carriage?" Indy asked.

"A carriage? How about an auto?"

"You got one?"

"Colonel Mandraki does. He left the key at the desk of the hotel. I can get it, and I can drive it, too. I know how."

"I don't know about stealing his car," Indy said warily.

"Why not?" Shannon said. "If we have it, he won't."

"But Mandraki will know what to look for."

"So what?" Shannon responded. "We'll get to Athens, ditch the car, and get out of the country as fast as possible. Besides, he was shot, remember. He's not going to be in any shape to go anywhere."

Conrad nodded toward Dorian, who now looked as if she was asleep. "What about her?"

"Leave her," Shannon said. "Let Mandraki take care of her. She deserves whatever she gets."

Indy thought a moment. "Nikos, can you drive the car here without letting anyone see you?"

"Everyone will see me," he said proudly. "They will see I can drive."

Indy nodded. "That's what I thought." He turned to Conrad. "Listen, why don't Jack and I go get the uniforms off those soldiers I tied up. We'll ride horses into the village and then take the car. You stay with Dorian, and we'll pick you up."

"Everyone in the village knows you by sight," Conrad protested. "You won't make a very believable soldier. Let's do it this way. You stay here. Jack and I will get the car."

"Good idea," Shannon said. "Besides, I'm starting to think you attract trouble, Indy."

"Okay. Okay."

"I'll get the car ready," Nikos said, and hurried out the door.

Conrad picked up the rifle from where he'd set it against the wall, and Indy returned the revolver to Shannon. Just then, Dorian moaned loudly. She rolled over, letting the Omphalos slip to the ground. She sat up and rubbed her face.

"You going to be all right with her?" Conrad asked.

"I'll be fine." As they left, Indy knelt down beside Dorian and slipped the Omphalos inside the knapsack.

She watched him closely, but remained silent.

"What happened?" he asked.

She opened her mouth, but didn't speak right away. "I thought I was dead."

"Why?"

"I was being suffocated, squeezed to death by a giant snake. A python. It was wrapped around me. It was horrible. I could smell its cold, acrid breath."

She hugged herself and shivered. Her black hair fell over one side of her face. She sat like a child, with one leg tucked under her, the other stretched out. "It seemed so real." She seemed neither professor nor killer. She was helpless, confused. He didn't want to feel sorry for her, but he did.

"Why did you fake the trances, Dorian?"

"Don't you understand, Indy? Don't you realize the power of Pythía?"

"Wait a minute. You said there was no Pythía, you were faking."

"I didn't say there was no Pythía. Just ask the king. He saw, and I'm sure he believes."

"And now that Panos is dead, your priest is gone."

She leaned forward and that transfixing smile held his gaze again, drew him closer. "Panos was not meant to be my priest. He was not the right one. It is you, Indy. You will be my priest... and lover."

Indy forced himself to move back from her. "No. I don't think so."

"Do you think I cannot be Pythía, that nobody will believe? You know yourself that the readings were almost always ambiguous, interpreted one way if a certain thing happened, and another if something else happened. It's a technique. I'll teach it to you. We'll invent our own way of communicating with gestures and key words."

She reached for his hand. "Think of it, we'll be two of the most powerful and well-known people in the world. Do you realize that?"

Indy pulled his hand back and stood up. "Sure."

She stood, and moved close to him. "Don't you want me, Indy? I'll be yours. It'll be worth it, I promise. Think about it."

He could smell her musky scent, and felt the pull of her eyes again. He took another step back. "Even if I was interested, there's the big matter of trust here, Dorian. You brought me here with the intention of using me as your fall guy in your crazy plot to kill the king. And you've got a history."

"No, that plot was not my doing. That was Alex's game. Same with Richard Farnsworth. He killed him; I didn't."

Indy's hands tightened into fists. His cheeks flamed with anger. "But you were part of his game. You didn't stop it."

"I couldn't. He forced me. Anyhow, you know that I went against him. I shot him, for God's sake. He should be dead. What more can I do to show you my intentions?"

"You killed Farnsworth's brother. He was on that train to Brindisi. You stabbed him with a pick from your tool kit, then you threw him off the back of the train while I was eating ice cream."

"No. That's not what happened. He tried to kill me. I was only defending myself."

She had an answer for everything and the answer always sounded reasonable. That was her gift. "There's one thing I still don't understand. If you were just faking it in the vapors, why did you fake this last fit when you took the Omphalos from me? What was the point of that?"

"No. I didn't fake that. I don't know what happened, and I don't want to think about it, either."

Now that she'd admitted the truth, Indy knew that he couldn't so easily dismiss his own experience with the Omphalos as a meaningless dream.

Just then a car horn honked. Indy slung the knapsack over his shoulder. "Good-bye."

"You're taking the Omphalos?"

"Yes. I'll see that it gets into a museum."

"Take me with you, too. I can't stay here now."

"No."

"Please." She grabbed his arm. "You don't know what kind of things Alex would do to me."

The car honked again. "All right. Under one condition. I'm taking you to the king's palace and you are going to confess to your part in the assassination plot and turn in Mandraki."

"Okay. I'll do it. Whatever you say."

They stepped outside the hut and both gazed toward Apollo's Temple. With his free hand, Indy reached into his pocket and pulled out his watch.

"It's eight minutes to four." The vapors should have been rising for three minutes now, but there was no sign of them.

"The pattern's broken," Dorian said softly.

23

Escape from Delphi

A shiny Pierce-Arrow was parked outside the ruins, and for an instant Indy thought it must belong to the king. Then he saw Conrad behind the wheel. "Is that Mandraki's car?"

"One of them," Dorian said as they hurried toward the car.

Back in the States, you could buy a flivver for two hundred eighty dollars or five dollars a week on the installment plan, but few people could afford an elegant Pierce-Arrow, and no doubt the cost for one in Greece was much higher. "He must have money."

"Lots."

"Let's go," Conrad said from behind the front seat as he eyed Dorian warily.

"Where're your uniforms?"

"The soldiers were gone." Conrad glanced over at Shannon. "We almost didn't get away. Jack told Nikos to go back to the hotel for his cornet, and while we waited half the village came out to see the car. I think word got around."

Indy peered down the road toward the village. "Let's get the hell out of here."

"What's she doing here?" Shannon asked.

"I'm taking her to the king."

Shannon smirked. "You're what?"

"She's going to confess."

"Sure."

"Well, I can't leave her here. Mandraki will kill her, if he's still alive."

"I heard two soldiers talking," Nikos said from the back seat. "The colonel is okay. The bullet hit his ammunition belt."

"Nice shot," Indy said to Dorian. "Nikos, you better get out. We've got to go."

"I want to go to Athens with you," he beamed. "My father gave me permission."

"Did he know *how* you were going?"

"Well, no."

"It could be dangerous."

"You think so?" he asked hopefully.

Suddenly, a military truck appeared on the road, coming from the direction of the village. Conrad cranked the engine, stepped hard on the accelerator pedal. It sputtered.

"It's flooded," Shannon yelled.

Conrad tried again.

The truck closed in on them. Indy jerked open the back door and grabbed Dorian by the arm. "Get in. Quick."

The engine revved to life.

But Dorian surprised him. She twisted her arm away and ran toward the truck.

"Dorian," he shouted, and leaped from the car. But

the knapsack snagged on the door. He pulled it loose, but it was too late. She was running directly at the on-coming truck, waving her hands and calling out to Mandraki. The truck braked.

She's dead, he thought.

"Get in, for chrissake," Conrad yelled as he started to drive away. Indy trotted after the car, and leaped onto the running board. He looked back and saw Mandraki embracing Dorian in the middle of the road.

"What the hell?" Indy exclaimed.

A dozen soldiers poured out of the back of the truck and opened fire. Conrad stepped hard on the ac-celerator as Shannon returned the fire.

Indy swung the door open and was about to slide into the back seat when he felt something strike him between the shoulder blades. He dropped face first onto the seat.

Shannon let out a whoop as they roared away. "I got their front tires."

Indy was gasping for breath. "Good. But I think they got me."

Nikos helped him shed the knapsack. Indy ex-pected blood and pain.

"You're not shot," Nikos said.

"What?" He rolled over and saw Nikos holding up the knapsack.

"See, there's the hole, but only through the back of it. The bullet hit the thing you found. It saved you."

Indy opened the knapsack and stared incredulously at the Omphalos. He considered picking it up to look for the bullet's mark, but thought better of it.

"You okay?" Conrad called over his shoulder as they raced down the mountain.

"Just fine."

"You're as lucky as Colonel Mandraki," Nikos said.

Shannon turned in his seat. "I don't understand Mandraki. The woman shoots him and he welcomes her like someone who had just saved his life."

Indy shook his head. "I don't get it, either."

The telegraph operator in the back of the truck finished tapping out the message. He waited until he received acknowledgment, then nodded to Mandraki. "They'll never make it to Athens," Mandraki said, and he smiled at Dorian, pleased with himself.

"Good," she said. "But we can't hide their deaths. Too many witnesses."

Mandraki frowned. "We can't admit to killing them, either. The king will use it against me."

"Relax, Alex. It will be no problem. They stole an officer's car, and an archaeological artifact, a national treasure. They were killed in a gun battle as they tried to escape. Simple as that."

"You are a complex woman, Dorian. But I like your simple solutions. Now tell me which one of them shot me."

It was twilight as they descended the hills to the outskirts of the capital. The lights of Athens were blinking on below them. Indy was tired, thirsty, and hungry, but most of all he was anxious to get to the presidential palace. It was the one place he felt that they would be safe for the night. *If* they could get through the front gate.

"You ask me, we should skip the visit to the palace and go on to Piraeus, and take the first boat out of here," Shannon said. "With luck, we could be in Paris tomorrow night."

"That wouldn't be luck. That would be a miracle," Conrad quipped. "But it might be a good idea to get out of here if we can."

Indy shook his head. "They'll be waiting for us at the port."

"But they're behind us," Shannon said.

"Mandraki won't be there, but his men will be watching for us. You can count on it."

"The port isn't the only place they're waiting," Conrad said. "Take a look at what's ahead."

Indy grimaced. "Swell. A roadblock."

Nikos leaned forward. "I bet this is where it gets dangerous."

Indy frowned at the impetuous kid. "At least one of the places."

"Look," Conrad said. "Let's reason with them. We'll explain we have to get to the presidential palace, that we have important information for the king. It's possible they're loyal."

There was no time to argue about it. He stepped on the brake and slowed. They were fifty yards short of the roadblock when one of the soldiers pointed. Several others raised their guns. They fired and the windshield shattered. "I don't think they're open to conversation," Indy said.

Conrad stepped on the gas pedal and veered off the

road. He headed along a slope, attempting to loop around the roadblock. The car tilted precariously and gunfire rattled off the roof. What happened next seemed to take only an instant. The hill was too steep; the car rolled over and kept rolling. Indy didn't know which way was up as he was hurtled about, but finally the car landed on its wheels again. Miraculously, they were on the road, and past the roadblock. But now Indy was behind the wheel, Conrad to his right and Shannon in the back seat.

"Hey, I'm driving."

Indy glanced into the mirror and saw soldiers in the road firing another volley. Bullets pinged off the trunk. They would be chased, but if the Pierce-Arrow could stay on the road, it could outrun any Greek military vehicle.

"We're out of range," he said, "and the city's just ahead. We're going to make it."

"We are?" Conrad asked. He looked glassy-eyed and stared straight ahead.

"Never would have guessed you could drive like that, Ted."

"I didn't, either. I was ducking under the wheel."

Indy looked over his shoulder. "Hey, what happened to Nikos?"

The kid rose up from the floorboards. "Wait until I tell my friends about this."

"How you doing, Jack?"

"I feel like my neck's broken, and I've got a fat lip. Guess I won't be blowing any tunes for the king tonight."

"Speaking of the king. Anybody know how to get to the palace?" Indy asked.

"I do," Nikos said. "It's by the new Olympic Stadium."

"Where is that from the Acropolis?"

"I'll show you."

Indy noticed people staring at the car as they cruised into the city. "Guess they're pretty impressed by the Pierce-Arrow." Then he saw the reflection of the car in the window of a shop. The top was flattened, the driver's side was smashed, and the entire vehicle was pockmarked with bullet holes.

"Lucky we're alive."

"Indy, here's the Platía Phlomouson Hetairae," Nikos said as they drove around a square. "You remember I told you about it?"

"The what?" Shannon asked.

"It's where the best tavernas in town are found," Indy answered.

"I could use a drink," Shannon said as they drove on.

"There's the stadium," Nikos said. "Turn left when you pass it."

Suddenly soldiers poured out of the stadium, charging into the road, blocking traffic and waving guns. "Maybe they're on our side this time," Conrad said hopefully.

A bullet glanced off the hood, another tore into the front seat between Indy and Conrad. "No, don't think so."

"This is getting old," Shannon groused.

Indy swung the wheel to the left, and drove rapidly along a winding narrow street until they reached a main crossroad.

Nikos pointed to the right. "The palace is down there."

More soldiers were hustling into the street where Nikos pointed. Instead of turning, Indy drove straight ahead and directly into a park. He barreled along the sidewalk, scattering the promenading citizens who cursed and shook their fists.

"Where are we, Nikos?"

"In the palace garden. Go that way," he yelled.

Indy veered to the right, and headed toward the boulevard that fronted the palace grounds. He swerved onto it, and now the palace was on his right. "We're going to make it," Conrad said.

"You're dreaming," Shannon answered.

Indy slowed as they neared the main gate. A couple of dozen armed soldiers stood guard.

"They're the king's men," Indy said. "They must be."

"You ask me, they look just like the ones who've been shooting at us," Shannon said.

Now Indy wasn't so sure. "I'm going around. Must be another way inside."

They circled the palace, but the only other entrance didn't look any more inviting. "What is that funny looking machine by the soldiers?" Nikos asked, his voice filled with awe.

Indy kept driving.

"It's called a tank," Conrad explained. "They started using them in the war. The first tank battle was fought in 1917 at Cambrai."

"Always nice to have a history professor on hand," Indy remarked. "I say we try the main entrance. What do you think, Ted?"

"We've got nothing to lose. No one shot at us when we passed."

"Definitely a favorable sign," Shannon said, his voice thick with irony.

Nikos pointed toward the main entrance. "Look, the gate is opening for us."

Indy turned the wheel. A safe harbor, at last. Suddenly, he slammed on the brakes. Another tank blocked the entrance. "I hope it's the welcoming committee." Indy looked around, assessing the situation. He was about to back up, but the first tank now was right behind them.

Soldiers surrounded the battered car, their rifles trained on them. "This doesn't look good," Conrad muttered.

Hands yanked at the locked doors amid excited yells and shouts of orders. Then everyone stepped back. No one fired. The soldiers stared as if the car were on exhibit.

"What's going on?" Shannon asked.

With the soldiers out of the way, it was obvious. The two tanks were closing in on them. A second later, they were greeted by a high-pitched screech of crushed metal as one rolled into the front, the other struck the rear.

"Goddamn," Shannon yelled, popping his door open. They dove out of the car and into the grasp of the soldiers. Indy was lifted by his arms and legs; the knapsack was ripped from his grip. "Hey, that's my bag. I need it back."

They ignored him. Behind him the tanks crunched the remains of the Pierce-Arrow.

*   *   *

"Your Highness," Dorian said, "the man is dangerous. We don't need foreigners like him. I think he and his friends should be immediately expelled."

The king leaned back in his thickly padded chair in the royal library. "If what you tell me is true, then expulsion might be too easy for them. After all, it's a matter of honor as well as justice when someone steals the property of one of our officers, and then opens fire on him."

"I understand your feelings, Your Highness. However, as you know, no one was injured."

The king stroked his chin and considered what she had said. "Why are you defending him, Dr. Belecamus?"

You'll never find out, she thought. "I feel partially responsible. This man is one of my graduate students and I brought him here."

"I've already met Mr. Jones, as you recall. I found him a bit odd, but that's not unusual for Americans. However, I didn't think he was a criminal, and I'd like to hear his story."

Exactly what she wanted to avoid. She glanced at Mandraki. *Say something, damn it.*

"I don't think it's going to be necessary to go to that trouble," Mandraki said. "You see, in deference to Dr. Belecamus, I don't want to press charges against Jones or the other men."

The king nodded, and motioned to one of his aides. "Prepare their exit papers. I want them on board the ship to Brindisi in the morning."

Dorian stood, feeling relieved, and extended a

hand. "Thank you, Your Highness. I appreciate this, and I apologize for the inconvenience it's caused you."

"I'll be happy to take charge of them until their ship leaves," Mandraki said.

The king shrugged, then waved a hand. "It's no trouble keeping them here tonight. In fact, I'd prefer it. I don't want to hear about any more wild escapades."

He said it with a tone of finality, and Dorian knew it would do no good to argue. She was about to stand up when the king changed topics.

"Now what about the artifact? It was the reason you pursued Jones and the others, wasn't it?" He glanced at Mandraki. "Besides the car, of course."

"Yes, it was, Your Highness."

"Well, do you want to take it with you?"

Just the thought of the Omphalos made Dorian uneasy. She never wanted to hold it again. But she couldn't say that to the king.

"I'd rather not right now. I'll send someone to pick it up in a couple of days."

"What is this thing, the Omphalos?"

"I believe it's a meteorite that was cut and polished and covered with a rope netting that's petrified. Its value was symbolic in the time of Pythía. Now it's mostly a curiosity."

"Why did Jones want it?"

She shrugged. "Who knows? I think he was a little deranged from breathing those vapors. I was speaking prematurely when I said they had no apparent effect. The fact is, they seem to have varying effects."

She smiled modestly, the humble servant. "I'm just pleased, Your Highness, that they affected me in a way that helped you. I don't recall what happened, but I understand that I was able to warn you of a threat against your life."

The king touched his hip, and she wondered if he still believed the vapors had healed him. "Yes, I want to thank you. It was a peculiar situation, but if I hadn't been warned who knows what would have happened." He stroked his chin, and nodded. Then he rose from his chair. "Well, now it's late."

Dorian said good night, and waited as Mandraki shook the king's hand. She smiled to herself as she heard the king murmur that he was sorry about what happened to his car. As she and Mandraki left the library, she spoke quickly under her breath. "I think we did just fine. He'll go to bed soon, and by the time he wakes up they'll be gone."

Mandraki didn't respond.

"What's wrong?"

"I'm not worried about Jones anymore," he said in a hushed voice as they walked down the wide hallway. "We've got to get that bastard out of power. The Agora is filled with refugees; more are arriving every day. The country is falling apart."

"He'll pay for his mistakes," Dorian said. "We'll see to it, and we'll do it right this time."

"And soon," Mandraki added.

24

IN THE PALACE

In a barren cell somewhere below the palace, Indy hovered on the border of sleep. He saw the eagle flapping its wings, soaring high above him, then Mandraki's face obliterated the eagle. The colonel smiled cruelly, then pointed the barrel of his gun in his face.

Indy jerked awake, pounded the hard mattress, and turned over. He knew that what had happened to him in the crevice had been more than a dream. But he didn't want to think about it, didn't want to give it meaning, because all he could see was death, his death obliterating his future.

He turned over again, trying to stop his thoughts, but couldn't do it for more than a few seconds. He counted backwards from one hundred. Ninety-nine, ninety-eight...He made it to eighty-five before the numbers muddled in his mind, and he drifted. Eighty-six, seventy-eight...He slept.

He blinked his eyes open.

Something had jarred him from his sleep.

He listened.

He heard breathing.

Shannon and Conrad.

But another noise had awakened him. He heard it again. Hollow, distant voices.

Growing closer.

Footsteps echoed in the hallway. He heard a jingle of keys. A voice like gravel growled, another grunted in response. Now what?

The door opened. In the dim light from the hall he saw two uniformed guards enter the cell. They looked around. One pointed at Indy and the other immediately jerked him from the floor.

"What's going on?" Shannon shouted as Indy was dragged toward the door.

"Where're you taking him?" Conrad stood, but he was pushed back down. The door slammed shut.

Hope this isn't the execution call, Indy thought. "Is it morning already?" he asked in Greek as he was led away.

The guards didn't answer. No one had told the prisoners anything. They'd been fed soup, bread, and water, and given a blanket and a thin mattress apiece. But their pleas to see the king or anyone who would listen to them were met with silence. In fact, they didn't even know the whereabouts of Nikos. They hadn't seen him since they left the car, and Indy hoped that somehow in the confusion he had managed to escape.

They reached a stairway, and the guards literally ran him up the steps. "Hey, boys, what's the rush?" He was ushered into a back hallway. He glimpsed a huge kitchen off the hall where men in white uniforms scrubbed the floor. He smelled the faint odor of food.

"Oh, time for breakfast already?" The guards' sullen expressions remained intact. "Guess not."

They kept walking, and soon they entered another hallway, but this one was ornate, suitable for a palace. His feet sank into the plush carpeting. The walls were mahogany and the cornices were trimmed with gold leaf. He had no doubt that he was now in the main part of the palace.

Halfway down the hallway they stopped in front of double doors tall enough for a giant to enter without ducking. One of the guards tapped lightly. Immediately, the door opened a couple of inches. A few words were exchanged, then Indy was escorted into a library filled with books that reached from floor to ceiling.

The royal library, he thought. Like in my dream-vision.

A large, muscular man in a suit pointed to a wooden chair and Indy sat down. He looked up glumly at the man, expecting an interrogation session. But why in a library? Maybe he was going to beat him to death with books. Joyce's *Ulysses* could kill him with a single blow.

"Hello, Mr. Indiana Jones."

Indy looked around and saw the king step into view. He was wearing a blue satin robe and slippers— just like in the vision—and he limped slightly as he walked.

"Your Highness." Indy stood up, but the guard shoved him back into his chair.

The king lowered himself into a swivel chair in

front of a fireplace. "I'm talking to you against the wishes of my advisors. They thought I should expel you from the country without another word."

"Really?" It was the best news Indy had heard since they'd left Delphi. "I'm sure my friends and I will accept that. But—"

The king raised a hand, cutting him off. "The reason I've decided to talk to you is that I feel I owe you at least that. You saved my life."

"I feel very fortunate to be here with you."

The king laughed. "You are fortunate to be alive, much less in the palace. If the reports I received were accurate, luck must be on your side."

Indy tried to answer, but his throat was dry and his voice cracked.

The king snapped his fingers and murmured something to a man who had been hidden by the bookshelves. Indy looked around, wondering how many other people were in the room. A moment later, the aide handed Indy a glass of water.

"Now, tell me why you stole an artifact from Delphi and an automobile from Colonel Mandraki."

Indy gulped the water down, and cleared his throat. "Mandraki was going to kill you. I mean, he wanted me to kill you."

"Wait." The king interrupted. "Start from the beginning. Why did you go to Delphi with Dorian Belecamus?"

Indy told his story, starting with his first encounter with Dorian. He told the king everything, from her ploy to become Pythía to the story of Richard Farnsworth. He hoped all the details would make his story about the assassination plot more believable.

The king listened closely, expressing astonishment at Belecamus's double dealings. "No wonder the miracle vapors didn't work. The cure didn't last any longer than the new Pythía."

He asked about Stephanos Doumas, and Indy told him that the dead archaeologist had been involved in the Order of Pythía, but not in the assassination attempt. "So you say that this supposed attempt to kill me had nothing to do with this mystical order, but was a military plot led by Colonel Mandraki?"

Indy nodded.

The king looked distracted. "I'm well aware that my political enemies are growing in numbers, and that everything has not worked as I had hoped. But until now none of them has attempted to kill me." He turned to Indy and smiled. "If what you say about Mandraki is true, I don't feel so bad now about his car being destroyed."

He got up and hobbled over to the fireplace. He rubbed his hands together over the low-burning fire, then turned to Indy. "I'd like to offer you and your friends a choice of staying in the palace as my guests of honor, or leaving and doing as you please."

"I think I can speak for my friends and say that the three of us are ready to go back to Paris." Then he asked about Nikos.

The king glanced to the side and the aide who had brought the water appeared again. The man watched Indy as the king spoke under his breath. He said something back to the king, then after another exchange the aide moved away. "I'm sorry, Mr. Jones," the king said, "but we know nothing about the boy. I hope he was able to get out of the car."

"Are you saying he never got out?" Indy raised his voice, and the guard by the door took a couple of steps toward him until the king motioned that it was okay.

"I'm saying I don't know. If I knew he was dead, I would tell you."

The aide returned carrying the knapsack and handed it to the king, who offered it to Indy. "I believe this is yours."

Incredible. He's going to give me the Omphalos, Indy thought. Again, just like the vision.

He shook his head. "No, it's not mine. It's the Omphalos. It belongs to everyone."

"It seems that there has been more attention given to this stone than it deserves," the king said.

"I'm not so sure about that, Your Highness."

The king reached into the knapsack and scooped out the cone with one hand. "Dr. Belecamus, for all her faults, is an authority on Delphi, and she told me that the Omphalos is really nothing more than a curiosity, a meteorite actually. I'm sure if it was of great value she wouldn't have left the palace without it. I'd like you to take it as a memento of your trip."

"Your Highness, I think you should put it back in the knapsack. If it's held too long, it may...you may..." Indy didn't know how to explain it. He really didn't believe it, but something had happened to him, and to Dorian.

"I don't see anything unusual about it." The king turned it over in his hands. "It feels warm."

He folded down into his chair. "I feel a little drowsy."

The knapsack dropped to the floor as he wrapped

his arms around the Omphalos. For several seconds he was motionless. Then his eyes grew wide, his mouth twisted in an expression of shock, and Indy knew that the artifact was working its spell. He rushed forward, but the burly guard caught him before he reached the king.

"Do something," Indy barked. "Can't you see he needs help? Get the stone."

The aide moved to the king's side, asked if he was okay. Carefully, he lifted the Omphalos and set it on the floor. "The doctor. Quickly," he yelled.

The king raised his hand. "No. I'm okay."

He ran his hands over his face. "Release him," he told the guard who still held Indy.

"I'm sorry, Your Highness. I tried to warn you."

The king stared down at the Omphalos. "I had the strangest experience. It was like a dream, but I was awake. I was surrounded by horrendous army ants, and they were picking at me. They were trying to carry me away."

Indy nodded, uncertain what to say.

"What happened to me?"

"I don't know," Indy said. "I think the artifact needs to be carefully studied by scientists."

"It needs to be locked away," the king retorted. "Or maybe lost again." A beat passed. "Well, if you're going to make the ferry on time, you better be on your way."

As the king accompanied him to the door of the library, Indy thought there was something different about him now. But he wasn't sure what it was.

He thanked the king for his help.

"Thank you for yours. Now, I have some army ants

to deal with this morning." With that, he turned and walked away.

As the door closed behind Indy, he realized what it was about the king. He no longer limped.

The city was just coming awake as they walked out a side door of the palace, and headed toward the street. A church bell pealed, a rooster crowed. The clatter of a horse and buggy contrasted with the rumble of a car engine. "I can't believe we're getting out of this nightmare alive," Shannon said.

As they reached the street, a soldier with a rifle approached them. "Now what?" Indy said wearily.

The soldier pointed to a new Cadillac waiting at the curb. "Your ride to the port."

As he closed the door after them, Indy couldn't help commenting on the irony. "That guy was probably ready to kill us yesterday."

"He's only doing his job," Conrad said.

"Yeah, just following the score," Shannon said.

"And what are we doing?" Indy asked.

"Playing it by ear."

"It's more interesting that way," Indy said.

"To some people," Conrad responded. He stared out the window toward the palace with a look of longing. "It would have been nice to stay at the palace for a few days. I might have gotten inspired for my novel."

Indy looked over at him as the car pulled away. "What about everything that's happened to you in the last few days?"

"Experiences are deceptive, Indy. A writer is much

better off working from the material of his inner self rather than from confusing experiences."

Indy mulled over that a moment. "If you ask me, people are confusing, not experiences."

Conrad didn't answer and they were each left with his thoughts. As they passed the remains of Hadrian's Library and neared the Roman Forum, Indy gazed out at the refugee shanties that were built on top of the ruins. Smoke was curling from a few rooftops and reminded him of the vapors rising from the crevice in Apollo's Temple.

Then he saw her moving through the gray dawn, her long hair tied in a braid. There was no doubt in his mind that it was Dorian Belecamus.

"Stop."

"What are you doing?" Shannon asked as Indy opened the door. "We've got to get to Piraeus."

"Listen, wait five minutes for me. If I'm not back, go on. I'll meet you at the ferry. There's something I've got to do."

"We don't have much time," Conrad warned.

"I know. I know."

He slammed the door without another word and hurried past a hodgepodge of shanties. She had been headed in that direction, and he thought he knew her destination. He passed by the ancient gate to the Forum, continued a ways, then saw the Tower of the Winds. She stood beneath it, gazing upward.

Dorian stared intently at the face of Lips, the southwest wind, who was speeding along the voyage of a ship. Jones and the others would soon be gone. The danger was over. And yet, she felt empty.

She would miss Jones. She had truly enjoyed his company, something he would never believe. He wouldn't understand the complexity of her life, and how forces beyond her personal life were directing her. She also knew that even if she had succeeded in breaking away from Mandraki and becoming Pythía, it would not have been any different. Those same political forces still would have driven her, and her fantasy about herself and Jones in the seat of power would have failed.

She didn't know what her future was. Maybe she would return to Paris. Maybe not. Nothing would be resolved until Mandraki acted. Her life was not really hers, and she detested that.

"Now I know why this is your favorite ruin."

She spun around, startled. "Indy!"

"You're just like it. Different faces for different winds."

"What are you doing here?"

"On my way back to Paris. Just saying *adío*."

She glanced around. Mandraki was inspecting the refugee situation and he would meet her here any time. "You shouldn't be here. *Fígete*."

He laughed. "Now you're telling me to get lost. I'm not leaving until you've satisfied my curiosity. Why did Mandraki take you back after you shot him? He doesn't exactly seem like the forgiving type."

She knew he wouldn't go away until she answered. "He didn't know who shot him. You can see through the vapors better than you can see into them. He only heard me call his name."

"That figures. You deceived him just like you did me and probably every other man in your life. And I thought for a while that I loved you."

She met his cold stare. "I'm not really a bad person, Indy. I do what I have to do. But you're a man. You wouldn't understand."

He shook his head. "Your gender has nothing to do with it. If every woman were like you, we'd all be in—"

"Just go. Please."

But it was too late. Mandraki stood just five feet away, and he was raising a revolver.

The gun seemed to move in slow motion. This couldn't be happening. The vision couldn't be true. What about all the adventures? Had his entire future, or the lack of it, depended on whether or not he left the car to follow Dorian?

"Jones, you're dead."

"No!" Dorian yelled, and she stepped between them.

"Get out of my way, Dorian. Now!"

"No. You aren't going to kill him."

"Move out of the way."

"You'll have to kill me first."

"Damn you, Dorian." The gun fired.

Indy caught Dorian as she collapsed. He felt the warmth of her blood seeping through his shirt and heard the soft, terrible wheezing as she tried to pull air into her lungs. He knew Mandraki was still standing there with the gun as he placed Dorian gently on the ground. He elevated her head so she wouldn't drown in her own blood.

"Dorian," Mandraki whimpered. "I didn't mean it. The gun just fired."

She tried to speak, but couldn't. She tried to lift her hand, but couldn't do that, either. Indy bent over her, touched her cheek.

"Get away from her," Mandraki yelled. "You did this. You killed her. Now you're dead."

Indy looked up into the barrel of the gun. Just like the vision. So this was it.

He heard a gunshot.

Mandraki staggered a couple of steps. *"Maláka,"* he cursed, and he dropped to the ground.

Indy recognized the guard from the king's library, standing in the clearing. As the guard moved toward them, Indy saw Mandraki lift his weapon and aim it at him again.

But the guard was ready. He pumped several shots into him. The gun fell from Mandraki's hand. Blood oozed from his mouth. This time he wouldn't get up.

When Indy looked down at Dorian, she was dead. Her eyes gazed vapidly at the blue morning sky overhead. Oddly, he knew he was going to miss her. In spite of her shortcomings, she had influenced his life. He would never be the same person again, and he knew that he had found the career that would be his life's work. He brushed a hand across Dorian's cheek, then closed the lids of her eyes.

"Indy, are you all right?"

"Nikos! What are you doing here?"

Nikos glanced anxiously around. "I hid in the palace garden all night, then I saw you leaving in the car.

I followed you in a taxi, because I wanted to say good-bye."

"I've got to get to the ferry."

"C'mon. The taxi's waiting. You can still make it."

He glanced once more at Dorian's frozen expression, and turned away.

The ferry's horn blasted as they arrived at the port. He shook hands with Nikos, and thanked him for his help. "Come visit me in Paris."

"I want to go to America too, and see a jazz band and the Grand Canyon," Nikos called after him.

"Why not?" Indy said, and smiled. Then he strode up the gangway. The horn blasted one final time, and the gangway rose behind him.

As the ferry edged away from the pier, Indy heard another horn. It was Shannon playing his cornet on the deck. He strolled over to him, nodding to Conrad. Shannon blew a few more bluesy notes, then lowered the horn.

"You just made it, Indy. What the hell were you doing?"

"I'll tell you later. We've got plenty of time to talk. But what was that tune? Don't think I've ever heard it."

"That's because you've only seen the lyrics. It's called 'Down in the Quarter.' Still need a singer, but at least I've got a new verse." He snapped his fingers, then tapped a beat on his cornet.

> *Took a trip to Greece;*
> *left the Quarter far behind.*

But Lord, never knew how I'd miss
that second home of mine.

"My sentiments, too," Indy said.

"Got something for you," Conrad said, and he handed Indy a package. "It arrived just before you got here."

"What's this?" Indy ripped open the envelope attached to the top of the package, and saw it was a note from the king.

Dear Mr. Jones—I hope you will change your mind and accept the Omphalos. Bury it at sea, if you wish, but please take it far from Greece and Delphi. The days of Apollo's Oracle are long over, and we Greeks must look to our future rather than try to revive our distant past. Thank you.

"What is it?" Shannon asked as the ferry pulled away from the pier.

"A piece of a falling star, I guess." Indy balanced the package on the railing.

"What are you going to do with it?"

He looked down at the dark blue sea. "I don't know. I'll have to think about it. But I know a museum curator in Chicago who would be very pleased to have it in his Greek collection...."

ABOUT THE AUTHOR

Rob MacGregor is an Edgar-winning author who has been on the *New York Times* bestseller list. He is the author of seventeen novels, ten nonfiction books, and numerous magazine and newspaper articles. In addition to writing his own novels, he has teamed with George Lucas, Peter Benchley, and Billy Dee Williams.

The adventure doesn't stop here—there's more
chills, adventure, and mystery ahead in the next
Indiana Jones adventure—

INDIANA JONES AND THE
DANCE OF THE GIANTS

Read an exciting preview of the next novel in the
series starting on the next page. . . .

Everywhere he looked, he saw figures draped in billowy black robes, their heads covered in cowls. They chanted a rhythmic drone, over and over again. It was endless. It was maddening.

He peered through the gray haze, trying to get his bearings. It was either dawn or dusk; he wasn't sure and it disturbed him that he didn't know. He could see that he was inside some sort of temple. It was immense and circular, roofless, with stone pillars arching toward the grey sky.

He didn't belong here; he was out of place. His head stuck out above everyone else's, and he was the only person who wasn't wearing a robe. He looked down at himself and saw that he wasn't wearing anything. Then he realized that he was standing on a flat rock and that was why his head protruded above everyone else's.

What was he doing here? How had he gotten here?

They were looking at him now. Every head was turned toward him. The droning grew louder. There was a rhythm to it, and it pounded against him. Why were they moving toward him? Why wouldn't his feet move? Why did his body feel like lead?

Now they were rushing at him. They were a sea of black. Their robes flapped at their ankles. He looked around frantically for an escape route. His arms pumped at his sides, his feet blurred beneath him, but he didn't seem to be getting anywhere. They must have drugged him; but who were they?

His head snapped around. They were almost on top of him. *Move. Move. Fast.* Air exploded from his lungs. A grinning face leered at him. The sky tilted. The pillars were toppling toward him. And suddenly he was awake, his arms twitching, his feet jerking, a scream poised at the edge of his tongue.

He sucked in his breath, looked around. But he could still hear the incessant chanting. He blinked his eyes, orienting himself. The train. Of course. The cars rumbled over the rails, the sound of the chanting, and someone was pounding on the door of his compartment. He sat forward, ran his hand across his perspiration-soaked brow.

"Who is it?"

The pounding stopped. The door opened and a slender, gray-haired Englishman wearing a conductor's uniform peered in at him. "Mr. Jones? Sorry if I disturbed you."

Indy rubbed his face. "What is it?"

The conductor held up a package. "It was waiting for you at the last stop."

"You sure it's for me?" Indy took the flat, rectangular box wrapped in white paper. On it was taped an envelope addressed: Indy Jones. "Yeah. Probably only one of us aboard." He thanked the conductor, who smiled thinly, nodded, and retreated.

Indy turned the package over in his hand. It looked like a candy box. It rattled when he shook it. He held it to his nose; it smelled faintly of chocolate. Who would send chocolates, he wondered as he slipped a card out of the envelope. The message was typewritten: *Have an enjoyable trip, and good luck on your new job. Henry Jones, Sr.*

He blinked, re-read it. Now how the hell did his father know he would be on this train? And since when did *he* wire him boxes of candy? Hell, they hadn't spoken for more than two years, not since he'd informed him of his switch in studies from linguistics to archaeology.

Then his frown vanished, and a smile curled on his lips. It was Shannon; it had to be. Jack Shannon knew all about his relationship with his father. The package was a goddamn joke, at least to someone with Shannon's jaded sense of humor. He shook his head, and set the card down on the box.

He stared out the window at the gray countryside drifting by. His thoughts turned back to his last night in Paris. A cloud of blue haze hung in the air of the nightclub as the black woman on stage swayed and sang, her voice deep and sonorous, a perfect accompaniment to the soulful sounds of the cornet being played in the shadows behind her. As the last notes of the song slowly faded away to the applause of the crowd, the tall, gangly cornet player with the goatee and unruly hair walked off the stage. He shook hands, nodded, smiled as he wove his way through the tables. Finally, he lowered himself into a chair in a table near the corner farthest from the stage.

"You're sounding real good, Jack. You *and* Louise," Indy said.

"Thanks. It's really come together in the last six months."

"I'll miss it."

Shannon studied Indy's face. "So you're really going to teach archaeology in London."

"At least for the summer. I'm leaving in the morning."

"I don't blame you for wanting to leave Paris. It's getting too hectic. The scene's changed." Shannon leaned forward and lit a cigarette from the burning candle on the table. "Sometimes, I look around and there's hardly a Parisian in the Jungle anymore. All tourists. Every night a new crowd. The regulars never show up until the last set, anymore. If they show up at all."

"Sorry I couldn't make it earlier."

Shannon waved a hand. "I'm not talking about you. It's everything. I guess I'm getting restless as well."

Indy put on his hat. "You know you're welcome to come and visit anytime you like."

"I may take you up on that. I'd like to see London again."

The rural countryside had given way to sooty brick factories and spewing smokestacks, and Indy knew that he'd be in the city in a few minutes. After leaving Paris earlier in the week, he'd spent a couple of days in Brittany, where he'd examined some of the megalithic ruins in the region. Then this morning he'd taken a ferry across the channel and boarded the train.

He ripped the paper from the package. He smiled. French chocolates from Paris. "Nice going, Shannon."

He was about to remove the cover and sample a chocolate when the train suddenly braked for another station and a book slid off the seat. He leaned over and picked up the book. The cover had flopped open to an epigraph on the first page of the 18th century tome, which read: *Felix qui potuit rerum cognoscere causes.*

"Fortune is he who can know the inner meaning of things," he muttered.

He closed the cover. The book was called, *Choir Gaur; The Grand Orrey of the Ancient Druids, Commonly Called Stonehenge.* He laughed to himself. He didn't have to look any further for the meaning of his dream. He'd been reading the book before he'd fallen asleep. Why black robes, though, he wondered. He was sure Druids wore white. But who said dreams made sense.

The train started up again. He tapped his fingers on the package. Trains were so monotonous, always stopping. Everyone was saying that airplanes would soon make trains obsolete. It hadn't happened yet, but he was all for it.

He lifted the cover off the candy box, and reached inside for a chocolate. It took a moment before he comprehended what he was seeing and feeling. Something black and hairy was crawling up his fingers, and it wasn't made of chocolate. His jaw dropped; he shouted and shook his hand. Then he gaped at the box. He saw a few chocolates, but the rest of the compartments were filled with walnut-sized spiders. At the same time, his knees kicked the box into the air. Chocolates and spiders spewed over him. He swept them off his legs, his arms. He leaped to his feet. He stomped on spiders, squashed chocolates, swept his arms and legs and body clean of the crawling creatures.

Finally, he examined his seat, then sat down again, but as he did felt one creeping inside his pants leg, and another on the inside of his collar. He nearly leaped out of his clothes. He shook his leg until the spider fell to the floor, and he squashed it. Then carefully he reached up to his collar and brushed at his neck.

He laughed nervously as a chocolate dropped to the floor. Relieved, he sat down, exhaled. But now he felt a tingling on his calf, and pulled up his pant leg. Dozens of tiny, newly hatched spiders were crawling over his calf and behind his knee.

"AW...AW..." His teeth chattered; he shuddered.

He brushed them off, swatted them with a rolled up newspaper. Then, carefully he inspected his leg to make sure none was left.

He picked up the box, examined it. It hadn't been a matter of spiders invading the chocolate box. Someone had planted them.

"Shannon?" he said aloud. Would he go to all the trouble for a joke that he wouldn't even see carried out? Maybe, but this was no joke.

He looked at the card again. Maybe it *was* his father? No, couldn't be. He wouldn't. Besides, it was addressed to Indy Jones, and his father never called him that. But Shannon knew that. If he was playing a joke, why wouldn't he have addressed it to Henry Jones, Jr. as his father's letters had always read when they were college roommates back in Chicago.

He heard a tap on the door. "Yes?"

The conductor opened it. "Is everything all right?" A frown creased his forehead. "I thought I heard a noise."

"You mind if I switch compartments for the rest of the trip? This one has spiders."

"Spiders?" The conductor's eyes shifted about the compartment. He twitched his shoulders as if the thought of spiders made him uneasy. Indy understood perfectly. Spiders usually didn't bother him as much as some things, but almost swallowing one is definitely an exception. He pointed to one.

The conductor backed out of the compartment. "Right this way, sir."

Indy gathered up his books, and the conductor carried his luggage. At the last moment, he grabbed the empty box and wrapper, hoping they'd hold some clue to the souce of the so-called gift. When he was settled in his new seat, he asked the conductor how he might find out where the package he'd received had come from.

"That's easy. Just look at the number in the corner of the wrapper."

Indy flattened it out. "Twelve."

"That's it. They always put a number on the packages so the sender can be notified by the telegraph office that the package was delivered if they request the service."

"So where's 'twelve'?"

The conductor smiled. "That's easy. It was sent from London."

Indy glanced over his shoulder as he passed through the stone gate of the university and caught sight of a tall, dark-haired man moving behind him. The guy had been following him for the last two mornings. At least, maybe it was just someone who was walking the same route.

He glanced back again, but the man had vanished into a crowd of students. Just his imagination, he told himself. Even though six weeks had passed since his first day of classes, he hadn't been able to put the incident with the spiders behind him. He wanted to think it was all a mistake, that the candy box hadn't been intended for him. But he knew it had. He just didn't know why. He'd been expecting something to happen, some indication of what the box had meant, but there'd been nothing.

Despite his efforts, he'd had no luck tracing the source of the package. Shannon had sworn that he knew nothing about it, and Indy believed him. Whoever had sent it had been careful not to leave a trail.

But he was too busy to spend much time thinking about it. He arrived on campus each day by eight, read over his notes in his office, and taught a two-hour class at nine, and another at one. Although his classes were over at three, his work had just begun. He would go back to his office or to the library, where he would take out his class syllabus, open his books, and begin preparations for the next class.

He yawned as he entered Petrie Hall. Much of the material he was teaching was new to him so he was a student as well as a teacher. At best, he was a week ahead of his students. Some days he was thankful for the syllabus, which provided him with a general outline of topics to be discussed for the week. But other times, he felt restricted by it. If he taught it again he could already see ways of improving the class. There was no guarantee of that: He wouldn't know for another couple of weeks, when the summer session ended, whether or not he still had a job.

Landing the job so soon after graduating had been a surprise. In fact, he would have been content to remain in Paris, and look for a position at one of the city's universities while he continued his part-time job in the archaeology lab at the Sorbonne. But Marcus Brody, an old family friend and a curator of an archaeology museum, had given him the lead for the job. The native Londoner had wired him that one of his contacts at the University of London had informed him about an opening for a summer teaching job in archaeology that could become full-time in the fall.

He hadn't thought he had much of a chance, but he'd applied, mainly to show Brody he appreciated the help. While the position was for an introductory course, its emphasis was on Britain's megalithic monuments, a topic which he'd examined only superficially in his studies. A week later he was asked to come to London for an interview, and a few days later he received a letter telling him that he'd been hired. Although the interview had gone well, he was convinced that Brody must have more influence in professional circles than he'd imagined.

As he entered the classroom, his eyes fell on the good-looking redhead who sat in the center of the front row. He soon discovered she was an engaging, intelligent woman a few years younger than him, but she also made him uneasy and aware of his limited knowledge of British archaeology. She spoke up often, too often, interrupting him with a question or comment, or answering questions he posed to the class as if she were the only one present. But that wasn't the only reason he was wary of her. Her name was Deirdre Campbell, and she was the daughter of Joanna Campbell, the head of the department and his boss.

"Archaeology is one profession where you can take pleasant walks in the countryside, and still be working," Indy began as he stepped up to the podium. "In fact, we have a name for it. It's called fieldwalking."

He looked over the rows of bowed heads taking notes. Deirdre, however, sat back in her chair watching him. He explained that fieldwalking involved looking for deviations in the landscape. Slight undulations could indicate the remains of an ancient ditch or the site of a medieval village. Changes in the color of the soil or the density of the vegetation is another indicator. If the boundary of a field shifted for no apparent reason or the shoreline of a body of water followed a peculiarly straight line, it might mean the presence of an ancient wall.

Indy looked up to see a hand raised in front of him. It didn't take her long to get started. "Yes, Deirdre?"

"What about Stonehenge?"

She spoke with a Scottish lilt, pronouncing it "Stoonheenge." Indy looked blankly at her. "What about it?"

"Well, fieldwalking (*field*-**wooking,** she said) didn't do much good there. People had walked all over Stonehenge and the surrounding area and didn't see the certain changes in the landscape because they were too close to them."

Thank God he knew what she was talking about. There was nothing in the syllabus about the use of aerial photography, but he'd been preparing for an upcoming lecture on Stonehenge and had read about the photos taken of the ruins.

"Good point," he said and quickly explained what she meant. Near the end of the war, a military airport was built a short distance from the ruins, and photographs taken by a squadron of the Royal Air Force in the summer of 1921 revealed some surprising details. It was discovered that the grain in an area leading away from the monument grew darker in colors than the surrounding grain. Yet, it was impossible to see the difference from ground level.

"Does anyone know what would cause this to happen?"

Of course Deirdre did.

"It shows that the ground had been dug up in those darker areas, and the roots of the plants were able to penetrate the tough layer of chalk that's just beneath the top soil."

"That's right," Indy said. "In September of '23, Crawford and Passamore began studying these darker areas, using the pictures as their only guide. They discovered the exact entrance to the ruin and a straight road which reached nearly to Amesbury, eight miles to the north. Stonehenge may very well be the first archaeological site anywhere that has taken advantage of aerial photography. I'm sure we'll see a lot more of it. But we can thank the Royal Air Force for furthering our knowledge of Stonehenge."

Indy looked up to see Deirdre's hand again. He knew most teachers would love to have a dozen bright students like Deirdre in class, but she was getting out of hand.

"What about the controversy with the military authorities?" she asked.

Even when she posed a question, she phrased it in a way that showed she already knew the answer. What the hell was she doing, testing him for her mother? This time he was at a loss. In spite of all the time he spent preparing his lectures, he knew there were things he was missing, and this must be one of them. "Sorry. I'm not sure what you mean."

"That's understandable," she said in a knowing voice. "You haven't been in England long, and I hear they don't report our British doings very thoroughly in your newspapers. But it was quite a controversy here. Near the end of the war, the authorities wanted to knock down Stonehenge, because they felt the stones might be dangerous to low flying airplanes."

"You're kidding."

"Not at all. It was quite a stink."

Indy noticed several heads bobbing in agreement. "Well, I'll have to look into it," he muttered and cleared his throat again. He was angry with Deirdre.

She was acting as if this were her class. He needed to straighten her out, and quickly.

She must have sensed his unease, because she only spoke up a couple more times during the remainder of his lecture. As the class came to an end, Indy said the next time he would be talking about Stonehenge. "We've already discussed menhirs and dolmens, and now you can add trilithons to your vocabulary. Your assignment is to read all the articles entitled, 'Excavations at Stonehenge,' by Colonel William Hawley that have been published in the *Antiquaries Journal* since 1920. Hawley, as you should know, is the archaeologist in charge of the current digging at Stonehenge. We'll talk about what he's found so far and the implications. By the way, does anyone know what he found under the so-called Slaughter Stone?"

After a few seconds, Deirdre raised her hand, but this time only to shoulder level. Indy waited a moment longer for other hands, but there were no others. "Go ahead, Deirdre."

"He's found some flint tools and pottery shards, and also stone mauls and deer-antler picks. But I think the item you're referring to is a bottle of port left by another archaeologist, Colt Hoare, a hundred years ago."

Everyone laughed.

"Very good. You stole my joke. See me after class, will you, Miss Campbell? Class dismissed."

As they filed out of the room, Indy gathered up his notes and thought about what he would say. When everyone but Deirdre had left, he remained behind his podium as if he were about to continue his lecture for a class of one. She approached the podium with her hands folded in front of her over a notebook. She was a petite woman, an inch or two over five feet. Her long auburn hair had curls that twirled down over her shoulders. Her skin was pale, and her eyes were the violet of heather. She wore just a touch of makeup. There was something contradictory about her appearance. She was frail, but savvy; innocent, but sophisticated. Looking at her for some reason made him think of an oxymoron his father used to quote when his mother was agitated about something trivial. "O heavy lightness, serious vanity!"

"You're Scottish, aren't you, Deirdre?" he began.

"Yes, I am."

"So am I. Well, I mean my father is, or was. He was born in Scotland." Bad start.

She stared directly into his eyes, challenging him, a slight smile on her lips. "Is that why you asked me to stay after class, so we could discuss our ancestries?"

He cleared his throat. He was nervous. She was the one who should be, but wasn't. "I want to ask you if you . . ."

"Yes?"

He looked down at the podium. ". . . if you would mind . . . Deirdre, why are you taking this class? I mean you seem to know the material, and your mother is certainly more knowledgeable about British archaeology than I am."

"But you're the one teaching the class. She's not. I can't get credits through heredity."

He knew that if he angered her it might get back to her mother and it could be the end of his chances for being rehired for the fall, but he had to say something.

"Deirdre, listen, I'd appreciate it if you would give the others in the class a chance to talk."

Her eyes blinked rapidly. "What do you mean?"

"I think you might be intimidating them."

"Oh? No reason for it. They're certainly free to say anything they like."

"Yeah." Indy looked down at the podium again as if his notes would give him an idea of what to say.

"Can I make an observation, Professor?"

Now what? "Go ahead."

"It seems to me that you are the one who is intimidated."

He shrugged. "Not intimidated, just a bit irritated."

"Why?"

"Look, this is my first teaching job. I've never been involved in any fieldwork here. I'm not English."

"You don't have to apologize to *me* for not being English. Remember, I'm not either."

Indy didn't join her laughter. "And your mother is my boss."

"You don't have to make an accusation out of that fact. If you want to know, I'm enjoying your class. I think you're doing a terrific job, and I've told Joanna, my mum."

"Why, thank you."

"She keeps teasing me about you." She smiled awkwardly, her face reddening. "I better go."

He watched her leave. He smiled to himself. A real oddball, that one. He liked her, he decided. But then he'd known that from the first day of class.